WAYNE STINNETT

RISING SPIRIT

A JESSE MCDERMITT NOVEL

Caribbean Adventure Series

Volume 16

2019

Copyright © 2019
Published by DOWN ISLAND PRESS, LLC, 2019
Beaufort, SC

Copyright © 2019 by Wayne Stinnett

Library of Congress cataloging-in-publication Data
    Stinnett, Wayne
    Rising Spirit/Wayne Stinnett
    p. cm. - (A Jesse McDermitt novel)

ISBN-13: 978-1-7339351-4-2
ISBN-10: 1-7339351-4-2

Cover photograph by Popoudina Svetlana
Graphics by Wicked Good Book Covers
Edited by The Write Touch
Final Proofreading by Donna Rich
Interior Design by Ampersand Book Interiors

This is a work of fiction. Names, characters, and incidents are either the product of the author's imagination or are used fictitiously. Any resemblance to actual persons, living or dead, businesses, companies, events, or locales is entirely coincidental. Many real people are used fictitiously in this work, with their permission. Most of the locations herein are also fictional or are used fictitiously. However, the author takes great pains to depict the location and description of the many well-known islands, locales, beaches, reefs, bars, and restaurants throughout the Florida Keys and the Caribbean to the best of his ability.

FOREWORD

In 2001, I moved from Florida to Travelers Rest, SC, in the foothills of the Appalachian Mountains. It was a big change for me, but it wasn't completely foreign. You see, as a nineteen-year-old Marine, I went through cold weather survival training in Fort Drum, New York. We worked and trained outdoors for the whole two weeks. At the time, the common belief was that the next big land battle would take place in the frozen wasteland of northern Europe, so we trained for it. The Cold War wasn't just a phrase about political attitudes.

Jesse went through that same training with me. So, I thought I'd take him back to a snow-covered mountainside and see if he'd lost his edge. Throughout this story, many characters kept telling Jesse that as a Keys charter boat captain, he was out of his element. On top of that, I thought I'd throw him a curve ball and bring back a couple of women from his past.

I enjoy putting my characters into unusual situations to see how they'll react. Unlike many writers, I don't create an outline for my work. I set the location, plop the characters into it, and they tell me the story from their points of view. I quite literally make it all up as it goes along and have no idea how it will end until I get there. In writing the story, I experience the twists and turns much the same way that my readers do. It took me four months to reach the end. I hope you'll find the read a little faster.

This one took a little longer to write than most of my stories. I started it in May and didn't finish until September. It was summer, I had a new boat, and the 30th annual Novelists, Inc conference was fast approaching at the end of September. Serving as the organization's 2019 president took quite a bit of time away from my work and my boat! But being elected by my peers to lead this very prestigious organization was very humbling. I like to think I did the job well.

While at the conference during the last week of September 2019, I was able to sit down with several team members. My editor, Marsha Zinberg, was there meeting new and old clients, as well as my narrator, Nick Sullivan, and my co-author in the Charity series, Kimberli Bindschatel. We all had dinner together and were able to discuss ideas and plans several times before and during the conference. Thanks for the companionship and friendship.

With every book, I thank the many members of my beta reading team. I call them that for lack of a better name, as they are the first ones to read my manuscripts after me. I have to say it again: without these folks, all experts in various fields, my stories would be far less accurate and enjoyable. Among this group are doctors, lawyers, pilots, boaters, locals, air traffic controllers, military, law enforcement, and spec-ops folks, and old friends from my teen years. Trust me, they know they can't hurt my feelings. They point out many flaws, give me great ideas that make the story better, and provide expert advice during the writing process. They have now all become my friends and integral parts of my team. Many thanks to Debbie Kocol, Thomas Crisp, Ron Ramey, Dana Vilhen, Katy McKnight, Torrey Neill, Mike Ramsey, Alan Fader, Charles Höfbauer, John Trainer, David Parsons, Drew Mutch, Deg Priest, Glen Hibbert, and Debbie Cross for helping to polish up the manuscript.

During the writing of this story, tragedy struck the Bahamas in the form of Hurricane Dorian. A member of my beta reader team owns the small resort where Jesse stayed on Elbow Cay in *Fallen Mangrove*. Yeah, that was a real place! We had been planning a week-long social event there for a small number of readers and friends, scheduled for March 2020. Most of the island and many others in the Abacos have sustained catastrophic damage and many people have died.

The small resort of Crystal Waters and Villas was among the damaged properties. Early photographs show that the resort's structures weren't destroyed, but damage was horrific and they likely won't reopen until sometime next year.

Look them up, book in advance for next year, and make a donation along with your deposit. I can promise it will go to those who need it most in the form of materials to rebuild.

Islanders are tough people and the Abacos will bounce back. It's been five weeks since the hurricane as I write this, and last night I watched a news story about a dog that was pulled alive from the rubble of a house, though severely malnourished and dehydrated. The Abacos are still in clean-up and recovery stage and it will be years before things are back to normal.

I'd also like to thank my incredible publishing team under the Down Island Press umbrella. Editor Marsha Zinberg of The Write Touch is slowly turning a storyteller into a writer with her insights and instruction. I've never claimed to be a writer, just a storyteller. But there's hope yet.

The last person to read my work with a critical eye to style is Donna Rich. She's been a part of this process almost from the start, when she was the second proofreader of my second novel. I couldn't think of releasing a new book without her eyes on the finished manuscript.

Veteran actor of stage and screen, Nick Sullivan, has been the voice of Jesse McDermitt since the beginning. He was the sixty-third audition I listened to and he had me with his rendition of Rusty Thurman. Now that he is a terrific novelist himself, Nick and I have brought our characters together in our stories. His friendship is very valuable to me, and his attention to detail in his narration really puts that last spit-shine on the story. The best way to find the little mistakes is to read a book aloud. But when Nick finishes, it's still not a book. It's just an ugly Word file that he's masterfully acted out on audio.

A book has a cover, and that's where cover designer Shayne Rutherford of Wicked Good Book Covers comes in. She's responsible for grabbing your attention and you've seen her work on many of my author friends' works.

What turns all this into a book that creates an enjoyable reading experience? Professional formatting and artistic flair. That comes from the desk of Colleen Sheehan of Ampersand Book Design, who formats the interiors of my books to make them much more than just words on a page.

Thank you all.

That sounds goofy.

Thanks, y'all!

That's better.

So, go grab a sweater, put another log on the fire, and let me take you to my ancestral home in the Shenandoah Valley region, where my 7th great-grandfather first settled in 1750, just below the Tobacco Row Mountains, south of the Valley. In Amherst County, Virginia, there are more Stinnetts than there are Smiths, Johnsons, Clarks, and Joneses combined.

Jesse's not out of his element, but I promise that by the end of the story, you'll be hip-deep in alligators once more.

One Human Family

To Debbie and her family, and to all
the people of the Abacos.

If you'd like to receive my newsletter,
please sign up on my website:

WWW.WAYNESTINNETT.COM.

Every two weeks, I'll bring you insights into my private life and writing habits, with updates on what I'm working on, special deals I hear about, and new books by other authors that I'm reading.

The Charity Styles Caribbean Thriller Series

Merciless Charity
Ruthless Charity
Reckless Charity
Enduring Charity
Vigilant Charity

The Jesse McDermitt Caribbean Adventure Series

Fallen Out
Fallen Palm
Fallen Hunter
Fallen Pride
Fallen Mangrove
Fallen King
Fallen Honor
Fallen Tide

Fallen Angel
Fallen Hero
Rising Storm
Rising Fury
Rising Force
Rising Charity
Rising Water
Rising Spirit

THE GASPAR'S REVENGE SHIP'S STORE IS OPEN.

There, you can purchase all kinds of swag related to my books. You can find it at

WWW.GASPARS-REVENGE.COM

MAPS

Jesse's Island

MAPS

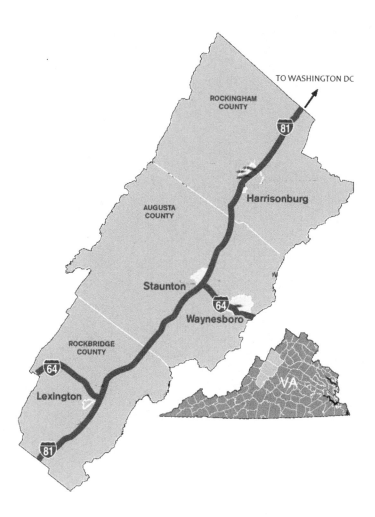

Shenandoah Valley, Virginia

PROLOGUE

The early fall air was crisp and cool as a light breeze out of the northeast rustled the leaves. Muted shades of orange, yellow, red, and green covered the far-away hillsides of the Shenandoah Valley.

The breeze seemed to swirl the colors around, some becoming more or less intense as the wind moved the many differently colored leaves.

It was the time of year when the sun began to relinquish control of the sky, yielding more and more time to the moon as the days got shorter following the autumnal equinox.

The sparsely planted trees along the town's busy two-lane streets tried to mimic those on the forested hillside. Their leaves were the same color, but they couldn't quite match the grandeur of the mountains surrounding the valley. All the buildings, cars, and people detracted from the splendor.

The town had been laid out long before traffic jams, malls, fast food, and rush hours, and the buildings had been erected with a smaller populace in mind. They were built in such close proximity that the streets would never accommodate more than two lanes of traffic, bordered by narrow sidewalks and minimal parking on either side of the busy thoroughfares—unless the mostly historic buildings were torn down. And that wasn't going to happen. So, the busy town endured the narrow streets.

The colonial-style building on the corner of Augusta and Johnson Streets in Staunton, Virginia had been built in 1901, when there were still hitching posts instead of parking lots. The *new* circuit courthouse had replaced the previous one on the same property. In fact, there'd been a courthouse of some kind or other on that corner since 1755. The current two-story, red brick building had a wide portico in front, supported by four brick columns painted a pale yellow.

Above and behind the courthouse entrance was a domed cupola, topped with a statue of Lady Justice, blind-folded and lifting her scales high to proclaim equal justice for all. At her side, she gripped the hilt of her long broadsword, a powerful representation of authority.

Kamren Steele stood on the corner across the street from the historic building, waiting for the light to change. "Imposing," he commented to the woman standing beside him.

"Arrogant, if you ask me," Sandra Sneed replied. "Built by slaves."

He smiled at her. "It's not quite that old."

"Built at the turn of the last century," she argued, staring venomously at the building across the street. "By freed black men who had been born into slavery and lived under Jim Crow laws for half their lives."

A young African-American couple hurried past the courthouse, crossed Augusta Street just as the light changed, and entered the Union Bank building on the opposite corner.

"The times, they are a changin'," Kamren responded, stepping off the curb after the crossing light signaled it was safe to walk. "Come on, let's get this done."

She stepped out beside him, shaking her head but smiling. "Only you would quote Dylan in a town like this."

Kamren Steele was the leader of Earth Now, an environmental group made up of like-minded people who abhorred overdevelopment, and the unadulterated stripping of the land. He was tall and ruggedly handsome, with black hair graying slightly at the temples. His face was clean-shaven, and at fifty-five, lines had begun to appear at the corners of his eyes. Equally comfortable wearing a business suit in a board room, or boots and jeans on a hiking trail, he'd opted for the former for this preliminary hearing.

Sandra Sneed was an attractive woman from the North Carolina coast. She was not as tall as his five-eleven, but she was close, with blond hair, a slim figure, and long, shapely legs. Like him, she was dressed con-

servatively; a gray pencil skirt and blazer over a light blue blouse, and modest heels.

She'd been a permanent fixture at Kamren's side for twenty years and was equally at home in the conference room or deep in the forest, though she much preferred the latter.

The two had met in 1999 at the dedication of James River State Park, east of the small town of Amherst, Virginia. At the time, she'd been divorced for nearly a decade; a single mother of two girls, aged ten and fifteen. Kamren had never married, had no children, and never planned to change either. The two had quickly discovered their shared passions for endurance hiking and protecting the environment, and regularly spent days together in the wilds of the Appalachian Mountains, her kids packed off to her parents or to boarding school.

With her girls grown and now living in Florida, the couple had more time to pursue their common interests. Earth Now was a growing organization, and Kamren found himself more at the forefront these days, wearing the suit. With Sandra at his side, Earth Now's ranks had quickly swelled to over five thousand members, mostly in Virginia, Maryland, and North Carolina. They worked tirelessly to raise awareness and funds for endangered species and the vital importance of wetlands and woodlands. They had picked up the slogan, *Think Global, Act Local*, and carried it into small towns and villages all around the tri-state area.

The judge who would be hearing their preliminary motion for an injunction would listen to both sides of a dispute over water pollution in the upper creeks and streams that flowed into rivers, and eventually reached Chesapeake Bay. It was commonsense legislation and both sides of the aisle were behind it.

The matter was quite simple, as far as Kamren and Sandra were concerned. All that was needed to stem half the pollutants flowing into the bay was for livestock to be kept out of the upstream creeks and rivers.

During hot summer months, roaming livestock sought out the cool water and often worked their way along the banks, eating the abundant grasses that grew down to the shoreline. The animals defecated in the water and their waste had been proven to be one of the largest contributors to pollution in Chesapeake Bay. All that was needed to reduce this pollution was for fences to be installed to keep the cattle out of the water. Some farmers adopted the new policy as a matter of course, but others couldn't be bothered. Those farmers were the reason Kamren and Sandra had come to Staunton.

Within five years of implementing the new policy, Earth Now's scientists predicted there would be a noticeable change in the amount of dissolved pollutants in Chesapeake Bay, and they projected that within twenty to thirty years, fish populations would return to pre-industrial numbers.

Kamren held the door for Sandra and together they entered the courthouse, armed with words and scientific data.

◆ ◆ ◆ ◆

An hour later the couple was back in their hotel room. Sitting on the edge of the bed, Sandra looked up at Kamren. "Let's get out of here and go up to the Trail. I didn't like the looks some of those men were giving us."

"It was a minor victory," Kamren said. "These people will just have to learn that the law is the law." He nodded at Sandra. "We're finished here."

"The car's packed with all our gear," she said, excitedly. "I'd rather not sleep in a hotel again tonight."

Kamren smiled at his common-law wife. "There's a beautiful twenty-mile stretch of the A.T. that I don't think either of us has hiked in years; we can be there in an hour."

Sandra smiled, rose from the bed, and flung her arms around Kamren's neck. "You really know how to woo a girl."

They changed into more suitable attire for hiking, gathered their things, and were soon on I-64, heading east. Traffic was light as they crossed the valley toward the eastern ridge and began the long, uphill grade. Exiting the interstate at Rockfish Gap, they drove east on U.S. 250 for less than a mile, then made the turn to access Skyline Drive, heading north. A few minutes later, Kamren turned off at the Rockfish Gap Entrance

Station—one of many entrances to the Appalachian Trail.

"God, I hated being around all those people," Sandra said, pulling her backpack from the trunk of the car. "Could you believe some of those backwoods farmers?"

Kamren looked around as he pulled his much larger pack from the trunk. The parking area was small, with room for only a dozen or so cars. It was nearly full. "This time of year, there won't be any shortage of people on the trail either."

"Yes," Sandra agreed, shrugging into her pack. "But at least they'll be *our* kind of people."

Kamren closed the trunk and took Sandra's hand, leading her toward an opening in the underbrush. "I think the judge's ruling might have made us a little unpopular in town," he conceded.

Sandra laughed. "You think?"

As the attractive couple entered the woods, they turned left, heading north on the famous trail.

A moment later, an old, blue GMC pickup pulled into the parking area and the driver steered into a vacant spot just past Kamren's rental car.

Two men got out of the truck, both of them starting to show signs of age. They wore jeans and work shirts and neither had a backpack, nor did they carry any sort of camping gear. One man had a shaved head. He looked around and, not seeing anyone, nodded toward the gap in the brush. The two men disappeared into the woods a few minutes after the couple.

CHAPTER ONE

I t'd been two years since the storm and nobody in the Florida Keys called it Hurricane Irma anymore. At some point in the future, I felt sure the name would return, as new storms filled more recent collective memories. In the Bahamas the general term now had a different meaning and a different name, after Hurricane Dorian destroyed much of the Abacos just three months ago. As had happened in the Keys, the media moved on to other stories, even though the devastation has only barely begun to be cleaned up. It would be years before those islands recovered.

But for now, here in the Keys, if someone mentioned "the storm," you knew which one they were talking about.

Though there were still signs of Irma's destruction everywhere, most of the folks who lived in the Middle Keys had returned to a somewhat normal pace. The outpouring of compassion in the first weeks and months after the storm had nearly evaporated, even though the need was still there. Some folks would simply never recover.

I'd done my part. I'd helped those who were hurt or displaced, I'd put people to work, injecting much needed cash into the community when most were out of work. Businesses closed and some never reopened. But the employees; the locals who'd lived here all their lives, or like me, who'd visited and decided to stay and put down roots, needed an income. They needed help. Anyone who could walk helped those who couldn't. Anyone with food or shelter shared it with those who had suddenly been left with nothing. I'd joined in, working for days before I even thought about starting on my own home.

That was when people came to help *me*. I could have handled it on my own. I'd built everything on my island once before and had planned to do so again. But they came by the dozens and offered help. I'd gladly paid them, though they were the kind of people who would have helped for free. And I didn't take "no thanks" for an answer. It had been a really simple matter: I had the money and others needed it. So, I hired anyone and everyone and paid them according to their need. None would accept a handout, but all were willing to work.

With the help of friends like Deuce Livingston, Rusty Thurman, John Wilson, and Jack Armstrong, along with dozens of others, we'd removed everything from my island that the storm had wrecked and begun the work of rebuilding.

Ambrosia, the primary research vessel for Armstrong Research, had remained anchored in the mouth of Harbor Channel for two months, just past Mac Travis's island. She served as the mother ship, with enough building material on board to get the job done, plus housing for the workers. At 199 feet, she dwarfed the biggest boat I'd ever seen in this part of the Gulf of Mexico.

The damage to my island hadn't been as bad as it had been just a few miles down island. The eye of the storm had passed just five miles to the west of my island, but it had crossed US-1 on Cudjoe Key, blasting it, Summerland Key, and Ramrod Key with winds in excess of 100 miles per hour.

My home, as well as the other three structures on my island, had been solidly built. Flood waters had damaged the other three houses, and all four had their roofs blown off. One bunkhouse had been swept from its foundation. But the walls, floors, and the heavy pilings the other three houses had been built on were mostly undamaged.

Sitting on the deck with Finn, I gazed out across my island. My daughter and son-in-law, Kim and Marty, had lived in one of the converted bunkhouses on the north side of the island. It had been ruined, and the other bunkhouse completely destroyed except for the floor and pier points.

The new houses we'd built on the existing pilings were higher and sturdier, built ten feet off the ground and to modern hurricane standards. Mine was four feet higher than the others, to allow room to dock my boats beneath it. The only structural damage to my house

had been the loss of the roof, the big doors to the dock area caved in, and some siding ripped away around the lower half.

Jimmy's house was rebuilt in the same way as the bunkhouses. He'd been my first mate for years aboard my charter fishing and diving vessel, *Gaspar's Revenge*. He and his girlfriend, Naomi, now split their time between my island and her place in Marathon. But Jimmy still came out to my island every day, while Naomi worked as the daytime bartender at the *Rusty Anchor*.

Kim and Marty had been transferred to a Fish and Wildlife office in Miami last year. They mostly lived on the mainland, in a small bungalow they rented in Coconut Grove, not far from their office. But they spent as much of their free time as they could down here. The western bunkhouse was now their home, a little two-bedroom house with a porch off the bedrooms that had a great view across the mangroves toward the setting sun.

The eastern bunkhouse was still just that, a bunkhouse for fishermen. It was a stipulation in the sale of the island that it be maintained as a fish camp for twenty years. The end of that term was fast approaching. It was purely a utilitarian structure, furnished with just the six sets of bunkbeds, an empty desk, and a bathroom.

Sara came out of my house and handed me a beer, taking a seat beside me on the bench. "What time do you want to head down there?"

We were going to the *Rusty Anchor* for a grand re-opening celebration and Thanksgiving dinner all rolled into one.

"We don't have to leave right away," I said, as Sara leaned against my shoulder. "I don't like being the first to arrive."

My friend, Rusty Thurman, had only closed the doors of the *Anchor* for two days; just before and immediately after the storm. Not even that long, really. He'd housed quite a few displaced people in his home and his bar all during the storm.

The *Anchor* was the hub for local business and gossip and had become the rallying point for the cleanup effort after the storm. It had sustained little damage, but Rusty and I agreed it needed some attention. His wife, Sidney, was all in favor of a complete makeover. But Rusty and I decided we wanted to maintain that old-time Conch vibe. Being part owner, I kicked in half the cost for a full renovation of the property. It'd taken two years, working on just one section at a time, so as to keep the place open during remodeling, but it was finally finished. The work on the bar itself, and the little open-air kitchen attached to the back, was performed at night, then cleaned and ready for business by morning.

"You just don't like being around a bunch of people," Sara said.

"Not true," I replied defensively. "I have friends I like to hang around with."

Sara Patrick and I had been together for a couple of years now. She was a widow when we met, and neither of us was looking for a relationship at the time. We'd become close friends and co-workers, enjoyed each other's company, and had eventually started a monogamous physical relationship that was satisfying to both of us. There were times when one of us would be called away for weeks, or sometimes months, and neither of us wanted the stress of an emotional relationship.

She playfully punched my ribs. "Deuce, Jimmy, Rusty, and my dad. Everyone else you simply tolerate."

"Also, not true," I said with a grin. "There are a lot of people I *don't* tolerate at all. But I guess we should go on down there."

Finn rose from the deck and stretched, then shook his big head. I thought he'd been napping, but as usual, he was just waiting on the *go* word. Finn was mostly Labrador Retriever, but he had a little Short-haired Pointer mixed in, as well. At ten years old, he wasn't as fast as he once was, but he still got around well. His favorite word was *go*; go fishing, go for a boat ride, go diving for clams, go to the *Rusty Anchor*.

"We're staying aboard in the marina tonight?" Sara asked, as we both rose.

Finn danced his way toward the door to the house, his claws clicking on the teak deck.

"Yeah. I don't want to come back out here in the dark after drinking."

"Good," Sara said, with a come-on look. "I like that big bed on *Salty Dog*."

When we re-entered the house, I locked the door behind us. Originally, there had been an exterior access door to the docking area under the house. But after an intruder got inside just before the storm, I decided to forego that luxury when rebuilding.

The exterior walls around the boathouse were concrete now, all the way down to the bedrock, and the only access to the lower level and my boats was from inside the house, and the big double doors at water level. In a pinch, I could swim under the outer boat doors, but they reached to within a couple of feet of the bottom. I'd had to do just that a few times already, having left my keys in the house.

I'd rebuilt my house to nearly the same proportions and design as it had originally been. My Pap often told me, "If it ain't broke, don't fix it," and the simplicity of my old house was what worked for me. It had one big open room in front, and a bedroom and bathroom in back, which together made up the total one thousand square feet, the same dimensions as the other three houses. *If it ain't broke, don't fix it.*

The front room was a combination living room, dining room, kitchen, and work area. It was slightly smaller than the original, due to the new stairs going down to the boathouse. They ran the length of the front room's back wall. The stairs were narrow, but Finn had no trouble with them. He couldn't climb the metal ladder the stairs had replaced, though.

Moments later, the three of us idled out from under the house. I clicked the button on the key fob and the big doors slowly closed as we motored into Harbor Channel. I turned northeast and brought the little Grady-White center-console up onto the step, navigating the narrow cut that ran out of the channel with ease. Then I turned south and increased speed.

Finn stood in front of the console with his front paws up on the casting deck, his ears flapping in the wind. He was a boat dog, and never tired of going for a ride.

It only took twenty minutes to reach the Seven Mile Bridge and another ten to swing around Sister Rock and turn into the canal to the *Rusty Anchor Marina*.

Part of the redevelopment of the property had been to dredge the canal back to its original depth and width and lengthen the seawalls on both sides. To do that, the wrecked boat ramp had to be moved further to the east. Rusty now had room for a lot more boats, and as we entered the canal, I could see that nearly every slip was taken.

My Formosa ketch, *Salty Dog,* was tied up at the near end, closest to the sea, with my amphibian airplane, *Island Hopper,* tied down on shore right next to her. The two had a combined age of 103 years, but both were in like-new condition and carried modern electronics.

I idled up to the dock, which extended a few feet beyond the *Dog's* bow and allowed Finn and Sara to step up onto the planks. She quickly snugged the line around the last dock cleat and waited for me to line the much smaller Grady up between the *Dog's* bowsprit and the dock. I shifted to reverse and turned the wheel to the right to swing the stern around toward shore. With no cleat to tie to, I just tied a line off to the cranse iron at the end of the bowsprit, while Sara secured the bow line. It was close, but there was at least a foot between the Grady's gunwale and the *Dog's* dolphin striker. I shut down the engine and used the bobstay to climb up onto the bowsprit, where I went aft to turn on the breakers so the air conditioning would cool the boat's interior.

After I joined Sara on the dock, we walked toward the newly renovated bar at the far end of the canal. Finn ran off toward the backyard, looking for someone to play with.

Rusty had expanded the outside deck, wrapping it around the side nearest the docks, and extending it farther out into the backyard. The new stage on the southwest corner of the deck was elevated two feet and covered with a big blue triangle of heavy sailcloth. When someone was performing, they didn't have to stare into the setting sun.

The side deck was also covered in sailcloth, arranged in alternating triangles of red and blue, while the back deck still had tables with individual white umbrellas, though they were newer. Rufus's partially enclosed kitchen was also enlarged, and Rufus had brought his niece from Jamaica over to work and train as his assistant.

Rufus was a wiry little Jamaican man, with a shaved head and gap-toothed smile. He'd been Rusty's chef since he'd retired from a five-star restaurant in Negril about twenty years ago. He'd seemed old and wizened then, but nobody knew just how old he was. I figure he had to be pushing the eighty-year mark.

The *Rusty Anchor Restaurant* could now serve about a hundred people outside, and another fifty inside, though the inside was primarily the *Rusty Anchor Bar*.

There was evidence of Sidney and Naomi's input here and there—Naomi was Sid's niece. Though still a locals sort of place, Sidney had convinced Rusty that "local" didn't have to mean just Marathon. With the number of people the two of them knew up and down the hundred-mile-long archipelago, they could draw in a much bigger crowd. Sidney booked entertainment and advertised the length of the Keys and soon, the *Rusty Anchor* had become a lot busier and more profitable than it'd ever been. But it still held firmly to that old Conch spirit. Rusty ran the bar, Sid ran the restaurant, and they both ran the marina.

As we strolled along the dock, we said hello to a few people we met and stopped to talk to Deuce and his wife, Julie, aboard their Whitby ketch, the *James Caird*. Julie was Rusty's only child, and she and Deuce now had a pair of tow-headed boys, who were nowhere in sight.

"Where's Trey and Jim?" I asked, accepting the offered beer from the cockpit.

The couple had honored both their fathers in naming the boys. Deuce's full name was Russel Livingston, Junior and that name was passed on to the oldest boy, who logically became Trey. Had Russ, Senior still been around, I think he would have liked being the Ace in the threesome. The younger boy was given Rusty's first name, James.

"They took off with buckets a couple of hours ago," Julie replied.

"Said they were going to find treasure," Deuce added. Then he turned to Sara. "How's your dad?"

Sara's father, John Wilson, had suffered a heart attack during the summer and had to spend nearly a week in the hospital. He'd stayed with me and Jimmy on the island during the rebuild, while most of our other friends and hired contractors went back to Marathon each night or stayed aboard *Ambrosia*. At seventy-four, he'd worked right along with us, setting a grueling pace for some of the younger workers who were half or a third his age. The heart attack was mild and it had happened quite unexpectedly the week after we'd declared the island fully habitable and he'd returned home.

"He's a pain in his doctor's butt," Sara replied. "Stubborn as a mule and twice as thick-headed. But he's doing a lot better, thanks."

Deuce and I owned a security consulting business in Key Largo. His dad and I had served together in the

Marines and Deuce was once a Navy SEAL officer. He and I had worked together for Homeland Security for a time. Both of us, along with the people we employed, also did contract work for an oceanographic research company on occasion, as did Julie, Sara, and John. But what we did for Armstrong Research seldom had anything to do with science.

Spotting Rusty on the back deck, I yelled and waved him over. He turned and shouted something through the open back door. Sidney came out, and together they made their way toward the *James Caird*, followed by Kim and Marty.

To say that Rusty and Sid were an unusual pair would be an understatement. Rusty was five-six and, though he'd lost a good bit of weight recently, he still tipped the scales at nearly three hundred pounds. His head had always been bald, and his bushy red beard was about half gray now. Sid was five or six inches taller, and a good hundred pounds lighter. She'd been a Playboy bunny in her early years, and still had the looks, with piles of auburn hair and a ready, gleaming smile.

"When's this party supposed to get started?" I asked, shaking my old friend's hand and pulling him in for a man hug.

"Jimmy's gonna open the gate in about an hour," Rusty replied. "But a lot of people are already here."

"I can see that," I said, nodding toward the end of the canal, where a segment was reserved for smaller boats.

It was crammed full of all manner of small craft, from dinghies to sleek flats skiffs.

Kim leaned over the rail and gave me a big hug, and then embraced Sara, as I shook my son-in-law's hand with a shoulder bump. After pleasantries were exchanged and we'd caught up, Kim nodded toward the end of the dock; her way of telling me she had something to share that others might not need to know. I followed her down to where the Grady was docked at *Salty Dog's* stern.

"Where's Eve?" I asked, worried because they apparently hadn't come down from Miami together.

"She's not coming, Dad. Something came up."

Kim's older sister and I didn't see eye to eye on a few things, but it wasn't like we were estranged. The first weekend of every month, Eve and her husband, Nick, would bring my grandson down, and Nick and I would take Fred fishing. Later, when Anna was born, it was just Nick and Fred who came down from Miami. I got to know my son-in-law a lot better when Eve wasn't around. He was more guarded when she was. Now that Anna was a toddler, Eve also made the trip and took her to see things or to the playground.

"Something came up?"

"Mom's in town."

"Sandy? Here?"

I'd talked to my ex-wife only three times since we divorced; about once a decade. Kim had come to the Keys to find me ten years ago, and Eve had done the same not long after that. They quickly learned I wasn't the kind of man their mother had told them I was.

"Not *here*, here," Kim said. "She's been staying with Eve for the last couple of weeks."

"Why? Is something wrong?"

"Kamren—the guy she's been living with since we were kids—well... he was murdered two months ago. According to Mom, she barely got away and has been receiving threats ever since."

"Kamren?" I'd known of him, but he'd always been called "the boyfriend" or something; never a name, and I'd never asked. "How? Where?"

"Up in Virginia," Kim said. "They were hiking, and she'd left the trail to look at something. Two guys came along and started roughing Kamren up, asking where Mom was. She'd hidden in the bushes and watched them knock Kamren to the ground and shoot him in the back of the head."

She said it without emotion. I'd never pried into Sandy's life with either of my girls. Was there something there, or was Kim in cop mode and simply digested the information weeks earlier?

"Have the police caught the guys?"

Kim shook her head. "No. Mom even recorded it with her phone. But the cops said the video doesn't show their faces. Dad, she got a threatening email to her private account, saying that she can't hide in Florida, either."

She went on to tell me that Sandy and her boyfriend had gone to Staunton, Virginia about an environmental problem concerning livestock waste polluting the headwaters of Chesapeake Bay.

I felt torn. Sandy and I had split up right after Kim was born. She'd left me on Christmas day after my unit had deployed to Panama unannounced. I'd hated her for years but understood why she'd left. Being married to a Marine infantryman wasn't an easy life.

I'd only had a few short conversations with Sandy since then—none recently. As a person, she no longer meant much of anything to me—just a stranger I once knew. But she was also the mother of two of my daughters, so anything that hurt their relationship would naturally appear on my radar. And if whoever was threatening my ex found her at Eve and Nick's house, that put them all in danger. Including my grandkids, Fred and Anna.

I looked out over the water to collect my thoughts. "What steps has Nick taken?"

Nick and his father, Alfredo, were a father-and-son law firm. We'd once been adversaries, but now we got along okay. The father was cordial, but I always sensed a respect born of fear. I'd long ago accepted their apologies and Nick had gotten past what had happened on Elbow Cay—men they'd hired to steal a treasure tried to kill me and my friends. Several people died as a result, and the original *Gaspar's Revenge* had been blown out of the water.

"He's filed a protection order," Kim replied. "Since the email sender wasn't known, that opened the door for a subpoena to the internet provider. The email address turned out to be bogus, and all the provider would say was that it originated from the Virginia area."

I didn't know a lot about such things, but I did know that emails could be tracked to a more precise location than just a state. And I also knew who could find that information.

"I'll make a call," I said. "See if we can't find out anything more."

"We?"

"She's your mom, Kim. Anything that bothers her affects you and Eve."

"And anything that bothers us, you kick the snot out of?"

I shrugged. "Something like that."

"I'm a cop, Dad."

I gave her a crooked grin. "Fish and Wildlife."

She knew I was kidding and that I was very proud of the path she'd taken. Kim was an excellent cop, in or out of the water. She and Marty were responsible for a couple of pretty big drug takedowns.

"You're still a knuckle-dragging Neanderthal, Dad."

I pulled her to my side, my arm around her shoulders. "Sometimes the world needs a knuckle-dragging Neanderthal."

CHAPTER TWO

We sat around Deuce and Julie's boat for a while longer, catching up on all the news and gossip. Finally, with a glance up at the sun's position, Rusty called Jimmy on a portable VHF radio and told him he could open the gate.

The entrance to the *Rusty Anchor* wasn't concealed, but there weren't any flashing neon arrows like on Bugs Bunny. In fact, there wasn't any kind of sign out there at all. Just a mailbox, which had been leaning since Hurricane Donna hit Marathon when Rusty was an infant. The "gate" was nothing more than a rusted chain between two posts. It effectively blocked the crushed shell driveway, which just vanished into lush tropical foliage like many other properties in the Keys. A casual passerby would think it was a private home. And it had been for a long time. Rusty's house was forty years older than the bar.

Jimmy's voice came over the speaker. "Cars are backed up on the shoulder all the way to Kmart, man. Must be a hundred of them. A bunch of people walked, and there's a good-sized crowd around me, man."

Rusty took Sidney's hand. "We'd best get to work, babe."

I rose and followed them, pointing toward the stage, where several people were working. "Who's playing?"

"Oh, we have something special lined up," Sidney said. "We're calling it 'Writers Circle.' A bunch of local song-writers will be onstage together, all unplugged."

"Anybody I know?"

Rusty chuckled. "Like you know *anyone*. Get off that rock of yours once in a while, bro."

"Scott's coming up from Key West," Julie said.

Sidney nodded. "And Eric's supposed to be here, but he called and said he'd be a little late. His motorhome was overheating up in Key Largo, and he's having to load his equipment into the car he pulls behind it. He's bringing a friend, too. Dan is already here, along with a few others; Todd Sparks, Jack Mosely, Sheree Cade, and Todd Trusty."

"Julie's gonna sit in, too," Rusty said.

"All onstage at the same time?" I asked, recognizing most of the names. "That sounds great!"

We walked together toward the bar as Sidney continued. "Harry Teaford and Gonzo Mays are out back setting up."

I looked to Rusty for help.

"Harry's with Radio A-1-A," he said, "and Gonzo's the *official* unofficial mayor of Key West."

"So, what are they setting up?" Marty asked as he and Kim walked hand in hand with us.

"Radio A-1-A will be doing a remote broadcast and it'll go out on Pyrate Radio," Sidney replied. "And Eric usually does a Facebook Live event when he plays."

"Going worldwide, huh?" I said. "That's a big audience."

"You know about that stuff?" Rusty asked me. "Streaming radio, the Facebook, and whatnot?"

"Jimmy and I listen to Pyrate sometimes," I replied. "We don't exactly live in a cave up there."

Since they'd replaced the cell tower on the north end of Big Pine Key, Jimmy and I were able to get a good signal on our regular cell phones. He had an unlimited data plan and streamed Pyrate Radio and other stuff from his phone to an excellent wireless speaker system on his porch. The two of us tried to play along sometimes, but neither of us was all that good. Mostly it devolved into an argument over what chords were being played. We both had tin ears, so figuring out a song took some time. It was just a way to pass the idle time, which we didn't have a lot of. Some of the songs Pyrate played made me want to sail away, and the few short commercials were for places all around the Caribbean, further reinforcing the urge.

As we reached the deck, pickups and a few cars started streaming into the new, enlarged parking area. Once inside, I saw there were already quite a few familiar faces. I matched most of them to the many small boats at the dinghy dock.

Dink was regaling a couple of the other guides with one of his outlandish sea stories and had just reached the end. "Then it jumped over the bow and spit that fly right into his tackle box."

The others laughed and Dink stepped back, nearly falling over a table. I managed to grab his shirtsleeve to keep him on his feet. Dink had perpetual sea legs. On his skiff's poling platform, he was like a six-foot ballerina, but the moment he stepped on shore, he was more ungainly than the proverbial drunken sailor.

"Thanks, Jesse!" Dink offered. "Haven't seen you around in a couple of months. Where ya been?"

"Off island for a while," I said, moving over to my usual spot at the far end of the bar. "Working a find in the Windwards."

"Hope it pans out for y'all," Dink said, and returned to his group of buddies.

Kim and Sara took the remaining two stools at the bar, leaving me, Deuce, and Marty standing.

Julie stepped up on her toes and kissed Deuce. "Gotta get to work."

"You're working?" he asked, apparently surprised.

"Why not?" she said, as she slid behind the bar and headed into the office with Rusty.

The front door opened, and several people came in. I recognized some from around Marathon and a few other faces seemed familiar, but most were people I'd never seen before. Glancing out toward the parking lot at the stream of vehicles pouring in, I knew the place was about to get busy.

"She always liked taking care of the guides, fishermen, and other locals," I told Deuce. "She's kept a lot of good ol' boys in line since she was tall enough to see over the bar. Next to poling across the flats, it used to be her favorite thing. But this place is filling up with people I don't know."

"Seems like mostly people from the Keys," he said, nodding to a couple who'd taken a seat at a window table. "Those two live at the same marina where we berth the *Caird*; Jason and Tammy something. I don't think they ever gave a last name."

I leaned over to whisper in Kim's ear. "Can you get your mom to send you that email and then send it to me?"

"I already have it," Kim replied. "What do you need it for?"

"So Chyrel can find out who it came from," Deuce said, leaning in with a grin. He shrugged his shoulders. "Julie read about what happened on the internet. When you step on one toe, we all say ouch."

"You knew?" I asked.

"Since about two weeks ago," he replied, then leaned in closer. "Tony and Andrew are watching Eve's home. Just as a precaution."

"Why didn't you say something?"

"And what would you have done?"

He had me there. "Put Andrew and Tony on her house."

"Just saving you the trouble. I'm sure it's nothing."

"Probably," I agreed. "Sandy pisses a lot of people off. But they're mostly loud-mouthed activists."

Kim pulled her phone from her back pocket. "How do you know?" she asked as her thumbs moved across the screen with a speed that I couldn't follow.

"I don't really. Just basing an opinion on past experiences."

When she shoved her phone back in her hip pocket, my own phone vibrated in mine.

"Thanks," I said, pulling it out.

"Chyrel's probably driving," Deuce said. "Just wait till she gets here."

I nodded.

"I've had a few pleasant enough conversations with her," Marty offered about his mother-in-law. "She seemed like a nice lady. A bit nervous, maybe, but Kim and I were both in uniform. I don't think she likes guns very much. Or maybe the uniforms made her jumpy."

I raised an eyebrow to Kim.

"Her stance on guns is her choice," she said. "One that she makes on her own. I choose my own way."

Rusty and Julie came out of the office and he moved behind the bar, coming to the end where we were. Julie grabbed stacks of menus and joined Naomi, passing among the tables and taking orders.

"Dad said to tell you good luck," Sara said to Rusty. "Not that you need it. He also said he wished he could be here."

"Just another day," Rusty said.

I looked around the room. It was already nearly as full as I'd ever seen it and people were circulating out on the deck, as well. This wasn't going to be "just another day" at the *Rusty Anchor*.

"You got anyone else working?" I asked. "It looks to me like you're getting slammed."

"Jimmy's gonna help behind the bar," Rusty said, placing a beer in front of Dink and making a mark on a pad beside the register. "And Sid's out back with Robin and Pam."

Robin was a flirtatious blonde who used to work at Dockside, back when I lived on my boat there. Since it was still closed from the storm, she worked at the Kmart and picked up shifts at half a dozen other bars whenever someone called in sick.

"Can you use another server?" Kim asked cheerfully.

"You wait tables before?" Rusty asked.

"Up in Gainesville."

"You're hired," Rusty said, with a sideways glance to me. "Fifty bucks for the night, plus tips, same as Pam and Robin, and all you can eat."

Kim reached across the bar and shook Rusty's hand. "Done."

"Julie and Naomi can cover in here. Pam's got the stage mostly. Ask Sid how to split up the rest of the tables outside."

"Let me know when you go on stage," Sara said, touching Julie's arm as she came back. "I'll cover your tables."

I spotted Eric Stone out on the back deck, talking with Dan Sullivan and another guy. I excused myself and followed Kim outside.

"Hey, Jesse," Eric said, as I approached.

Dan turned and grinned. "What's the craic, boyo?"

"Looks like you'll have a fine crowd," I replied, feigning a snap left jab at Dan's face.

His head bobbed to the side and his hand suddenly appeared where my fist stopped. He lightly tapped my knuckles with his forefinger, then pointed at his ear. "Over here."

Dan and I sparred together now and then. He was quite good and had lightning-fast reflexes.

"I'm getting by," I said, shaking hands with both men.

"Have you met Don?" Eric asked, introducing the other man.

He was a big guy, younger than me, with a goatee starting to show a little gray. The lines around his mouth and eyes reflected a fun personality.

"Not sure if I want to after that greeting," he responded, then stuck out his hand and smiled. "Don Middlebrook."

I recognized the name and shook his hand. "I've heard your songs. Name's Jesse McDermitt."

"You play, Jesse?"

"Learning," I replied. "I wouldn't quite call it playing yet."

"Took me a while before I could put two chords together." He chuckled. "Then I wrote some two-chord songs."

"Get you guys anything?" Pam asked.

They told her what they wanted, and she hurried off. Pam Lamarre worked at the local bank during the day and managed a couple of my trust funds. She returned quickly and explained, "I only have you guys and the two tables by the stage, so just nod if you need anything."

I spotted Chyrel walking from her car. "Good meeting you, Don," I said, leaving the group and waving at her as I hurried across the lawn.

"Hey, Jesse," Chyrel said as I got near. "Good to see ya."

She gave me a quick hug and stepped back. "What's up?"

"Did you bring your computer?"

"No, but I have my phone," she replied, digging into her bag. "What do you need?"

"I have an email from someone in Virginia. I need to know…"

"The email to your ex, threatening her? I already have it."

"You do?"

She took my arm and started for the door. "Buy me a drink and I'll tell you all about it."

CHAPTER THREE

The Thanksgiving feast and celebration continued through the evening, quieting only for sunset. There was never a water view of the setting sun from the *Anchor*; it never occurred far enough to the south to be visible even from the back of the property. But watching the sun come up over the bight happened almost year-round, except for a few weeks around the winter solstice, which was fast approaching. Still, people paused and looked toward where the sun slipped below the mangroves that lined the far side of the canal.

Chyrel told me that the email to Sandy had originated from a rural part of Virginia, not far from the town of Staunton, but cautioned me that the area identified might not be where it came from at all, since IP addresses sometimes changed. It being a rural area, she explained, she felt certain she'd isolated it to one of several farms clustered in the area.

There were more people at the *Anchor* than I'd ever seen before. The crowd did seem to be primarily Keys people, mostly local, but I met others from all up and down the hundred-mile archipelago. There were also a few tourists, but they didn't seem the cruise ship or fly-in type. Most could have passed for locals; the women were tanned and the men scruffy-faced. It was lobster season and a lot of Floridians traveled to the Keys every weekend to dive for the crustaceans. And Thanksgiving weekend meant four days of diving instead of two.

The friend Eric brought with him, he'd introduced as his fiancée, Kim. She struck me as a very upbeat, happy woman, with a touch of an accent. Upper-Midwest or even Canada, I figured.

He'd also brought along a young woman by the name of Isabella Stefania and her dad. She looked like she could still be in high school, and since she was with her father, she might have been.

As the musicians went around the circle, each spoke about song writing, and played and talked about songs they'd all written. The others played and sang along, all knowing one another's work.

When it came to her turn, Isabella described a song she'd written about a Sea Ray boat. As she talked, Julie brought out her guitar and took a seat next to the young woman. The two of them played and sang the song in harmony; a positive tune that the crowd really enjoyed.

While Julie sat in, Sara attended to her tables, keeping drinks filled and faces smiling.

Deuce leaned in and whispered, "What are we going to do about this thing up north?"

"We?" I asked.

"We're all family," Deuce said. "What affects one affects all."

"I was thinking *Island Hopper* needs to stretch her wings."

"You're going up there?"

"Yeah," I replied. "Just to poke around."

"Who's going with you?"

"Just me," I said.

As Julie and Isabella finished the song, the crowd cheered loudly, complete with a few whistles and cat-calls. The two women's voices blended well and even I knew some of Isabella's songs. When Julie started to rise, the other musicians asked her to stay a bit longer. She looked toward Sara, who waved her back to her seat.

"I'd feel better if you'd let me or one of the guys go with you," Deuce said, as his wife joined Isabella in another of her songs.

Marty leaned in. "I have a week's vacation. Be more than happy to tag along."

My son-in-law used to be a Monroe County deputy, but like Kim, he now worked for the Law Enforcement division of Florida Fish and Wildlife. He was quick-witted, reliable, honest, and capable.

"Thanks, Marty, but like Deuce said earlier, it's probably nothing. Just some irate farmer. I'll be gone three or four days, max."

"And I assume you're leaving in the morning?" Chyrel asked.

"Right after Sara flies out," I said, as Sara approached the table, smiling.

"This is fun," she said. "Reminds me of my college days. I've already made ten dollars for Julie."

I grabbed her around the waist and pulled her close. "Don't have too much fun, galley wench."

She cupped my face and turned it upward, smiling sweetly. Then she kissed me deeply. "I get off later tonight, sailor."

"Me too," I whispered with a lewd grin.

Julie asked if she could play a song that she'd written herself, and before the others on stage could say anything, the guides and other locals in the audience started chanting, "Way Back, Way Back."

"The stage is yours," Don told her.

She started playing a simple melody. Those who frequented the *Anchor* back in the day knew the song well. She'd written it about the back country many years ago, when she was a teenage flats guide.

Within a few strums, Eric and Sheree had the rhythm and began playing along as Julie sang about the sun, water, sandbars, and islands. Many people in the audience sang along.

Trey and Jim came running, Finn dancing along beside them. The boys crowded around Deuce, and Finn plopped down beside me, his tail wagging. The boys watched their mother sing and play and they really seemed mesmerized by all the attention she was getting.

"Who is she?" I heard someone at the next table ask.

Trey's head jerked around at the question. Dink was standing behind the man who'd spoken and leaned in. "She was once one of the best flats guides in the whole Keys, man."

Trey looked up at his dad. "Mom was a guide?"

"That was before I met her, son," Deuce said, tousling Trey's mop. "Uncle Jesse knew her then."

Both boys looked up at me expectantly, as I absently scratched Finn's neck. "That's right," I told them. "When your mom was no bigger than you, Trey, she could out-fish any boy on this island."

They turned and listened to Julie singing the words to a song I know I'd heard a thousand times as she'd worked on it. She painted a picture with words and melody, describing a place that was no longer a part of her life. I could see in the two boys' eyes that they were not just hearing but seeing and feeling what she described.

The song ended to a chorus of applause. Julie blushed and rose from her seat. "Thanks, y'all," she said with a big smile. "But I gotta get back to work."

Sara made her way toward the stage and brought Julie to our table. "Sit down a bit, while I check on your tables."

"Wow, Mom!" Trey shouted, as both boys hugged their mother tightly. "That was so cool!"

In the Keys, the traditional Thanksgiving meal of turkey and dressing was always accompanied by fresh seafood and Rusty had pulled out all the stops. Rufus had put the turkeys in his new smoker at noon and had been preparing since sunrise. While the music played, platters of grilled mahi, grouper, snapper, hogfish, lobster, and stone crab claws were placed around the birds for the revelers to help themselves. All the seafood had been supplied by local fishermen. Most people took a little of everything after paying ten dollars for a meal ticket. Stubs allowed seconds.

After midnight, as the crowd started to diminish, Sara and I made our way down to the *Salty Dog*, Finn trotting ahead of us.

"What were you and Deuce talking so seriously about?" she asked, as she stepped up onto the *Dog's* side deck and ducked under the Bimini.

How does a guy tell his girlfriend he's taking up his ex-wife's cause? I decided that with Sara, the truth was the only way.

"Kim and Eve's mother is being threatened," I said. "Her boyfriend was murdered up in Virginia. I'm gonna fly up there to poke around."

"Will you need help?" she asked, as I unlocked the hatch and opened it for her. "I can take some time off."

I followed her down the companionway and slid the hatch closed, pulling the double doors shut and latching them. I wasn't sure what kind of reaction I'd get, but the one I got wasn't one of them. Over the last couple of years, I'd learned a lot more about Sara. She didn't talk much about herself or her past, but I knew her to be quite capable with many weapons or no weapon at all.

"No need," I said. "I'm only going to be gone a few days; just sort of a recon mission to see what's going on and what isn't."

Sara turned to starboard, heading down to the aft cabin. She stopped with one hand on the companion-way rail and looked back at me. "And your ex is staying with your daughter in Miami?"

That was more the response I'd figured on.

"Yes, she is," I replied. "Sandy is Eve and Kim's mom. I can't just ignore a threat that might put Eve and her family in jeopardy."

She smiled. "I'll take 'Good answer' for $1,000, Alex."

With that, she took my hand and dragged me toward the master stateroom and the huge bed that occupied most of it. Well, *dragged* might not be the right word, but there did seem to be a sense of urgency to get there.

CHAPTER FOUR

I woke to the smells of bacon and coffee. Either scent would be enticing, but combined, they were downright overpowering. I rose from the bunk and pulled my skivvies on, then padded barefoot up the steps to the galley.

As I worked the kinks out of my neck and shoulders, Sara looked up from the stove and smiled. "We need to work on your stamina when I get back."

My mug was already sitting beside the coffeemaker. I filled it and took the first sip. "You're an insatiable woman, Sara Patrick. What time's your flight?"

"The company plane is coming from Baton Rouge to pick me up in less than an hour."

I took another sip of Rusty's greatest discovery to date; the Tarazzu blend from Hacienda la Minita.

"Need a ride over to the airport?"

"Julie said she'd give me a lift. She's taking the boys in her car and Deuce is going to solo their boat. When are you leaving?"

I slipped my arms around her narrow waist from behind and kissed her neck. "I was hoping we'd have a little more time this morning."

She turned inside my embrace and kissed me. She was wearing nothing but a T-shirt. "Can't," she said, breathing in my ear.

"Why not?"

I already knew the answer. The job.

She pushed me away, though I could tell she didn't want to, and turned her attention to the stove. "*Ambrosia* will be weighing anchor at noon and I have to meet a helicopter in Port of Spain. It will take me out to the ship as she comes out of the Orinoco River." She slid an omelet from a skillet onto a plate already piled with bacon. "Sit down. You need protein."

Sara nibbled on a couple strips of bacon from my plate as I devoured the rest. For some reason, I was always hungry when she was around. We talked about everything except what was on both our minds; my trip to Virginia and hers to Belize.

Armstrong Research conducted oceanographic studies all over the world, primarily focused on cleaning up the environment and on more efficient and safe ways to get oil from the ocean floor. Sara was first mate on *Ambrosia* and she was a skilled mariner, working hard to make the ocean a cleaner place. On certain occasions I was called on to clean up *other* problems. So, we were often apart.

Together, we washed up the dishes in the galley and put everything away. As we stepped out into the sunshine, Sara's phone rang. She answered it, as Finn trotted off toward the shoreline to see what might have floated up during the night.

"I'm on my way," Sara said, then ended the call.

"That was Rick," she explained, as we walked toward Deuce and Julie's boat. "They're twenty minutes out."

Julie stepped up out of the cabin of their ketch and waved. "You ready?"

"Yeah," Sara shouted back. Then she turned toward me. "Be careful up there. There's no water for you to hide in or escape to, just woods and mountains."

I had to grin, thinking back to similar mountainous training areas covered with dense woodlands. "I'll be fine," I told her, slipping my arms around her waist. "I'll call you when I get there and when I get back."

She looked past me toward my plane, *Island Hopper*. "Three or four days, right?"

"Yeah," I replied. "Piece of cake."

"We'll be on station off Belize by then."

"I could come down when this is over. Great diving if you can get away for a day."

"We'll play it by ear," she said, kissing me softly. "Once we're on station, I can probably get away for a few days."

As she turned and walked away, Julie waved to me and joined her. Finn came trotting up as Sara and Julie climbed into Julie's yellow Cherokee. He nudged my hand and I scratched absently at the side of his face.

After they drove off, I headed up to the *Anchor* with Finn. When I entered, Jimmy and Naomi sat on opposite sides of the bar, chatting.

"You taking off, dude?" Jimmy asked, slipping Finn a small piece of ham.

"Yeah," I replied. "Thanks for taking care of Finn for me."

"He's the one takes care of me, *hermano*," Jimmy said, rubbing Finn's neck. "Right, *mi amigo?*"

"I should be back Monday. Tuesday, at the latest."

Rusty came out of the back office. "You sure you don't need to take someone with you?"

"Just a simple recon mission," I said, rolling my eyes at my old friend. "Anyone else would just slow me down."

"Uh-huh. You know you're not twenty-five anymore, right?"

We said our goodbyes and then I headed out to the plane, grabbing my bags and locking up *Salty Dog* on the way.

Thirty minutes later, having done a complete inspection of the plane, I started the big radial engine and taxied down the new boat ramp and into the water, raising the wheels once she was floating.

I planned to follow the coastline all the way to Wilmington, North Carolina, not just for the view, but also because the Intracoastal Waterway afforded a lot more and safer emergency landing places than highways or airports. Not that I anticipated trouble, but knowing

I had a place to bring the old girl down easy was comforting.

From Wilmington, I planned to turn north for the last leg up to Virginia. I called Miami Flight Center and requested flight following, then repeated back the squawk code they gave me as I entered it.

The engine in the deHavilland Beaver roared as I advanced the throttle, and the old amphibian gathered speed quickly. The floats made a smooth, whooshing sound on the calm water, which diminished as the *Hopper* rose higher on the surface, then disappeared completely as we became airborne.

I turned out over Key Colony Beach and kept the long ribbon of U.S. Highway 1—Useless One as we called it—to my left. I adjusted the tinted visor to block the morning sun, just ahead and off to starboard.

Island Hopper had a range of about 450 miles with a ten percent reserve. The airport northeast of Staunton was just over a thousand miles away, going the route I was taking. With an added fuel cell, I could make it with one stop, but I planned to refuel in St. Augustine and Wilmington just the same. That would put my arrival close to sunset.

Settling in for the long trip, I leveled off at 3,500 feet as the many islands that make up the Florida Keys slipped past, one by one, in a slow curve toward the mainland. Nearing Biscayne Bay, Miami diverted me farther out over the water to avoid air traffic at one of the busiest airports in the country. Once clear of their airspace, I flew along the white, sandy beaches of the Gold Coast at 4,500 feet.

Beyond the sparkling beaches, I could see I-95 and the Florida Turnpike, which ran parallel to one another. Both were crowded with holiday traffic; people heading home after the obligatory Thanksgiving dinner at grandma's house.

My mind drifted to my ex-wife, Sandy. We'd met just after I'd returned to Camp Lejeune from Okinawa. I'd just turned twenty, and she was nearly eighteen, fresh out of high school. She'd been a beautiful girl; tall, with long, wavy hair the color of honey, and a bright smile. She was a lot of fun to be with in those days.

She'd promised to wait for me when my unit deployed to Lebanon just four months after we'd met. I remembered not holding out much hope for that. It was a four-month deployment and that was a long time for a pretty eighteen-year-old girl.

But she did wait and we'd resumed our relationship with a new fervor when I returned. Sandy became pregnant and we'd married in a small ceremony on base. I reenlisted two weeks later and was subsequently promoted to sergeant.

Less than a month after we married, my unit was rotated back to Lebanon for what was to be another four-month tour. It turned out to be a little longer. During that deployment, a suicide bomber in a truck full of explosives destroyed our barracks in Beirut and killed 220 of my brothers. I'd been one of the lucky ones, out on a mounted patrol near the airport. We'd had to fight our way back to the barracks to set up a perimeter, allowing the clean-up to proceed. I could still remember the smell.

When I'd returned home after the bombing, I'd sensed a strain in our relationship. I knew that I had changed after the attack. Many of those who perished were friends; it would have jaded anyone. I'd tried to hide it, to shield Sandy from the pain I felt, the loss of people she barely knew. In the last months of her pregnancy, Sandy hadn't known if I was one of the 220 Marines killed or not. She'd only found out through the chaplain, who'd asked her help in notifying the other wives.

When Eve was born, just six weeks after my return and three days after Christmas, it changed everything in my eyes. I became a father and was suddenly confronted with what that meant as a Marine. I learned to change diapers efficiently and sanitarily in either boots and utes or in my dress uniform. I stayed up when Eve was cranky and Sandy worn out. More than anything, fatherhood gave me a greater sense of my own mortality, and a sense of what would happen to others should anything happen to me.

When Eve was just three months old, the Corps transferred me to the drill field, and we moved to Parris Island, South Carolina for Drill Instructor School. My days were very long then; out of the house a couple of hours before sunrise and not returning home until late in the evening. When I picked up my first platoon of recruits, I stayed in the squad bay on duty every fourth day. Sandy and I rarely saw one another during those two years. They were tough times.

While on the drill field, I was promoted to staff sergeant, and at the end of my tour we'd been transferred back to Camp Lejeune. Sandy seemed to like that. She was happy to be back in familiar surroundings, with family and friends close by. I reenlisted again, figuring things were going well. And they did go well for a couple of years. My job became routine, there wasn't a whole lot going on in the world, and I started to relax and enjoy life with my little family.

We were expecting our second child when I received orders to report to the battalion landing team of the newly reformed 1st Battalion, 9th Marine Regiment— the Walking Dead. I was with the BLT's recon platoon, where I felt most at home. Late that spring, we received orders for a WestPac—a West Pacific cruise. Looking back, that was probably the lynch pin of our breakup.

WestPacs were typically six-month deployments aboard naval warships, and I wasn't there when Kim was born.

Just weeks after returning to Camp Lejeune, I was transferred to the newly formed Fleet Anti-terrorism Security Team. FAST Marines were highly trained individuals, ready to deploy at a moment's notice to protect Navy and Marine Corps assets from terrorist attacks anywhere in the world. That was just before Thanksgiving in 1989.

Just days before Christmas and a week before Eve's sixth birthday, my team was ordered to Panama. No planning, no discussion, no phone calls, just grab your gear and go. Sandy didn't even know I was gone until the next day. By then, we'd already been inserted and my squad had made first contact with enemy forces. From there it quickly deteriorated into a waiting game for Noriega.

When I got home, the house was empty. I found out from neighbors that Sandy had packed up and left on Christmas Day. I felt lost and lived on autopilot, pouring my soul into the job. That summer, I was promoted to Gunnery Sergeant, eleven years and three days after first stepping on the yellow footprints at Parris Island. It was to be my last promotion.

I'd only talked to Sandy a few times since then. Her father had hired a hot-shot lawyer from Raleigh and in my absence had managed to get her full custody and a restraining order; hard to overturn in North Carolina. I tried.

After refueling the plane in St. Augustine and again in Wilmington, I started my overland leg up to Shenandoah Regional Airport, with the sun falling away to the west. Looking off to the northeast, my eyes followed the sweep of coastline and I could just make out Onslow Bay and Cape Lookout, where Sandy and I had spent many weekends.

The rest of the flight was uneventful, and I landed at Shenandoah Regional just as the sun slipped below the

hills. On approach, I saw what looked like a fl ying boat parked on the grass just off one of the private aprons north of the runway. I got another glimpse as I taxied toward the fi xed base operator.

It was a Grumman Goose with U.S. Air Force markings. Probably owned by a collector. I would have loved to have one of those old fl ying boats one day. Unlike *Island Hopper* with her big Wipline fl oats, a fl ying boat was just that; the fuselage was a boat hull and the wheels retracted into the sides for water landings. They had small floats on the wingtips to keep the wings out of the water, but they fl oated on their hull-shaped fuselage.

CHAPTER FIVE

At his desk in his home office, Aiden Pritchard was just finishing a brief for a case in which he would be representing the Commonwealth of Virginia over the coming weeks. It was a slam dunk as far as Pritchard was concerned; the forensic evidence was overwhelming and indisputable.

As he reached for the desk lamp to turn it off, his phone rang and he picked up the receiver. "Assistant Attorney Pritchard."

"It's Lou," a man said on the other end. "We have a problem."

Pritchard sat back in his chair and glanced at the open door. He could hear the TV in the family room and his wife rattling around in the kitchen, preparing dinner. "Is it concerning what I think it is?"

"Yeah," Sheriff Louis Taliaferro replied. "The judge is breathing down my neck wanting results. He wants to know where the witness disappeared to."

"I know, Lou. He's giving me a hard time, as well."

"You need to do something, talk to them."

"I will," Pritchard said. "I already called Luke. He's getting the others together for a meeting after dinner."

"Good," the sheriff said. "We don't need that kind of problem."

"I'll take care of it, Lou. See you tomorrow at brunch."

"Maybe we can swing some clubs afterward?"

"I don't see why not," Pritchard replied, grinning. "See you then."

After dinner, Pritchard told his wife he had to meet someone in town and would be back by ten, then headed out to his new pickup in the driveway.

The drive was a short one, but it wasn't into town. Instead, he turned onto a dirt road that led up into the mountains west of his property. He found the spot halfway up and parked next to Luke's pickup. Jeb's truck was there, also, but not Stuart's.

He'd better have ridden with one of the other two, Pritchard thought, stepping out into the darkness.

He reached behind the seat, took a long, black flashlight from a pouch and switched it on before striding toward the trail head. The meeting place he used with these men was easy to find. But the lights of anyone who came up the mountain would be visible to them and they'd hear another vehicle for miles.

After a hundred yards through the woods on the worn path, he could see the light of the small fire. The two men sitting on logs around the well-used fire pit rose as Pritchard approached them.

"It's me," he called out to his two nearest neighbors.

The flickering light of the small flames played across the men's faces and cast dancing shadows around the campsite as all three sat down.

The two men Aiden had come to meet were older than him by a couple of decades, with gray stubble on their chins. They had been friends of his father. Though dressed in appropriate attire for a wilderness camp—jeans, flannel, and a light jacket against the promise of the fall's first frost—Aiden was clean-shaven, with a recent haircut. His demeanor exuded authority.

"You know why I called you up here," Aiden said.

"Yeah," one of the men admitted, poking at the fire with a stick. "Look, Aiden, I didn't know Stuart was gonna shoot the guy. You gotta believe that. We was just gonna rough 'em up and let 'em know they wasn't welcome 'round these parts."

"Water under the bridge," Aiden said. "We can't go back and change that now." Secretly, Aiden didn't care that Stuart had shot the tree-hugger. As far as he was concerned, Stuart and Jeb should have found the woman and killed her, also. The two strangers had come for one thing only; to stir up trouble.

Again, water under the bridge, Aiden thought.

Aidan Pritchard looked at the two older men, fixing them with penetrating, dark eyes. "I don't need to remind you that we have a lot on the line here. We don't need a bunch of environmental activists sending DEQ up into the hills to inspect your fencing."

Pritchard, though only thirty-six years old, was one of the wealthiest and largest landowners in the Shenandoah Valley. As an attorney and officer of the court, he was very familiar with the comings and goings of agents who worked for Virginia's Department of Environmental Quality. But what concerned him more was what those agents might stumble upon if they lost their way on the slopes of the Blue Ridge Mountains and ended up on his property.

"We know that, Aidan," the first man said. "We sided with your pa long before you were born. But you know how Stuart can be sometimes."

"He's your cousin, Jeb," the other man said, turning to his old friend. "You was there. You shoulda never let that boy carry a gun."

"I got no control over him," Jeb fired back. "Hell, Luke, he used to be married to your niece. You know damned well nobody tells Stuart what to do." Jeb poked at the fire with the stick and muttered, "Boy's nuts ya ask me."

"Why isn't he here?" Pritchard asked. "He's late."

"He was making a run down to Lynchburg," Jeb replied. "A hundred gallons at a good price. Won't be back till near midnight."

Pritchard stared at Jeb until the older man looked up. "So, where is the woman now?"

"Miami," Jeb replied, still stirring the embers. "Staying with kin." He tossed another log on the fire, sending sparks flying up into the night air. He looked up at Aiden. "Stuart's a bit hotheaded sometimes, but the

Army trained him with computers and stuff real good, and he's a smart boy. Said the bitch left a paper trail a blind man could follow."

"Judge Whitaker is pissed," Pritchard said. "He's been all over Sheriff Taliaferro to get to the bottom of this and he's leaning on my office, too. Lou's one of us, but he can't stall the new judge forever."

Aiden pronounced the sheriff's last name *Tolliver*, though it was spelled completely differently. It was a common name in central Virginia, going back to pre-Revolutionary War days, and the pronunciation had become more Americanized over the ensuing two-and-a-half centuries. Pritchard's own family had settled the valley in the early 1700s, as had the two older men's ancestors. Nearly everyone in the valley was related through marriage or birth if you looked back far enough. Those that weren't were newcomers to the valley.

"Does Stuart know where in Miami the Sneed woman is staying?"

"Yeah," Jeb replied. "He knows. She musta hid out here for a coupla weeks, then flew out of Shenandoah Regional, headed straight to Miami."

"What should we do?" Luke asked.

Pritchard's eyes moved from one man to another. "Finish the job."

Jeb swallowed hard. "You mean..."

"When Stuart gets here," Pritchard said, rising, and brushing the back of his jeans, "tell him to pack. He's going to Florida in the morning."

CHAPTER SIX

C hyrel had arranged a rental for me, a green Ford four-wheel-drive pickup. I didn't have anything to haul—it would just be less conspicuous where I was going than the typical rental sedan.

There was a bite in the air as I exited my plane. I'd dressed for the woods and brought a jacket, knowing it would be considerably cooler in central Virginia than in the Keys. Just a few years ago, I didn't even own a jacket. But Armstrong Research sometimes sent me places where one was needed.

After refueling *Island Hopper* and tying her down, I gathered my gear and carried it to the private fixed base operator's building. There, I received the keys to the pickup from a pretty twenty-something FBO agent and headed outside.

I stowed my gear in the small backseat of the extended cab pickup and climbed into the driver's seat. The truck was nice, but I doubted it would have the off-road capability of *The Beast*, my ancient-on-the-outside

International Travelall. But it *was* equipped with a navigation system.

On my phone, I pulled up the addresses that Chyrel thought Sandy's threatening email had come from. I punched the information into the GPS and the mechanical voice told me to proceed to the route and the guidance would start.

Before leaving, I called Sara to let her know that I'd arrived okay and was going to be checking into a local motel soon, but she didn't answer. Not unusual. She never carried her personal cell phone with her when she was on the bridge, and *Ambrosia* was probably miles out to sea by now. So, I left a message and told her I'd call again before I left Virginia.

I knew I wasn't going to be able to just walk up to a farmhouse and ask the owner for their ISP address or if they'd sent a threatening email to my ex. I'd have to snoop around the three farms and see if I could figure it out.

The GPS told me the first address I'd entered was thirty-five miles away, straight down I-81 and north of Staunton. I left the airport and was quickly headed south on the interstate.

Less than an hour later, I was driving west out of Staunton on Virginia Highway 254 toward Buffalo Gap. It was a two-lane blacktop that passed houses, farms, and fields, but little else. Turning southwest on another state highway, the GPS told me that my first waypoint was half a mile ahead on the left. With no other vehicles on the road, I slowed as I approached the first address.

There was a heavy gate across the entrance, barbed wire extending from it in both directions, and a cattle guard below the gate. A cattle guard was nothing more than a trench with a wide grate made of pipes across it to support vehicles. Cattle wouldn't walk on it, so it served as a barrier to keep them in when the real gate was left open.

There was only a number on the mailbox. I debated checking the box to see if I could get anything from an envelope, but at this late hour, I was sure they'd collected any mail. I already had the names of the landowners, anyway. Chyrel had given me a brief report on each one. None had much of a recent criminal background, save a few traffic citations and a bar fight or two, and one was a lawyer. She said she'd dig deeper and would send me an update.

Far down the track, I could see buildings, a couple with lights on, but I couldn't tell if they were barns or homes. All three addresses were on this same road, so I started watching mailboxes for the next one.

Ahead, a car turned out of a sideroad on the right, going the same direction I was. I slowed to let it get farther ahead, as I continued to look for the next mailbox.

When I got to the second address, it was where the car had pulled out of, so I decided to follow the car. Again, the entrance was gated, with barbed wire fencing and a cattle guard. This one appeared a bit more upscale, with a sign over the gate that said, "Pritchard's Ramble" and fresh paint on the gate itself.

Aiden Pritchard was one of the names on the list, a lawyer and wealthy landowner who worked in the prosecutor's office.

The vehicle ahead turned out to be a pickup, though I didn't get close enough to determine what make it was. I let it get half a mile ahead, in case the driver got nervous. After two miles, the brake lights came on and the pickup turned off the road to the right. As I got closer, I could tell it was a dirt road by the glow of the truck's tail lights in a rising plume of dust.

Slowing, I reached back and grabbed my tactical backpack and set it on the front passenger seat. Then I pulled out my night-vision goggles, turned them on, and perched them on my forehead. When I reached the spot where the other truck had turned off the main road, I doused the headlights and pulled the night optics down over my face.

This road wasn't gated, so I figured it was a public road, but I didn't want to take any chances. The tail-lights of the other truck glowed in the gray-green light of the night optics, subduing my visibility when I looked toward it, as it adjusted to the brighter light. I lowered my head, so that the lights wouldn't interfere, and the optics adjusted again, providing better visibility of the road ahead. Every now and then, I looked up to see where the truck was.

After ten minutes, the truck's brake lights came on and it turned to the left. When I reached the place it had turned, I found that it was just a curve in the road, deeply rutted. Ahead and higher up, I saw the truck turning back to the right; a switchback. A quick glance at the GPS told me that the road zig-zagged up the side of a mountain.

Steep mountains would be impossible to drive straight up, so roads are often built to follow the contour of the land, rising less steeply along the flank and turning back in the opposite direction to continue the climb.

I followed the truck at a safe distance for the next thirty minutes, until it pulled off the road. The reverse lights flashed as the driver put it in park, then the inside light came on.

Finding a safe place, I slowed and idled off the road, using the parking brake to stop, so no light would come on. I put the Ford in neutral, mashing down hard on the parking brake. Before I opened the door, I made sure the inside lights were in the off position.

Exiting the pickup with my tactical pack, I quickly shouldered it. My Sig Sauer P229 was holstered under my shirt, behind my back. I moved quickly up the hill toward the truck, not really knowing what I'd find or who.

When I reached the other vehicle, it was parked with two more pickups. The one I'd followed was a newer model Dodge Ram, but the other two were at least ten years old and showed a lot of wear; work trucks or farm trucks.

Approaching cautiously, I didn't see anyone or any movement. I scanned the area slowly. There was a faint glow coming through the trees and I occasionally saw a light bouncing and swinging from side to side.

I felt the hoods of the other two trucks, they were both warm. All three had just arrived. Moving as quietly as possible, I followed a foot path that didn't get a lot of use. As I got nearer, I recognized the glow as a campfire. The guy with the flashlight was moving toward the fire and I could hear voices.

I moved off the foot path, making my way quietly through the dense woods and rocky terrain. The trees were mostly hardwoods—oaks, maples, and sycamores— but as I started up out of a dry creek bottom, there were occasional stands of pines, which I recognized as hickory pines. I tried to keep close to them as I made my way toward the fire, flanking the guy with the flashlight. The dense cover of sound-dampening needles and lack of undergrowth allowed me to get ahead of him. It was still slow going, and as I neared the fire, I moved quickly and silently from tree to tree.

The man I'd followed approached two other guys, who were sitting around a small fire, the light from which would mean the three wouldn't be able to see more than ten feet beyond its soft glow, as they subconsciously stared into the flames. I moved to a position behind a deadfall, where I could peer under the trunk

and see all three men quite clearly from just fifty or so feet away.

The two men saw the flashlight approaching and stood. I hunkered down to see what happened next. Men didn't meet in the middle of the night in the woods to discuss the weather.

CHAPTER SEVEN

When I got to a hotel on the outskirts of Staunton at 2300, I was still digesting all that I'd heard up on the mountain. I checked in and got a room with a patio that had a southern exposure; I needed to talk to Deuce on the sat-phone. Before I could get it out of my pack, my encrypted Armstrong cell phone rang. I pulled it out of my pack instead and answered it.

"Hey," a voice said. "It's DJ."

"DJ Martin?"

I could hear salsa music in the background and the sounds of people talking and laughing. DJ had been one of a group of new operators I'd met aboard Armstrong's big research vessel when I'd first signed on. He'd later helped me and John Wilson take down a murderous cult in the BVI. I remembered he was a former Army spec-ops guy, who'd lost a leg in Afghanistan. I also remembered that not hampering him during his training with Armstrong.

"I was wondering if I could ask your advice," DJ said.

"My advice? Are you drunk?"

"Pretty much," he replied, unashamed. "Do you remember Jerry Snyder? He and his wife were with us on Norman."

"Yeah," I replied. "John was trying to recruit him."

"Well," DJ said, drawing the word out slightly. "I've been partnered with him for an op."

"He seemed capable," I commented, wondering where this was going.

"He is. That's not the problem."

"So, there is a problem?" I asked.

"I don't know if you noticed, but he's kind of a stick in the mud when it comes to rules and shit."

"And you like working alone," I said, starting to understand.

"Not so much that," DJ said. "We're just polar opposites, man. I'm more of a door-kicker. Ask a question and if the answer isn't forthcoming, break a finger."

"I see," I said, grinning.

The man was a lot like myself in my younger days. Hell, even more so after I left the Corps. I've bent and broken my share of rules.

"He's stifling, Jesse. Everything's gotta be straight from the book. Ever met anyone like that?"

A younger Deuce Livingston immediately flashed into my mind. When we'd first met, Deuce, as well as the two SEALs with him, Tony Jacobs and Art Newman, were the consummate professionals, everything according to the prescribed rules of engagement.

"Yeah, I have, DJ. You just described my partner Deuce."

"The big SEAL guy that was with you on *Ambrosia*?"

"One and the same," I replied.

"How did you guys make it work?"

"It takes time," I replied. "Just like a relationship with a woman. You have to give and take, accept and demand, until both people become more like the one in the middle."

"You sound like that old blind guy on Kung Fu."

I laughed at the comparison. "How long have you guys been working together?"

"Just one op, but where we're headed next, I don't see any way around busting some heads."

"Then bust them," I said. "You'll know when negotiations have ended before he does. Sometimes, that knowledge will be only seconds ahead of incoming fire. Easier to ask forgiveness than permission."

"I've gone that route once already."

"He's a smart guy," I said. "He'll pick up on things; sometimes it'll be after you, and hopefully before the shit storm starts. Give it time, brother."

"Thanks, Jesse," DJ said. "I just don't want to see the guy get hurt, if there's something I could have done to prevent it."

"Keep in mind," I said, "it's a two-way street. There may come a time when you think the only way forward is to bust someone's head, but Jerry knows a way around.

You'll both make mistakes. Talk out the situations afterward and learn from them."

"Thanks, again," he said and ended the call.

I put the Armstrong phone back in my pack, removed my personal satellite phone, and went out to the small patio to call Deuce on the video link.

"Get to Virginia without any problems?" he asked, when his face appeared on the screen. I could tell that he was aboard his boat and out on the water.

"Yeah, and I already identified three of the players and the killer."

Deuce's face leaned in closer to his phone. "What?"

"The triggerman is a guy named Stuart Lane. His name was one of the three Chyrel gave me."

"How do you know that so fast?"

"Dumb luck," I replied. "The three addresses were clustered together and as I did a preliminary drive-by this evening, a pickup came out of one of the driveways, so I followed it. It came from the property Chyrel identified as belonging to the assistant prosecutor, Aiden Pritchard. He met with two of his neighbors. One was Luke Wright, another one Chyrel identified. The third man is Jeb something, not one of the three addresses."

"Better lucky than good," Deuce said.

I grinned. Pap used to say that a lot. Said he got it from a baseball player named Lefty Gomez who had played ball when Pap was a kid.

"Who's watching Eve's house now?"

"Tony is there until midnight."

I looked at my watch, surprised at how much time had passed. "It's nearly that now. Pritchard told the other two to tell Lane to pack, he was leaving for Florida in the morning."

"Andrew will take over at midnight and be there until noon," Deuce said. "I'll have Paul back him up first thing in the morning, and Tom can back up Tony in the evening, so two will be there."

"Thanks," I said.

It made me feel better knowing that the guys were already on the alert. They'd be able to keep an eye on Eve's house without them even knowing. Tony Jacobs had served under Deuce when he'd commanded a SEAL team. Paul Bender used to be on the presidential detail of the Secret Service, and Andrew Bourke was a burly former Maritime Enforcement specialist with the Coast Guard. The last man, Tom Broderick, was once my commanding officer in the Corps. He'd been injured in Afghanistan and lost his hearing. His ability to read lips made him a valuable asset in a lot of circumstances—stakeouts being one. All were very capable, highly intelligent, and some of my closest friends.

"What are you going to do now?" Deuce asked.

"They're up to something up here," I replied. "And it doesn't sound like anything legal. The three men met way up on a mountain road, then hiked to a campsite. I overheard Pritchard tell the others that he didn't want Environmental Quality agents snooping around."

"Any idea what it might be?"

"I overheard that Lane was delivering a hundred gallons of something at a good price. In this area, that probably means only one thing."

"Illegal liquor."

"You got it," I said. "I got a room for the night and tomorrow I'll see if I can single one of those guys out."

"How do you plan to do that?" Deuce asked.

"No idea," I replied. "Hoping for more luck."

"You're due."

"Let's hope it holds out," I said. "You sailing alone?"

"Sailing *now*, yeah," Deuce replied. "The wind died to nothing right after I left the *Anchor*. Been motoring most of the day. It finally picked up about an hour ago, so I killed the diesel. I'm about five miles from the marina. Be there in less than an hour."

"Julie'll be worried."

"Just got off the phone with her before you called," he said with a chuckle.

"I just got off the phone with DJ Martin. Remember him?"

Deuce's laughter became a bit heartier. "You don't say. Is he having a problem with his new partner?"

"How'd you know?"

"Jerry Snyder called me a couple of hours ago. Said he needed some advice on how to handle a loose cannon, and since you and I are partners, he figured I could give him some tips."

It was my turn to laugh. "DJ was asking how I dealt with such a stick in the mud."

Deuce's face turned serious. "Think they'll make it?"

I half grinned in response to his earnestness. Deuce hadn't changed a whole lot, but he was a bit more liberal with force today than he used to be. I knew that my association with him has made me a better man.

"I'm counting on it," I said. "These are the guys who will take the place of the dinosaurs."

"You're the dinosaur," he said. "I'm still a young man."

"You shoulda brought Trey," I said grinning back at my friend. "He's a better navigator."

He laughed and we ended the call. It was a long running joke between us, that went back to before we even met. Deuce had been an officer and I was an enlisted man. It was often said around Marine squad bays that the most dangerous thing on the battlefield was an officer with a map and compass. It was all in jest, though. Deuce was one of the best tacticians I'd ever known, even better than his dad, whom I'd served with decades ago.

I knew Deuce would take care of things there and would have Chyrel working on the four men, digging up anything and everything she could that I might use or exploit. Which basically meant everything there was to know about them. Things that their own mothers wouldn't know. Things that were illegal for her to know and pass on to me. But we'd all decided a long time ago to play by the bad guys' rules—none.

Chyrel didn't look for evidence to use in court, and a lot of what she did was illegal. But only if she got caught. And she never got caught. She'd once hacked into the

CIA's main computer, which she said was easy. It was getting out and closing all the firewalls that was hard. I had no idea what she'd meant, but it was the CIA's computer. That alone meant something.

If Stuart Lane showed his face anywhere near Eve's house, the guys would quietly pick him up.

There was something stinking in the Shenandoah Valley, and it was bigger than cows crapping in the water. I could feel it.

Taking my laptop from its case, I powered it on and stripped down to my skivvies while I waited for it to boot up. Then I spent the next thirty minutes learning what I could on my own about the men I'd seen up on the side of the mountain.

Stuart Lane had a Facebook page and was friends with both Aiden Pritchard and a guy named Luke Wright, who looked just like the guy at the campsite. Looking through all three of their friends lists, I didn't find anyone named Jeb. And here I thought I was the only one who didn't use "the Facebook" as Rusty called it.

"What's Jeb short for?" I mumbled to myself.

Jebediah, maybe. I didn't see that name either.

I dug into each man's profile, reading their recent posts and going through their profiles, page by page. Both Luke and Stuart were farmers, judging by the pictures they posted. Luke liked trout fishing and they were both hunters, too. That presented problems, but nothing I was overly concerned about. They were both divorced—no big surprise there—and that would make things easier if I met up with one of them. No innocent bystanders.

This was way beyond any sort of environmental problem. Since hearing Jeb utter the statement about shooting Sandy's lover, my mind shifted to tactical mode. A man had been murdered and the apparent leader of this bunch of wack jobs was a well-placed attorney who had just ordered another hit. On my ex-wife. I saved Pritchard's Facebook page for last.

He was married and had two kids. He hadn't entered very much on his personal Facebook page, or he had privacy settings that prevented me from seeing it, but he also had a separate professional page, which was apparently public. His boss had just been reelected for another term, which I guessed meant that Pritchard would still have a job. At least for the foreseeable future. He hadn't posted anything new on his public page since the election three weeks earlier. Before that, he was touting his boss's successes almost every day. In the Corps, we called that brown-nosing, a deeper form of kissing ass.

A ping alerted me to an incoming email. It was from Chyrel. She said she had Lane's preliminary workup complete. I opened the attached file; it was pretty lengthy for a rush job. She'd probably already started with the three landowners upon identifying where Sandy's email had come from. The file contained all the basics, stuff that was readily available to the public, if you knew where to look. I decided to set up the little coffee maker and get a shower before delving into Stuart Lane's background.

Ten minutes later, I returned to the computer and carried it to the bed, along with a steaming cup of java in a paper cup. I stretched out, placed the computer on a pillow I'd propped on my legs, and then took a sip of the coffee.

When I opened Stuart Lane's file, I found a picture at the top with a physical description. He was a big man—six feet tall and 245 pounds. His head and face were shaven and his eyes were sullen, set deep in his skull, which made it look as if he had dark circles around them. Beneath his heavy, pronounced brow, his nose seemed a little crooked. A cruel-looking mouth with thin lips completed the picture.

In his younger days, Stuart Lane had had a few encounters with local law enforcement. He was forty-nine now and had remained fairly clean for the last few years. Before that, he'd had countless traffic citations, two charges of trespass involving domestic violence, two charges of vandalism occurring at about the same times as the domestic violence charges, and five for drug possession, going back to his seventeenth year. All but one of the possession charges had been dropped. He had done three months in the county lockup for simple possession, pleaded down from a felony charge of possession of ten pounds of marijuana with intent to distribute. He'd also been charged with several counts of disorderly conduct, public drunkenness, and assault and battery. He'd been a person of interest in the disappearance of a nineteen-year-old girl five years ago. All those charges were dropped as well.

Pritchard had been his lawyer, prior to moving over to the prosecutor's office. I knew Chyrel would find all the ways these men were connected. It was just a matter of time.

Lane owned the property he lived on, free and clear. He'd inherited it from his parents, who were both deceased. Property records went back more than two hundred years, with the land remaining in the same family name since 1810.

If Lane's tax statements were to be believed, he lived just below the poverty line, showing a loss for three of the last five years.

The man had to have a side gig; something that paid cash and was probably illegal. The "hundred gallons at a good price" that Jeb had mentioned was obviously moonshine and that was where Lane made his undeclared money. Even at just ten dollars a gallon for rotgut, that was a grand in income that I'm sure he didn't report on his taxes. With little or no overhead, a thousand a week could go a long way. If all four men were involved, it could be pretty lucrative.

I pulled up Google Maps and found that Lynchburg was seventy-five miles away. That got me thinking as I finished my coffee. A 150-mile round trip in the mountains was a long way. Only two reasons came to mind for going that far to make a grand—one being that he was cautious and didn't want to sell moonshine locally. Lane's criminal record showed that he hadn't been a careful man.

What had changed four years ago to make him toe the line? Maybe that was when Pritchard became involved in the operation, keeping him in check. His uncle Jeb couldn't do it. He'd said so himself: "Nobody tells Stuart what to do."

But Pritchard was a different kind of animal. I could see it in his eyes and the way the two older men kow-towed to him. He was dangerous in a different way than Stuart Lane.

Another reason for delivering to Lynchburg, one that fit in with all I'd learned so far, would be that if they had a large distribution system, Lynchburg was just one place they delivered. If Stuart had just been making his routine weekly run, Pritchard wouldn't have needed to know *where* he was going. A moonshine pipeline, as opposed to local selling, probably meant more produc-tion than a hundred gallons a week. My guess would be that they made a similar run several times a week, maybe daily. Both Jeb's and Luke's trucks were worn out, but not old.

High demand usually meant a good product. Ten bucks a *quart* was still cheap whiskey, but if it was half good, it could easily bring that, and if they were produc-ing a hundred gallons just two or three times a week, there could be $10,000 a week changing hands. Jack Daniel's Tennessee whiskey could run up to thirty dollars at a liquor store for less than a quart.

Maybe that was why Pritchard didn't want DEQ stumbling around on his property. He had the means to build a high-tech distillery. Who would suspect an assistant prosecutor? If his property was large, he could hide a state-of-the-art still in a barn or something. One large enough to produce a higher quantity of top-shelf corn whiskey—with a good distribution system to several locations—might be a $50,000 a week operation. Even to an assistant prosecutor, that was big money.

I went back to Lane's file. He'd served in the Army for two-and-a-half years. That sent up a red flag. Normal enlistments were six years, usually four years active duty and two years in ready reserve.

His MOS—his job in the Army—had been Information Technology Specialist, but he'd been charged with theft of government property—several computers—and sentenced to three months at hard labor, forfeiture of all pay and allowances, and given a general discharge.

I closed the computer and placed it on the nightstand. Setting my alarm for 0600, I decided to get some rest. I wanted to get close to one of these guys, but not Pritchard. The others would have guns, and I'd rather go up against an armed man than an unarmed lawyer. For now.

CHAPTER EIGHT

When my phone vibrated its alarm, I rose and turned it off. After setting up the coffee-maker, I dressed and repacked my stuff. I wouldn't be returning to this room. I tried to make it a habit to stay in different places whenever I was away from home. Ten minutes later, I shrugged into my jacket and was out the door, coffee in hand.

I remembered not having passed anything that looked like a restaurant after I'd turned off the bypass the night before. The motel I stayed at was at the east end of the loop, so I drove back around to the north side of town and, instead of turning north on US-250, turned south toward downtown.

I found a small diner on the edge of town, just a couple of miles from the loop road. Though it was early, there were already a number of vehicles in the parking lot. Most of them looked like farm trucks. I backed my rental into a corner spot, aimed straight toward the exit, and got out.

From my pack, I pulled out a worn Caterpillar hat and put it on. My boat, *Gaspar's Revenge,* has twin Cat diesels, and a mechanic who'd worked on them a year ago had left it aboard. Caterpillar also made heavy equipment and was once the leader in heavy truck-engine manufacturing. The hat was a suitable disguise for this part of the country.

The air was crisp and cold, not a cloud in the sky. A light breeze from the north carried the scent of burning firewood. I looked around. A maple tree in the corner of the lot, between the spot I'd chosen and the one adjacent to it, had shed most of its leaves. They covered the small patch of grass and a good bit of the two parking spots. The winter solstice was just a few weeks away and soon this part of the country would get its first snow. As I strode toward the diner's entrance, I hoped the weather would hold off until I left. I hadn't seen snow in a long time. That was one of the reasons I'd decided to retire to the Keys.

When I opened the door, warm air and half a dozen pairs of eyes greeted me. I scanned the inside of the diner, as if looking for a table. I didn't see any of the three men I'd observed the night before up on the mountain. The early diners were all men—farmers, by the look of them. Men who worked with their hands and backs, growing food from the soil. As one, they assessed me and then returned to their meals and conversations. I wore jeans and a flannel shirt under a denim jacket with work boots on my feet. My hair was short, there was a three-day stubble on my chin, and my skin was dark from long days in the sun. I didn't stand out among this group of men. Had we all been shirtless, it would probably have been different. I doubted their tans went below the neck.

There was a long breakfast counter lined with stools against the wall to my right. It ended before reaching the back wall, where a hall led to the right—I assumed toward the restrooms and kitchen. There were two more stools on the far end. I moved toward that spot and took the one next to the flip-up access for the waitress. A quick look down the hall revealed the kitchen entrance, two doors marked *Men* and *Women*, and a third marked *Private*.

A matronly-looking woman with graying hair piled on top of her head came over and asked if I needed a menu. Her name tag read *Madge*.

"No, thanks," I replied. "Three eggs, over medium, double bacon, hash browns, toast, and coffee."

As she scribbled on her pad, she asked, "What brings you to town?"

It was an innocent question. Small restaurants in towns like this had a regular clientele. The other men in the place had probably been coming here every morning for most of their lives. It was the nearest diner to the farms north of town. Which was why I'd chosen it. Although I blended in physically, I was an obvious stranger.

"Just passing through," I said, with a crooked grin. "Delivering parts south of here in a couple of hours."

She poured coffee from a stained pot. "Mountain Valley Diesel?"

"Yeah," I lied.

"They usually open around eight," she said. "Sometimes nine. I'll get your order right in."

"Thanks, Madge."

I scanned the patrons once more and saw nobody I'd consider a threat. The door opened and two men came in. They greeted several of the others by name, stopping to talk to one older man before taking a table near the opposite wall.

My breakfast arrived quickly, and it was good. I ate slowly, then lingered over coffee. A while later, the door opened again. Jeb and Luke came into the diner together. They said hello to a few people as they made their way to the breakfast counter. Both men were taller than I'd first guessed; probably close to six feet.

Jeb stopped to talk to the same older man the earlier two men had talked with. I used my phone and subtly took a picture of the man. He was probably in his sixties or early seventies, clean-shaven, with close-cropped silver hair and a distinguished-looking face.

Jeb joined Luke at the counter, a few stools down from where I sat. Both men nodded a greeting. I nodded back, taking a sip of my coffee. I was hoping Stuart Lane would stop here for breakfast before heading to the airport.

The waitress approached, stained coffee pot in her hand, and I nodded. I liked coffee. At times, I liked it strong enough to float a horseshoe. In my early years as a Marine, I would often turn the hot plate on to heat up the previous day's remaining brew, instead of wasting it. Day old Marine lifer juice would float a battleship.

The waitress poured more of the steaming, dark liquid into my cup and left the check. The meal was a good bit cheaper than I'd expected.

Luke looked back at the older man who seemed so popular, then said in a low voice, "Why you suckin' up to him?"

I pretended to be studying the check as Jeb looked around. "He's the new judge. Never hurts to be on the good side of the law."

"He's just another newcomer," Luke grumbled. "Ain't been here for more'n twenty years."

"That may be so," Jeb said, "but he's the law now. You get Stuart to the airport on time?"

"As if I don't get up early enough as it is," Luke replied, smiling as the waitress approached. "Yeah, he was on the first flight to DC."

Both men placed their breakfast orders, then the waitress came back to where I was finishing my coffee. "More?"

"No, thanks," I replied. "Gotta get going. The food was good."

As she started to turn away, I reached across and touched her arm. "Say," I said, whispering just loud enough for Luke and Jeb to hear, "is there a liquor store around? One that's open in the morning? I need to pick up a gift for a friend."

"What kinda gift would you be gettin' in a liquor store?" she asked.

I grinned and laid it on a little heavier, as I covered the check with a twenty. "My boss likes to sample local stuff. You know, legal moonshine?"

"Stay on Highway 250 toward the interstate," she replied. "There's two ABC stores before you get to it. One about a mile-and-a-half from here on the left, and another on the right just before the interstate."

"Thanks," I said, pushing the check for the ten-dollar meal toward her, along with the bill. "Keep the change."

She picked them up and smiled before moving down the counter to the register. I tipped my mug to my lips, though it was empty, and made a show of getting ready to leave. The bait was dangling.

I pulled my coat and hat on, looking around the restaurant once more. As I passed the two farmers, Luke looked up and nodded. "Couldn't help overhearing," he said in a quiet voice. "I might can help you out, without having to go through Virginia ABC."

The bait was noticed. Time for the teaser.

"There's a closer liquor store?" I asked. "I'm a little pressed for time."

Luke looked at Jeb, who glanced around the restaurant before leaning in closer. "Not exactly," Jeb whispered. "And not really what you'd call legal 'shine, neither."

"You mean—"

Jeb moved his hand in a downward motion. "Not so loud. You got another twenty?"

"I do," I said quietly, leaning closer to the two men. "But I'm not interested in rot gut from a car radiator."

"This ain't like that, mister," Luke said. "Best corn squeezin' in the valley."

"Thanks," I offered. "But like I said, I'm in a bit of a hurry. I have a delivery to make."

"Got a coupla jugs right out in the truck," Jeb said, with a wink.

"Is that right?" I offered, grinning crookedly, setting the hook.

Luke's chair scraped the floor as he stood up. "Won't take ya but a few seconds," he said. "And best of all, no taxes to the guvment."

"Lead on," I said.

"Be right back," Luke told Jeb.

I followed him toward the door. It didn't escape my attention that he stayed far from the judge's table.

Outside, I spotted Jeb and Luke's trucks, parked nose in, a few spots from my own. Luke walked straight toward the blue one.

"You ain't the law, are you?"

"The law?" I asked, shaking my head. "Nah, I just deliver parts. Got a drop-off at Mountain Valley Diesel as soon as they open, then back to Norfolk. But if I was the law, wouldn't I say I wasn't?"

Luke opened the passenger door to his truck, then looked around the parking lot. "Maybe, maybe not." He opened a box behind the seat and pulled out a quart jar. "But they're supposed to say if you ask 'em."

"Is that right?" I said, amazed at the guy's ignorance.

"This is made local, from local corn. Try a snort."

The lid to the mason jar was on tight. I screwed it off and held the jar to my nose. The liquor had a faint caramel color and a powerful smell. I took a small sip. It was stronger than the rum I usually drank. It had a good taste just the same, with a hint of oak and cherrywood.

"Oh, that's good," I said, putting the lid back on. "Tastes like it was aged a bit?"

"Not long," Luke said. "Just enough to add some color and flavor. That's from last year's run. Eight months in a cherry barrel, then finished a couple more months in charred oak. That's a-hunert-and-sixty proof hooch right there."

I pulled my money clip from my pocket. "Ten bucks, you said?"

The man smiled, showing yellow, stained teeth. "No, it was twenty, was what I said."

"Oh, yeah." I took a bill from my clip and handed it to him while stuffing the jar under my jacket. "Ya know, my boss might be interested in getting more of this. Ever been to Norfolk?"

"We can deliver down there," Luke said, pulling a cheap cell phone from his pocket. "Minimum's ten gallons and the price is the same. More'n ten gallons, it's only fifty bucks a gallon, though."

"How can I reach you?"

"Get your phone out and call me," he replied, holding his phone up. "Then I can save your number as a trusted customer."

He was careful, I gave him credit for that. If the law ever checked his phone records, they'd see that I had initiated the calls.

My cell phone was a little different than most. It had a second number that Chyrel could make disappear. Since I was coming up here, she'd changed the second number to a Virginia area code. I pulled it out of my pocket and when I touched the phone icon, I quickly switched it over to the burn number. Luke gave me his number and I punched it in, then hit the *Talk* button. His phone rang and he looked at it.

"Says Newport News," he said, looking up from his phone.

"Yeah, that's me. Name's Stretch Buchannan. Newport News is just across the James River from where I work in Norfolk."

Luke tapped the screen a few times, saving my burn number. I'd have Chyrel delete it later.

"All set," Luke said, pocketing his phone. "Give me a call and we'll work something out. When you call, tell me how many gallons of 'gear oil' ya want, and I'll know what ya mean."

Luke turned and headed back to the diner.

"Thanks," I called out after him.

I got in the truck and immediately called Chyrel. She answered right away, as if she had her phone in her hand.

"Can you pull up my burn number and put a trace on the last number I called?"

"Deuce's oldest boy can do that, Jesse."

"I keep forgetting who I'm talking to," I said, starting the truck's engine. "Is there a way you can patch any calls to or from that number to my phone, so that they can't hear me?"

"Well, Trey can't do that yet, but yeah, I can. Who is it?"

"His name's Luke Wright; one of the three landowners you said Sandy's email might have come from."

"Deuce told me this morning that you already ID'd the guys and learned which one killed your ex's boyfriend. That's fast work, even for you."

"I got lucky," I said. "Also, I'm going to send you a picture of a guy. I think he's the local judge. See what you can find out about him."

"You think he's involved?"

"No, just the opposite. But I want to be sure first. These guys seem to be involved in a pretty large-scale moonshine business."

"We call it white lightning back home."

Chyrel was an Alabama girl, but had worked for Deuce for many years now. Before that, she'd been a computer analyst for the CIA.

"I just bought a quart from Wright for twenty bucks."

"I'll get the call forward set up and get to work on the judge's background. I emailed you a file on Wright and the other guy—Pritchard? Is Luke Wright close to the third man, Jeb?"

"Yeah," I replied, putting the truck in gear. "They were just having breakfast together. They seem close."

"Good. I can cross-reference calls from Wright's number and probably find his last name. Then I can get some intel on him, too."

I drove out of the parking lot and turned right. "He's likely the least interesting of the bunch. Nothing about him strikes me as anything other than he appears; a farmer."

"I'll get right on it. If Wright makes or receives a call, your alert tone will be the theme song from Cops. You know, '*Bad boys, bad boys, whatcha gonna do?*'"

"Sometimes I think you enjoy your work too much," I said, then ended the call.

I drove fast. Jeb and Luke would take at least fifteen or twenty minutes to eat breakfast. I could stretch that to twenty-five if I hauled ass. That would be plenty enough time to get to one of their houses, locate a computer and email Chyrel to check the IP address.

The rental Ford ate up the miles quickly and I braked hard for the turnoff. With no other vehicles in sight,

I got to Luke's driveway and turned in. The gate was closed, so I jumped out to open it.

Back in the truck, I drove quickly down the double ruts of the driveway, keeping track of the time. I left the gate open, knowing I'd only be there for a few minutes and the cattle guard would keep any livestock from straying. My biggest concern was a dog.

The road led to a small farmhouse. There wasn't anyone around and there were no other cars parked outside, or in the covered carport beside the house. I turned the truck around and left the keys in the ignition before jumping out and running straight to the front door. If anything would get a dog going, that would.

I banged hard on the door and waited a few seconds. Wright made it too easy. The door was unlocked. I swung it open and called out in an urgent voice in case there was anyone there. No answer.

And no dog.

Moving quickly, I checked out the living room in the front of the house. It looked like it didn't get much use. Same with the kitchen. Luke probably ate every meal at the diner. The dining room table seemed to be the catch-all for mail and magazines. That room was where I found a desktop computer on a small desk in the corner.

When I moved the mouse, the screen came to life. I opened a browser in private mode and typed in a web address. When the page loaded, I signed in and composed a quick email and hit *Send*. Then I logged out and exited the browser. Being in private mode, there would be no history, and even if there was, Wright would have to know my login information.

When I got back outside, I climbed into the truck and started it up as I fumbled with my phone. After hitting the *Talk* button, I put it on speaker and headed for the open gate.

"I got your email," Chyrel said, instead of the usual hello or hiya.

"Is it a match?"

"No, Wright wasn't the one who sent the email to your ex."

"Damn," I said, as the truck bounced over the uneven terrain. "He and the Jeb guy were at a diner I just left when I talked to you earlier. I doubt if I have time to check Jeb's house. Besides, he doesn't strike me as the computer type."

"Speaking of," she said, her tone becoming serious. "You couldn't have been more wrong about that guy. His name is Jebediah Long. He did a fifteen-year stretch at Virginia State Penitentiary in Richmond, from 1975 to 1990, for involuntary manslaughter. The prison was built in 1800 and closed down in 1991. It had a rep for being a real hell-hole."

"Really?" I said, bringing the truck to a stop just outside the gate. I got out to close it, grabbing up the phone as I slid off the seat.

"Yeah, and the third guy, Stuart Lane, he was a person of interest in another murder in 2014. That one is still unsolved."

After closing the gate, I returned to the truck and headed back in the direction of town. "Any details on Long's conviction?"

"He served fifteen years of a twenty-year sentence for the beating death of a man named Justin Kiernan, who had been dating Long's older sister. She committed suicide a couple of weeks before the murder and Long blamed Kiernan."

Ahead, a blue truck was coming toward me. I pulled my hat down lower and held the phone to my ear, turning my head slightly to the right until the truck went by. It was Jeb Long, not Luke.

"And the unsolved murder in 2014 that Lane was a suspect in?"

"A local woman, Grace Masterson. She was twenty-one at the time of her death; a known prostitute and crack addict."

"Any interesting details in that murder?"

"The lead investigator at the time was Louis Taliaferro."

Chyrel had pronounced the name exactly as its obvious Italian origin would dictate.

I mocked a Virginia drawl. "That's pronounced Tolliver around these parts, thank ya ma'am."

"For real?"

"Same as Staunton being pronounced without the U," I said. "Families here go back to not long after the Pilgrims and the local dialect is...well...local."

Lou's one of us, I remembered Pritchard saying about Sheriff Taliaferro.

"Find out anything you can on him. He's the sheriff now."

"Will do," Chyrel replied.

"Anything yet on the judge?" I asked, turning back onto the main road toward town.

"Judge Oliver Whitaker," Chyrel said. "Originally from Pittsburgh, where he was a prosecutor for ten years before retiring and moving to Staunton. He ran for circuit court judge four years ago after the death of his wife and was just reelected by a landslide. He's spotless. His wife was killed in a drive-by and the police suspect it was gang-related; still unsolved."

"That's a lot of unsolved murders and disappearances for such a small town. Got an address for Judge Whitaker?" I asked.

"Sending it to your phone's GPS now."

"Thanks, Chyrel."

"Anything else?"

"Stuart Lane was on the first flight out of Shenandoah airport this morning, connecting in Washington. Can you find out what his arrival time will be and let Deuce know?"

"Already got it pulled up," Chyrel responded. "He's connecting through Dulles and Newark, arriving Miami at 3:20 this afternoon. I'll let the guys know."

"Thanks," I said and ended the call as I approached the ramp for the bypass.

I pulled over onto the shoulder and opened the GPS app. I saw a flashing bullseye just north of downtown, not far from where I was. It looked like it was only a couple of miles from the courthouse and about the same distance to the diner.

I made another phone call. It went straight to voicemail, as I'd hoped it would. I left a quick message and then hit the *Directions* button on the GPS app.

Judges don't usually work on Saturday, so I figured he'd be home at some point after having his breakfast.

CHAPTER NINE

The phone in Aiden Pritchard's home office rang just as he was about to leave for the barber shop and meet with Lou Taliaferro afterward. He returned to his desk and picked up the receiver. "ACA Pritchard."

"It's Lou," came his friend and cohort's voice over the phone. "Can we push back our appointment an hour or two?"

Pritchard sat down and checked his date book. "Sure," he said, scanning his calendar. "How about noon?"

"Same place?"

"Yeah," Pritchard replied. "But I won't have time for a round afterward."

"Sorry," the sheriff said. "Can't be helped."

"See you there at twelve, then."

Pritchard hung up the phone, wondering why the sheriff would change the meet time. The two of them met at least daily during the week to discuss pending cases, always at the end of the day. But this meeting was about personal business.

He picked the receiver up again and called the barber shop to reschedule his haircut from ten to eleven, the time he'd originally planned to meet Lou, so he could take care of both tasks in one trip. Then he left the office, taking his coat from the rack by the front door.

"Tell Lou I said hello," his wife said from the living room, where she was playing a board game with the kids.

"That was him on the phone," Pritchard said, pulling his coat on. "He moved our meeting to noon, so I'm going up the hill to check on things at the old barn before I go to the barber."

Sylvia Pritchard looked up at her husband. She knew what was going on at the old barn. At least she thought she did. He'd confessed to her that he made a little sipping whiskey for his own use and to give to friends.

"Be careful," she told her husband, as the kids ran to him for a hug.

Pritchard picked up his daughter and tousled the boy's hair, pulling him close to his side. "You kids be good while I'm gone and I'll bring you back something from town."

He placed the toddler back on the floor and his son took her hand and led her back to where they were playing.

"I'll go on into town when I finish up at the barn," he told his wife as he opened the door. "I should be home by three o'clock."

The air outside was crisp and cool, though it was mid-morning, and the sun was shining brightly. He got into his new Dodge pickup and started the engine, waiting a moment for it to warm up. His property extended well up into the mountains and it would take him twenty minutes to reach the old barn.

When he arrived, a white cargo van was parked just outside. Pritchard walked past it and entered the old structure. On the outside, it looked like a typical ramshackle barn, but inside, it was well lit, with concrete walls and floor. The ceiling was lower than most barns, with heavy insulation above it.

The old barn had been reconfigured for another purpose.

In the front part of the structure, separated from the rest by another concrete wall, were burlap bags of corn from the summer crop and winter rye from the previous winter. A man in a white lab coat looked up from a clipboard he was holding, surprised to see him. The man wore reading glasses and had graying hair, the only physical attribute attesting to his age. Otherwise, he could probably pass for half his fifty-five years.

"Good morning, Mister Pritchard. I wasn't expecting to see you until tomorrow."

"Hello, Walter," Pritchard said. "I suddenly had a couple of hours free this morning, and thought I'd check in early. How are things going?"

"Very smoothly," Walter Brown replied. "We started the extraction process last week and now have enough to begin the distillation process. Care to see?"

"Yes, I would. How much have you produced so far?"

"Nearly two liters," Brown said, unlocking the fire-proof door at the back of the room.

Pritchard followed him into the hall, where Brown closed and locked the door behind them. They passed two open doorways, through which Pritchard could see the two copper stills that made corn liquor. Exhaust fans in the ceiling moved the hot air out through underground ducts where the cooled air was released through stone chimneys that resembled old water wells.

At the end of the hall, Brown unlocked another fire door and opened it. Pritchard followed him inside to find another man at work. He also wore a lab coat, a hair net on his head and protective goggles covering his eyes.

"Hi, Mister Pritchard," the younger assistant said.

"Hello, Frank," Pritchard said. "What's with the goggles?"

"My eyes are a bit sensitive," Frank replied. "The fumes from the distillate make them water something fierce."

Pritchard looked to the senior botanist for an explanation.

"Not to worry," Brown said. "The fumes aren't harmful, though it does tend to irritate the eyes of some people."

Pritchard went over to the equipment, where a single jar sat beneath a dripping faucet. The liquid coming out was clear, producing a drop perhaps once every four or five seconds.

"Slow process, huh?"

Brown looked at his employer and smiled. "Yes, it's very exacting. The fungi grow only on the rye seeds and are only visible through a microscope. It's from those microscopic spores that we extract the ingredient and it takes nearly two kilograms of your winter rye seed to make each of those drops."

Pritchard stared intently at the scientist; the concern evident in his eyes. "It takes four pounds of rye to make just one drop of this stuff? What's that monetarily?"

"Each drop represents about ten dollars."

Pritchard whistled low. "That's not bad. About $120 a minute."

"Yes," Brown said. "Last year's rye has a high amount of ergot fungi. What we have on hand now should produce somewhere between eighteen and twenty gallons of lysergic acid."

"That's good," Pritchard said. "I have a buyer."

The old chemist looked at Pritchard over his reading glasses. "I'm sure I don't have to remind you to be careful. From just your rye alone, you can get somewhere north of one million dollars."

"From just *my* winter rye?"

"Yes, sir," Brown replied.

"And to think we all just plowed it under in the spring. It was good ground cover in winter and wasn't worth much on the open market."

The chemist grinned broadly. "I've checked samples of Mister Wright's and Mister Long's crops. They have similar amounts of the fungi per kilogram of rye, but

Mister Wright's farm produced about twice what yours and Mister Long's did last winter."

"Four million dollars?"

"Probably closer to five," Brown said. "Of course, these are just preliminary estimates."

"And you already ordered more seed?"

"Yes, sir. It should be delivered to all three of your farms well before planting. You're very fortunate to have these fungi growing naturally here."

"Walter," Pritchard said, "I'm giving both of you a raise."

Both men smiled. "That might be a bit premature," Brown said. "It will take several months to remove the fungi from all the rye and even longer to produce the finished product from it. I doubt you'll see a profit until late spring or early summer."

"Doesn't matter," Pritchard said. "Your work is well worth it. How is the whiskey distillation going?"

"Turning a daily profit of over two thousand dollars."

"Good, good," Pritchard said, rubbing his hands together. "I'm happy to hear that. I'll leave you gentlemen to your work, then."

Brown led the way back through the hall and unlocked the outer door. Once he closed it, he turned toward Pritchard. "There is one thing, sir."

"What's that?"

"I'm almost reluctant to mention it due to the vast difference between the products, but the alcohol volume going out isn't consolidating with the revenue coming back."

"What do you mean?"

Brown looked down at his clipboard for a moment. "You hired me to produce these two things, and you're already paying us quite well. So, I feel obligated to bring something to your attention."

"What is it, Walter?"

"Either all the liquor isn't being sold, or your delivery people are skimming the till."

"How much?"

"It varies," Brown said. "Anywhere from one hundred to three hundred dollars per shipment. Like I said, it's nothing compared to the income potential of the back room, and there could very well be a valid reason. These roads are rough—maybe some jars were broken. Perhaps they're lowering the price to sell more. I just thought you should know that the numbers aren't matching up."

"Thanks, Walter," Pritchard said.

Pritchard turned and went to the outer door, then stopped. "Does Frank know about the discrepancy?"

"No, sir. Only you and I."

Pritchard turned without a word and left the old barn.

CHAPTER TEN

It only took me fifteen minutes to get to the judge's house. He lived in an upscale neighborhood of mostly two-story homes. The yards were well-manicured with trimmed shrubs and old growth trees. There was a newer model Buick sedan in the judge's driveway. The car was parked in front of a two-car garage and I remembered having seen it at the diner, also.

I planned to play this conversation by ear with the judge. He was evidently clean and would probably want to know of any corruption in the legal system in his county. I also knew that if there was any doubt about the sheriff, he wouldn't want local law enforcement doing an investigation. I reached into my pack and pulled out three wallets. The first held my false, but very realistic, CIA shield and ID. The second one was the one I was looking for, and I stuck it in my shirt pocket, then returned the other two before getting out of the truck.

The front door of the house opened before I reached it. "Can I help you?" the same white-haired man I'd seen in the diner asked.

"Yes, Judge Whitaker, I hope you can. My name is Jesse McDermitt."

"I saw you at the diner, son. What can I do for you?"

He'd seen me pull up and remembered my face, though I was no longer wearing the Caterpillar cap. He was obviously a sharp man and I didn't think there was much that got past him.

I handed him the wallet from my shirt pocket, and he opened it, checking my credentials with a critical eye. This one wasn't a phony.

"Private investigator?"

"My company has been secured to investigate something that happened here recently," I said, taking my wallet back. "Does the name Sandra Sneed ring a bell?"

"Why don't you come inside, son. Care for a coffee?"

"Thanks, Judge." I followed him inside. "Don't mind if I do."

The interior of the house was immaculate. A woman's touch was obvious everywhere I looked. The decorations complimented the furniture nicely, though it was all a good decade out of date.

"We can talk in the kitchen," the judge said, leading me toward the back of the house. "The woman you mentioned is a material witness in a murder investigation. The Commonwealth Attorney would like to speak with her."

"That's the reason I'm here, Judge."

"Just call me Ollie," he said, getting two big porcelain mugs from a cupboard and filling them from a pot that was half full. "Nobody calls me judge when I'm not wearing the robe."

"Please just call me Jesse, then," I said, accepting the offered mug.

"My late wife would have had a fit over my not offering you a saucer," he said. "But to me that's just one more thing to wash and you don't strike me as a man who dwells much on social niceties."

"The mug's fine," I said with a genuine smile. I liked the man.

He waved a hand toward a small dinette against the wall, which had a tray with condiments on it. "Have a seat. There's sugar there, and I have regular milk, if you need it."

"Black is fine," I said, moving toward the table.

We both sat down, and I tasted the coffee. It wasn't off the shelf, that I could tell. "Good coffee," I commented.

"Thank you. There are some things in life that a man shouldn't count pennies on. A good cup of joe is one of them."

I studied the man closer. I knew he was seventy-two, but he didn't look it. Too young for the Second World War or Korea. "Joe" was a term soldiers used. Vietnam maybe.

"So, Sandra Sneed sent you?" Judge Whitaker asked. "Where is she?"

Not a man to beat around the bush. I liked that.

"She didn't really send me," I replied. "She's down in Miami and *she* would have pitched a fit if she knew I was here. We used to be married."

"Ah, the plot thickens. But why did she disappear in the middle of the sheriff's investigation?"

I didn't know any other way to say it and wasn't prone to beating around the bush either. "Your sheriff and assistant state attorney are dirty."

"Commonwealth," he corrected me, unflustered by the accusation. "There are only four states in these United States of America that refer to themselves as commonwealths—Kentucky, Massachusetts, Pennsylvania, and Virginia. The distinction is only in the name and really the four commonwealths are just like any other state, and there aren't any differences in their relationship to each other or to the nation."

His explanation seemed like a delaying tactic while he pondered my accusation. "I didn't know that," I said.

"It took me a while to get used to it."

I wasn't ready to tell him everything yet. "Sheriff Taliaferro and Assistant *Commonwealth* Attorney Pritchard weren't directly involved in the murder," I allowed. "But they are trying to sweep it under the rug."

"And you have some proof of this?"

Judges were only interested in evidentiary proof, not supposition. I took my phone from my pants pocket and pulled up the video recording I'd taken the night before.

"This isn't admissible," I said. "I'm only here to see you as a courtesy to your office. My investigation will proceed regardless of the outcome of our meeting."

Judge Whitaker watched the short video clip, where Pritchard instructed the other two men to send Stuart Lane to Miami to finish what they'd started.

When it ended, he played it back again, then pushed the phone across the table. "Not admissible," he agreed. "And wholly conjecture."

I nodded. "Yes, it is. This meeting took place last night. What would be your conclusion on what you just heard?"

He held my gaze firmly with eyes that were bright and clear, conveying an abundance of wisdom gained through many years. "I would conclude that ACA Pritchard wants Stuart Lane to go to Miami."

"Were you aware that the sheriff's office has a video of the murder that took place on the Appalachian Trail?"

His eyes never wavered, and he didn't blink. If he played a friendly game of poker with his neighbors now and then, they probably left with empty pockets.

"I know of no such evidence," the judge replied.

"I believe you, sir. I don't think that—"

"Ollie," he reminded me.

I nodded slowly, not breaking eye contact. "I believe the video evidence of the murder was kept from you, Ollie."

"Do you have that evidence in your possession?"

Flipping through the files on my phone, I pulled up the video that Chyrel had pulled from my ex-wife's phone without her knowledge. I slid the phone back across to the judge.

Ollie watched the video of Kamren Steele being executed three times, showing no reaction at all. I imagined that during his time as a criminal attorney in Pittsburgh, he'd seen a lot.

Finally, he pushed the phone back to me. "The shooter is Stuart Lane. I know the man well. The other man never faces the camera, but I believe it to be Jeb Long. If this video had been presented to Sheriff Taliaferro, an arrest would have been made."

"And if it was presented to the sheriff and no arrest was forthcoming?"

The judge pondered that a moment as he looked out the back window. I followed his gaze, noting a beautifully landscaped backyard and garden with a patio of rough-cut stone and black metal furniture.

"My wife and I used to spend hours out there," Judge Whitaker said. "She tended the garden herself and I did all the lawn work. I hire people to do it for me now; I tell folks it's mostly on account of my age. The truth is, it hurts in other ways to be out there with her flowers. But looking out there, I can almost see her smiling among the plantings." When he looked back at me, I could see the sadness in his eyes. "I was elected over four years ago, less than a year after my wife was murdered."

"I'm sorry to hear that, Ollie. I know how you must feel."

"Do you, son?" he asked bluntly. "Do you know how it feels to lose the woman you've loved and would give anything to have back?"

I took a slow drink of my coffee, then looked him straight in the eye. "I didn't have the many years you and your wife had. But my third wife was murdered on our wedding night."

"Third wife?"

"Sandy was my first," I said. "She couldn't cope with military life and I was a career Marine. I had a brief second marriage that ended in divorce. And then I met Alex a couple of years after I retired from the Corps. She was raped and beaten to death by arms smugglers just a few hours after we married."

The judge's eyes moistened as he again fixed me with them, boring into my soul. "Josie meant everything to me, Jesse. She was killed in a drive-by shooting—never solved. The sheriff thinks it was gang-related."

We stared at one another for a long moment. Finally, the judge asked, "So, you're here to gather evidence to have Lane arrested? He's got quite a history with the law."

I continued to hold his gaze and didn't blink. "Not just Lane."

"That would be an uphill battle," Ollie said.

"Sandy is staying with my oldest daughter. Do you have kids?"

"Josie and I had a daughter and a son, both grown with families of their own now. Phil lives in Boston and Candice in Seattle. I rarely see my grandkids."

"Stuart Lane is on his way now to murder my ex-wife, Ollie. That puts my daughter and her family in jeopardy. I'm not here to *arrest* anyone."

The implication of my statement wasn't missed, nor did he react. "Yet you're here and they're there."

"They're safe. When Lane arrives, friends of mine will put him on ice until I return."

The judge drained his mug. "You must trust these friends a lot."

"With my life, many times over," I replied. "Lane will most certainly fail."

"Why did you show me that second video?" he asked. "Do you want me to turn a blind eye?"

"The sheriff and the ACA are working with three others. They make moonshine and distribute it all over eastern Virginia and don't want people meddling in their affairs. Sandy and her boyfriend worked for environmental causes. They came to Staunton for that reason and would soon bring agents from DEQ with them."

"I'm aware of that," he said. "I heard the preliminary injunction and found in their favor. That doesn't answer my question."

"Besides Lane, there are two men by the names of Luke Wright and Jeb Long, who you mentioned. These men handle the deliveries. All under the protection of the law. There may be others." I paused, then added, "I'm here to shut them down and if need be, administer justice."

"I think you and I have differing opinions on that word, son."

"I don't think so," I said. "I think we both feel very strongly about justice and the reality of what it takes to live in a just and fair society such as these United States. You and I administer it in different ways is all. Blind eye, or eyes wide open, it doesn't matter to me. I'm going to stop them cold in their tracks."

I knew the judge could have me arrested for what I'd just said. It was a clear threat to his sheriff and assistant prosecutor. But I also felt there was more to the story of his wife's death than he let on. I was gambling pretty heavily on that, in fact.

"Where do you live, Jesse?"

"I own a small island in the Florida Keys, where I run a fishing charter."

"Fishing? I hear that's quite a fisherman's paradise down there. Maybe when all this is over, I'll go down there and you can take me out to catch a marlin. I've never hooked one of those before."

I took the last sip of my coffee. "I'd be honored to do that."

"I'm not going to offer to refill that mug, Jesse. In fact, I'd prefer if you didn't come around here or my courthouse ever again. I'm sure you understand."

I did. Being a sitting judge, I knew he couldn't take a stand in a law enforcement matter, and definitely not in a manner that might be seen as illegal.

I nodded my understanding and slid a business card across the table with the skull and crossed fishing hooks logo of my charter service on it. "Come on down to Marathon some time, Ollie. I'll see that you boat that marlin."

CHAPTER ELEVEN

W hen I got back into the truck, I called Chyrel again.

"How'd it go with the judge?" she asked.

It didn't surprise me that she knew I was at the judge's house. The phone's GPS worked both ways.

"I laid it out to him," I replied. "I get the feeling that he's suspected the corruption all along. Would you dig into the death of his wife for me? Anything you can come up with might help. I think there's something there."

"On it. And I emailed you a file on the sheriff, as you asked. He looks clean on paper."

"Yeah," I said. "But who writes the paper?"

"Good point. I took the liberty of listening in on the sheriff's private cell phone. He's meeting Pritchard at noon."

"Hm, I'd sure like to be a fly on the wall there."

"Where are you going now?" she asked.

"I'm gonna shake some trees and see if any snakes fall out."

"Be careful, Jesse. You're a little out of your element there and you don't have any backup."

"I'll be fine," I said. "I'll call you this afternoon with an update."

Backing out of the driveway, I headed toward the loop road around Staunton. I found I-64 and headed east toward Richmond. Soon the highway started up a long gradual grade, with a view to the southwest that was unbelievable. Shenandoah Valley stretched away to the far-off horizon and the autumn colors in the distance were diminished slightly by a light blue haze. It was that nearly ever-present haze that gave the Blue Ridge Mountains their name.

Chyrel, and it seemed a lot of others, had the notion that because I lived in the Keys and was born in southwest Florida, that mountains weren't in my wheelhouse at all. The fact was, I trained a lot in very similar terrain and often visited the mountains of western North Carolina when I was stationed at Camp Lejeune.

Soon, I pulled into a small parking area on the Blue Ridge Parkway that allowed access to the Appalachian Trail. It was the same place where Kamren Steele was shot down.

There were only three other cars parked there, one an unmarked police car.

I parked in front of Sheriff Taliaferro's cruiser and got out. Circling to the back of the truck, I nonchalantly dropped the tailgate and hopped up on it. I just sat there, looking back at the sheriff, and waited.

The rental was in the name of my alias, Stretch Buchannan. Stretch was a rather colorful south Florida character involved in quite a few illegal activities. All created by Chyrel, of course. After hearing the message I'd left him, the sheriff probably knew all there was to know about Stretch and was calling in the truck's tag number.

Finally, he opened the door and got out, adjusting his utility belt and holster. It didn't escape my attention that the snap on the holster was released and tucked behind his belt.

"Mister Buchannan?"

I grinned at the man. "Guilty as charged, officer."

"That's sheriff," he corrected me. "Sheriff Louis Taliaferro." He, of course, pronounced his name the Virginia way—Tolliver.

"But it's spelled like it's an Italian name," I said, still grinning.

He walked up and leaned against the fender of the cruiser. "You left me a message that you had information about a shooting that happened here. You said to come alone. Well, here I am."

"Yeah, I did," I said, dropping quickly to the ground, with my hands wide on the tailgate. The sheriff flinched ever so slightly, but other than that, he didn't react.

"What kind of information, Mister Buchannan?"

"The expensive kind," I replied, my voice low.

"I don't think I follow you."

"That's probably on account of you being in front of me, Sheriff."

He straightened, resting his right hand on the grip of his pistol. While Sheriff Taliaferro might think himself a dangerous man, there was no doubt in my mind that I could close the gap before he could draw, disarm him, and slap him around a little, if I chose to. The good sheriff was the one who was way out of his league, and he had no clue about it.

"What do you know about the shooting?"

"I know Stuart Lane pulled the trigger."

That got his attention. His nostrils flared and his pupils dilated slightly. I wondered if he ever played poker with the judge.

To his credit, he kept his cool. "And just how did you come up with that?"

"Ah, that's where things get expensive, Sheriff."

"You know I can arrest you right here, right now, for withholding evidence in a capital murder investigation?"

I slowly took two, measured steps, closing the distance between us. My eyes never left his. "No," I said flatly. "You lack that ability."

"Would you like to bet your freedom on that?"

I was taller than Taliaferro by several inches. At six-three, I was taller than most people, and I used that to my advantage. He was looking up into my eyes as I scowled down at him. His downward peripheral vision was lessened and mine increased.

"I've bet my *life* on that fact many times," I said. "Against men who were far more competent; men who would frighten the hell out of the best of your deputies. And I'm still here."

He blinked, and before his eyes reopened, my left hand was already moving. The knuckles of my fist caught the inside of his right wrist, just above the palm. I knew from experience that the strike would cause momentary numbness in his whole hand. Before he even knew what was going on, I unholstered his Glock and had it leveled at his midsection.

"You can't—"

With my free right hand, I slapped him hard across the face. "Oh, yes, Sheriff. I absolutely can."

Before he could utter another word, I pressed the release to drop the mag from the grip and stuck it under my arm. Then I racked the slide to eject the round that should have been in the chamber but wasn't. In one fluid motion, I pulled the trigger, unlocked the slide and pulled it off. Dropping the lower assembly to the ground, I compressed the recoil spring in the slide, lifted it, and let it fly off into the grass. Removing the barrel, I tossed it into the ditch, and threw the slide over his patrol car.

Taliaferro's left hand went to his cheek. "I'll see you rot in my jail, Buchannan."

I slowly thumbed the cartridges from the magazine, letting each one fall to the ground, where they rolled in different directions. "Is that any way to talk to a future business partner, Lou?"

"What's that supposed to mean?" he growled, watching his ammo roll under his car.

"I want in," I said, tossing the empty magazine over my shoulder. "You and your people are sloppy. Call Luke and ask if he knows my name. He'll say no, but my number is saved on his phone and a quart of y'all's moonshine he sold me is sitting on the front seat of my truck."

"I don't know anything about that," he lied. "And I don't know anyone named Luke."

"You're a liar," I said, spitting venom. "After you talk to Luke, call Pritchard and tell him I'll be wanting to meet him, as well. In fact, I think I'll just drop in on your twelve o'clock meeting and we can all talk about how sloppy you people are. How's that sound?"

"Who the hell are you?"

"See ya around, officer," I said, walking around and getting back into my truck.

I knew there was a chance that he had a backup weapon. But I also knew that as dirty as he was, he was now more curious than angry. I got in, started the engine and turned directly through the grass, the rear tires kicking up sod as I headed back toward the interstate. It'd take him a few minutes to gather up the pieces of his Glock and by then I'd be miles away. But I didn't know where the meeting was to take place.

When I turned west on the interstate, I gunned the engine and headed back toward Staunton as I called

Chyrel. She was already listening to his phone, so tracing it wouldn't be any trouble at all for her.

She was laughing when she answered. "It sure doesn't take you long to shake out the snakes."

"It's a gift," I said. "Some people just take me the wrong way."

"I'll say. The sheriff just talked to Pritchard and told him all about Stretch, including his colorful background."

"Did they say anything about where they were meeting?"

"No," she replied. "But Pritchard sounded interested in meeting you and told the sheriff they'd keep the appointment, but to have Luke across the street with a rifle just in case."

"That won't leave me much time. Can you send both their GPS locations to my cell phone? I'll get to where the two converge at about the same time and then locate Luke before I meet with them."

"Pritchard also mentioned that the manufacturing process was going well in his old barn."

"Ah, so that's where they're making your *white lightning*, huh?"

"You're really nuts, you know that, Jesse?"

"I blame Paul," I countered. "He's given me a very good understanding about how these people think."

Besides being a former agent with the U.S. Secret Service, Paul Bender had a PhD in forensic psychology and had shared his vast knowledge of the inner workings of the criminal mind.

"The sheriff's moving," she said. "He's headed toward Staunton about ten miles behind you. Sending the GPS info to your phone now."

I thanked her and ended the call. Modern technology was a wonderful thing. I'd once shunned it, but over the last few years, I'd found how useful something as simple as a cell phone could be.

There were two blinking bull's-eyes on my screen. One was behind me on I-64, and the other was north of Staunton. The one to the north was moving slowly toward the southwest. The GPS didn't show it to be on any named road, but I knew there were a lot of 4x4 trails up in those hills.

My cell started playing the Bad Boys song. I clicked the *Accept* button and held the phone to my ear, hoping Chyrel was right and the highway noises couldn't be picked up.

"Hello," a voice I recognized as Luke's said.

"It's Lou," the sheriff replied. "Who is Stretch Buchannan?"

There was a moment of silence before Luke answered. "Never heard of him, Sheriff."

"You sure about that?" Taliaferro yelled. "Because he just disarmed and belted me, saying he bought a quart of 'shine from you this morning."

"Oh," Luke said, sheepishly, "that guy. I'm sorry, Sheriff. It was—"

"Never mind! We have a job for you. Drop whatever it is you're doing and bring your hunting rifle to the stadium. Do you know where the new townhouses are being built near the south end of the ball field?"

"Yeah, I know where it's at."

"I want you to go there and get up on the second floor of the easternmost townhouse. It faces the field and it's the only one where you can see the infield clearly. Aiden and I are meeting this Buchannan guy there. If he gets a wild hair, I want you to drop him. Can you do that?"

"Whatcha mean by a wild hair?"

"I'll signal you by taking my hat off. When I do that, shoot him in the leg."

There was a moment of silence. Then Luke said, "Okay, Sheriff. But it'll take me thirty minutes to get there."

"That's perfect, Luke. The meeting isn't for an hour."

There was silence for a moment and I thought I'd lost the call. Then Luke said, "There's one thing, though."

"There's always one more thing with you," the sheriff said.

"If I gotta pull the trigger," Luke began, "even if it's just a shot in the leg, I'll want a grand."

"Five hundred and not a penny more."

"Okay," Luke agreed.

The call ended and I pulled up Chyrel's number. She answered almost instantly. "There are two ball fields there. Only one would qualify as a stadium. Sending the directions to your phone now."

"Thanks," I said. "I'm headed that way. I should have plenty of time to find and incapacitate Luke."

"Be careful," she said.

I chuckled. "Five hundred dollars is an insult. He should have asked for five thousand."

Ending the call, I pulled up the navigation app and found that the stadium was less than ten minutes away. I could get there ahead of any of them.

CHAPTER TWELVE

The map on my phone showed identifying tags for roads and landmarks. It showed the baseball diamond, a quarter mile ahead. The stadium was the home of the Staunton Braves, a collegiate baseball team. There was also a football field and track to the east of the diamond, but it had a different name. The GPS told me to turn right just before the football field, but I continued ahead to get the lay of the place.

Apparently, the road the GPS had wanted me to turn onto was the main entrance and parking area. The road I was on went along the south side of the football stadium, where the visitors' bleachers were located.

As I neared the baseball stadium, the road split. I took the right fork, which went between the left field wall and a construction site. As I passed the first building, I could see that it was still in the early stage of construction. Directly across the street, I could see the infield through the fence.

I turned down the next street to the left, where other multi-family homes were being built, and parked on the side of the road so my truck wouldn't be visible from the first building.

When I got out and headed around the building with my backpack, I glanced back. I was glad I'd rented a pickup. The F150 had some drying mud on the fenders and bumper and looked like it was in exactly the place a working man's truck should be.

Glancing at my phone, I saw that Chyrel had added a third blinking bull's-eye, which I assumed was Luke. He was close and the sheriff would reach my location just a few minutes behind him. I hoped the sheriff would pull in the main entrance and not do a recon of the area. He knew my truck and tag number. Not that it mattered a whole lot. By the time he got to the field, his shooter would be napping.

Luke was turning down the road by the football field as I slipped into the back entry of the easternmost town home. There were no windows or doors installed yet. Bare electrical wires hung between wall studs and a stack of drywall lay in the front room. I crossed the room and stood facing the wall opposite the stairs to the second floor, so I could just see out the window opening adjacent to it.

The first blinking marker on my phone was only about a hundred yards away. The next one still two or three miles. Hearing the wheezing sound of the truck, I put the phone in my pocket and stood closer to the wall, facing it. Brakes squeaked and the gasping engine died. There was complete silence in the crisp air. I heard the truck's door protest as it opened and after a moment, it closed and I could hear the crunch of boots moving quickly across the dry dirt.

The instant Luke came through the door opening into the gloomy interior, I stepped back from the wall and spun to my left, unleashing a long right hand that connected solidly with the side of the man's head.

Luke never saw me, nor anything else. His eyes didn't have time to adjust to the gloom after being in the full brightness of the midday sun. As he crumpled to the floor, I took the rifle from his hand and propped it up by the door.

Dropping my pack beside the inert body, I pulled a pair of nylon zip ties from a pocket and quickly bound his hands and feet. A roll of duct tape from my pack eliminated any chance of his calling out when he woke up. Finding his wallet, I removed his driver's license and slid it into my shirt pocket. Then I grabbed the rifle and went back out the rear of the building.

After stashing the Winchester in the back of my truck, I pulled my phone out. One of the markers was stopped at the turn into the main entrance, while the last one was just approaching the main road that ran alongside the fields.

A moment later, the two markers converged and then turned into the main entrance. I had no intention of going through the stadium's gate to reach the field. With both cars out of sight on the far side, I sprinted across the road to the fence and quickly scaled it. The left field bleachers had an open system of legs and braces that supported them. It stood close enough to the fence that I could reach over and grab a diagonal brace from the top of the fence. From there, it was an easy forty-foot climb to the top, where I dropped down into the cheap seats in left fi eld.

Taking a small pair of binoculars from my pack, I took a seat and scanned the fi eld, looking for an opening. There were the typical egresses at the dugouts and another in the center fi eld wall. Not seeing either the sheriff or Pritchard, I moved laterally to center fi eld and then down to the fi rst row of seats, just above the door that probably led to the bullpen. I took a seat, slumped down low, and waited.

A few minutes later, Sheriff Taliaferro stepped out of the home team dugout and walked toward the pitcher's mound, his head on a swivel as he scanned the whole fi eld. The rangefi nder binoculars told me he was nearly one hundred yards away. The top of the center field wall was in front of me, just below my eyes. I doubted he could see the top of my head from that far away.

Aiden Pritchard stepped out onto the fi eld from the visitors' dugout and started toward where the sheriff stood on the mound. "Is he here?"

The sheriff shook his head, still looking around.

I took my phone out and called Chyrel. "Start audio recording," I said, as the two men met on the mound.

I dropped my phone into my shirt pocket, with the mic end sticking up, and waited a moment while they talked and looked around. When both men were facing home plate, I stood and vaulted the low wall, dropping ten feet to the ground. I rolled and came quickly to my feet, right in front of the door to the bull pen. Both men were still facing away from me.

"Show time," I said, raising my leg and kicking back hard against the door with the heel of my boot. Then I strode confidently toward the two men.

Confusing the enemy was always a good tactic, in whatever way you could accomplish it. Anything that got your foe off balance gave you an advantage. Adding a bit of misperception as to how I managed to get onto the field was simple enough. All it took was a boot to the door.

Both men turned at what I'm sure they both assumed was the slamming of the door and the sheriff stepped slightly away from Pritchard, his hand hovering close to his sidearm. It had probably taken him a while to locate the little firing pin and spring in the tall grass.

"You must be the mysterious Mister Buchannan," Pritchard said, when I reached the pitcher's mound.

"Nothing mysterious about me. I'm an open book," I replied with a shrug, then nodded toward the sheriff while holding Pritchard's gaze. "I'm sure by now, Lou has learned things about me that I've forgotten." Then I turned toward Sheriff Taliaferro. "How's the jaw?"

Taliaferro started to take a step, but Pritchard's hand on his chest stopped him. "Never mind about that," he said. "Lou was telling me that you know more than you should, Mister Buchannan."

With mock indignation, I said, "Aw, Aiden, if we're gonna do business, you're gonna have to call me Stretch. But yeah, I have people everywhere. They hear things and tell me what they hear."

"What kind of things?" Pritchard asked.

I reached for my shirt pocket, and the sheriff dropped his hand to his sidearm.

"Really, Lou?" I said. "You wanna do that dance again? If I wanted to hurt you, I could have done it three times already, and there wouldn't have been a damned thing you could have done to stop me." I slowly removed Luke's license from my pocket and showed it to the sheriff. "You can take your hat off any time you like."

Taliaferro looked at the license, then whipped his hat from his head. I dropped the license onto the mound, folded my hands in front of me, and just watched him. He was furious.

I grinned. "You could try waving it around," I suggested. Then I fixed him with a stony expression. "But that'd just be a waste of time. Luke can't see you."

"What'd you do with him?" Pritchard asked, a bright shade of red crawling up from his collared shirt.

I was getting under their skin. People made mistakes and acted irrationally when they were off balance.

"Relax," I said. "Luke will be just fine. But I'm keeping his hunting rifle."

"What the hell do you want, Buchannan?" the sheriff asked.

I ignored him. "Here's the deal, Pritchard; you and your people are careless amateurs." I jerked a thumb toward the sheriff. "This Muppet couldn't pour water out of a boot if the instructions were written on the sole."

The sheriff started to take another step, but I turned fully toward him and dropped my left shoulder slightly. "Ya know what, Lou," I growled menacingly. "I hope you do go for it. I'm sick of waiting for you to try. Now pull that Glock out of that holster and either try to use it against me or toss it toward second base."

He hesitated.

"Do it now!" I shouted, taking a small step toward him.

Most of my weight was on my trailing right foot. He was well within range of a powerful hook kick, and over the past couple of years, I'd been getting much better at hitting a moving target. There was no doubt in my mind that if he drew, my left boot would collide laterally with his gun hand before he got it halfway up.

Pritchard nodded, and the sheriff slowly lifted his sidearm from the holster, not taking his eyes from mine. I could see the hatred in the man's face. His left jaw muscle twitched. We were three feet apart; it was all about reaction time at that distance. I didn't play poker either, for the same reason he shouldn't. I knew his cop mind picked up on the confidant resolve of my expression.

I also knew what thoughts were going through the so-called lawman's head. He was wondering if he'd remembered to chamber a round after reassembling the pistol, or if he'd even put it back together correctly.

Finally, he tossed the Glock toward center field. The weapon landed in the dirt about halfway to second base.

"That's smart," I said. Then I turned back to Pritchard. "I want in. In fact, you might say I'm taking over your whole moonshine operation."

"What moonshine operation?" Pritchard asked.

For a moment I saw a flash of relief in his eyes, then it was gone. I wondered why he'd be relieved that I knew about their operation. *There must be more going on.*

"Don't play coy with me, Aiden," I said. "You know exactly what I'm talking about."

"I'm an attorney, Mister Buchannan. Do you have any proof of these allegations?"

I was losing my patience with the guy and stepped closer to him. "You want proof? How about I tell Susan what you're doing? I bet Aiden Junior would be real proud."

My words somehow calmed the man. "You know my wife and kids' names. A simple Google search would tell you that, Buchannan. I'm a public figure."

"More public than you know," I said, grinning slightly. "I have video of Stuart Lane shooting a man, with Jeb Long standing there watching him do it. That's enough to send those two to death row. The dead man's girlfriend shot the video while hiding in the woods. Lou saw it and did nothing. I'm sure that's a violation of some law. But I'm not a lawyer."

Some of the color leached out of Pritchard's face.

"I also have video of you, Counselor. It was shot last night when you told Luke and Jeb to send Stuart Lane to Miami to kill the woman."

Pritchard's face paled as he tried to remember his exact words from the night before. So, I let it rip. "I know you make moonshine in your old barn on the back of your property. I know you age it in oak and cherry barrels. Not long, but it's good stuff. I know you have it shipped all over the state, but don't sell any of it around here. All these things are documented and I'm not the only one that has the information."

"What is it you want, Buchannan?" the sheriff asked again.

I glanced over at him, then back to Pritchard. "I can do one of two things here. My first option would be to just knock both your asses out right here and now, which I'm becoming more and more inclined to do, then truss you both up like I did Luke, and dump all these things that I know, along with the videos, into your boss's lap."

Pritchard swallowed hard. "And the other option?"

"I'm a fair man, Aiden. But I *am* taking over your operation. Make no mistake about that. And, I'll be bringing in my own people for distribution."

"You really think you can take the both of us?" Taliaferro said.

"Not really," I replied, raising my hands, palms up in a passive gesture, as I turned toward the sheriff.

Suddenly, I lunged toward him, bringing my right hand over and down onto the base of his skull; the sensitive spot where the trapezius muscle joins the neck. The blow paralyzed him instantly and then he passed out before his knees buckled and he dropped like a bag of feed, face down in the dirt.

I turned back to Pritchard. "As a rule, I take out the noisy one first; the one who can't make the decision."

Pritchard had no reaction to my swift attack on the sheriff. Maybe it happened too fast for him to understand what had occurred.

Slowly, he looked down at his fallen cohort, then back up at me. "What do you hope to gain by this?"

"Money," I replied. "You and your people will continue making liquor just the same as you have been." I pointed to the inert Taliaferro. "You'll continue to pay the good sheriff whatever protection money you two agreed on, though it's my belief that whatever the amount is, it's too much. I'll take everything you make off your hands at five bucks a gallon."

Pritchard only stared at me. Finally, he shook his head. "Five isn't good enough. It costs more than that to make good liquor. I'll sell you all I make at ten dollars a gallon."

I smiled at the man. He knew he was beat. Now it was just a matter of how bad. "We could dicker back and forth until Lou wakes up. But like I said, I'm a fair man. Let's call it seven."

"You think you can handle the delivery?"

"I can have my people here in less than twenty-four hours," I replied. "By Monday, *I'll* start moving *your* product. This could be a good thing for you, Aiden. It eliminates most of your risk and decreases your shipping expense."

"The people we deliver to don't like strangers."

"Being anti-social is their problem, not mine," I said. "If they don't want to deal with my guys, they can shop elsewhere. I have contacts in south Florida that will buy up anything you make."

"Florida?"

"That's where I'm from," I replied. "Those good ol' boys down in the 'Glades do love their liquor."

The sheriff started to stir and moaned softly.

"Should we shake hands?" Pritchard asked.

I had to hand it to him; he took defeat easily. Maybe too easily.

I just grinned at him. "I wouldn't want to sully the good reputation of the assistant commonwealth attorney. Why don't you just help the sheriff to his feet and go back to your cars?"

Pritchard's eyes cut to where the Glock lay in the dirt, twenty feet away.

"I'll keep the sheriff's gun, too," I said.

"How can I reach you?" Pritchard asked. "To arrange the pickup."

"Don't worry about that," I said. "I'll have a truck come to your barn at sunrise, Monday morning. You just make sure you have the distribution list ready, with names, addresses, quantities, and prices."

Pritchard's face suddenly showed fear. He hadn't shown any sign of it earlier, so I knew there had to be something else going on, and it had to do with the barn. There was something he didn't want me to see in that barn.

The fear left his eyes as quickly as it had appeared. "I produce three fifty-gallon barrels a day and we deliver five days a week, using a three-quarter ton cargo van."

"Not a problem," I said. "How many of those barrels are you currently aging?"

"Two hundred are in various stages of aging."

I did the math in my head and smiled at him. "So, you've been making and shipping a hundred and fifty gallons a day for a while, huh?"

"I would have thought you already knew that," he replied. "You seem to know everything else."

"If I'm going to do business with a man, I'd as soon know from the source."

"Yes," Pritchard said. "Lou told me about what a capitalist you are down in Florida."

"See, I'm no mystery at all."

He knew there was no way out. He could try to kill me on Monday or next year, but the copies of the evidence would prevent that. So, his only option was to open negotiations in a businesslike manner.

"You understand supply and demand economics, Stretch." He even offered a smile. "My customers demand a certain product; they want something unique. Aging for just a few months gives them that. And to be honest, I was planning to replace the men I have doing the distribution anyway."

"Luke, Jeb, and Stuart? Why?"

"One or all of them have been skimming," he said. "The amount is peanuts, but I won't tolerate people stealing from me."

"Really?" I said in a mocking tone. "Because from where I'm standing, it looks like I'm ripping you off."

"Semantics," he said, waving a hand as if brushing aside the idea. "You're right. Dealing with you might be less stressful than with these idiots."

"You're making and shipping a hundred and fifty gallons a day, five days a week?" I asked, to get him to confirm their output. "And you want to go into business with me on the terms I laid out, voluntarily?

"Yes," Pritchard said. "I'm not at all fond of the first option you mentioned, and as you said, I have a lot more to lose in not doing so."

"My crew can handle that." I said with a nod.

"Stuart did most of the driving," Pritchard went on. "He usually carried empty one-gallon bottles to fill for customers and brought back any empties they had. They buy anywhere from ten to thirty gallons each and they're filled straight from the barrels."

"Hence, the van," I said, nodding.

"My van isn't part of the deal. You'll have to get your own vehicle. I'll have the barrels on a pallet, ready to load into whatever vehicle you bring."

"Anything else?" I asked.

"Bring cash every day," he said flatly. Then I saw a glimmer of hope in his eyes; an idea. "One thousand and fifty dollars, plus another fifty for the bottles. Sunrise is at 7:15 on Monday. If you're five minutes late, I'll load it into my own van and move it out. My customers also like punctuality. You lose all rights to any days' shipment if you're late in picking up. Is that acceptable?"

Sheriff Taliaferro rolled over and slowly pushed himself to a kneeling position.

"I'll be there," I said, then pointed at Taliaferro. "Now take him and leave. Luke's tied up in the first townhouse being built across the street."

Pritchard helped Taliaferro get to his feet and the two started toward the home team dugout. I waited on the mound until they both went down into the dugout and out the back door.

Then I picked up the sheriff's Glock and started toward the outfield wall as I pulled my phone from my shirt pocket and held it to my ear. "You get all that?"

CHAPTER THIRTEEN

I t was already dark when Stuart Lane's plane landed at Miami International Airport. It'd been dark when he'd left his house fourteen hours earlier, too. In all, he'd spent less than five hours in the air on the three connecting flights. But he'd sat longer than that in the terminal at Dulles. A shorter layover in New Jersey threatened to turn into days; there'd been talk of canceling the flight due to an approaching snowstorm. Stuart had rarely seen snow so early in the year, but the folks up there seemed to expect it.

Once he'd found his backpack in the luggage carousel, he left the massive airport terminal and stepped out into the sweltering heat of a late November night in Miami. Outside was a cab stand and he approached the first one, showing the driver an address, he'd written on a sheet of paper.

"You know any hotels near here?" he asked the black man, hoping he spoke English.

"Coconut Grove? Yeah, there's a few, man. But I don't know if any are close to where you wanna be."

"Take me to this address so I'll know where it is, then take me to the nearest place where I can sleep."

"You gonna sleep in Miami on a Saturday night, man?"

"Just take me there," Stuart ordered, getting in the back seat.

"Whatever you say, man."

Stuart wished he'd been able to bring a gun. But even in a checked bag, he knew that would have been risky. With a gun, he could have finished this tonight and been back home tomorrow. Without one, he'd have to find a way to get close. Maybe wait for the woman to go jogging or for a walk. He'd have to play it by ear. It might even take him a couple of days to get close enough to strangle the life out of the pain in the ass woman.

He remembered how she'd appeared in the court-room back home; arrogant and snotty—looking down on them because they were farmers. But she wasn't a bad-looking woman. A few years older than he preferred; Stuart liked younger women. But still... she was hot.

Maybe I can make it last a while, he thought with a lecherous grin.

Thirty minutes later, the cab driver turned onto a residential street. He pointed to the GPS on the dash and said, "Your address is right up here on the right, my man. Want me to stop?"

"No," Stuart said. "Just drive by slow."

The cab driver did as he was told and slowed as they passed a white van parked in the street in front of the house next door to the one the woman was hiding out in. The lights were on inside the house. The neighborhood was nice, upscale, with sidewalks and fenced backyards.

"Okay," Stuart said, as they passed on by. "Find the nearest hotel."

The driver stopped for a moment and stabbed at the GPS screen with his finger. "There's a Hampton less than half a mile away."

"Perfect," Stuart said. "Take me there."

The driver circled the block to get back to the main road, then turned in the direction they'd come—back toward the city.

Stuart had learned that the meddling woman was staying with her daughter, Eve Maggio, and her husband, who was a lawyer. Stuart didn't much like lawyers and thought maybe he could just barge in and make it a trifecta. No witnesses.

How much of a fight could a couple of women put up while I squeezed the life out of the husband?

Stuart was a big man and knew his capabilities. His muscles were powerful from working in the fields since he was a kid. He'd killed with his bare hands before. Usually young hookers in the towns where he made deliveries.

Stuart memorized the name of the main road they'd turned onto and the name of the next street they passed, where the woman was hiding.

He continued to recall how she'd looked in court. She'd struck him as a snobby librarian with her shirt buttoned to the neck under her business coat. But Stuart saw a nasty streak, too. He could tell by the fit and shortness of her skirt that she could be a wild one. Her legs were long and very shapely. She probably ran every day to keep her body looking so tight at her age. He wondered if the daughter would be as good-looking.

She's younger, Stuart thought, *so probably hotter.*

The two women might be able to put up a fight, while he took care of the husband. Stuart had been in more than a few bar fights with big, powerful men, and had taken some solid licks and not gone down. He could just punch the lawyer's lights out, then restrain the women so he could finish the guy off.

I'll add a day, he decided. *Do the lawyer quick, and the women slow.*

Five minutes and just three turns later, the cab pulled into a fancy hotel. Stuart had memorized each turn and would have no trouble getting to the house on foot. Maybe later tonight.

"Pull around to the back," Stuart said. "I just texted a buddy and he's meeting me in the parking lot."

"Good idea," the driver said, his shaved head bobbing in agreement. "Hit South Beach. You can get anything you want on a Saturday night, man."

The driver again did as he was told, as Stuart pulled open his pack and took out a long, thin guitar string and a pair of heavy leather gloves. He put the gloves on and wound the guitar string around his protected hands.

"Right up there," Stuart said. "Park next to that white pickup. How much do I owe you?"

The driver took two parking spaces next to the white truck, so he could more easily back out, then put the car in park. As he started to reach over to stop the electronic meter, Stuart looped the G-string over his head and pulled back hard, pressing a knee into the seat back in front of him. The driver writhed and clawed at the strong wire as it cut into his flesh. He made a few gurgling noises, but soon stopped struggling.

Stuart liked the G-string. And not just for the titillating name—it was the third string on the guitar and the thickest of the three that were single, solid steel wires. The low E, A, and D strings were thicker, but they were wound strings, not a single wire. He'd won a few bar bets by breaking the thinner B and high E strings just by stretching them with his hands. But the G—no man could break the G-string.

Reaching over the driver's body, Stuart stopped the meter and cleared the entry, then searched the man's pockets until he found the roll of cash that he knew would be there. Getting out of the car, he looked around, stuffing the dead man's money into his pants pocket. There wasn't anyone in the parking lot that he could see.

Stuart shoved the makeshift garrote and gloves back into his pack. Then, using a handkerchief from his pocket, he wiped down everything he'd touched and reached through the driver's window to turn off the cab's headlights and shut off the engine. With any luck, nobody would find the body until the next day. As if nothing had happened and he was just another weary traveler, Stuart shouldered his pack and walked around to the front of the hotel.

Ten minutes later, he entered a very nice room that looked out over the parking lot. He turned on the bathroom light, nothing else. Then he tossed his pack onto the bed.

The heavy curtains that could be drawn over the window were gathered to the sides, but the sheer ones behind them were closed. He opened the nearly transparent fabric wide enough to see down to the parking lot. It was mostly dark; only a few lights. If anyone looked in the cab, the driver would appear to be sleeping. If anyone called the cops, they'd come with their lights on, alerting him. The air conditioner below the window hummed and the window itself wasn't the opening kind, so the lights would be his only warning.

He was hungry, but Stuart had been able to go without food for days and could ignore the pangs for now. There was another hunger that was becoming more urgent as he thought about the meddlesome environmentalist woman.

Taking his phone from his pocket, he tried to connect to the hotel Wi-Fi, but realized he'd left it on airplane mode. When he was able to sign on, he opened Facebook first, to see if the Sneed woman had an account. It was a pretty common name, but he already knew where she lived in North Carolina, and he found her easily enough.

Her posts were primarily about environmental crap and most of her pictures were of flowers, birds, and trees. There was one of her dressed in shorts and a tank top, carrying a backpack. The straps seemed to pull her shoulders back, poking her boobs out like a stripper. Stuart liked the pose. The date of the picture was only three years ago. Yeah, she was hot, all right.

He searched for the daughter's name in Miami and found her right at the top of the results. Her profile was private, so all he could see was the one profile picture. She wore a slinky, white dress that clung tightly to her body. She was with a man and two little kids; a boy about six and a girl who was probably just walking. The husband was also dressed for a night on the town. Eve Maggio was young, dark-haired, tall, and built like a brick shithouse. Just like the hookers he prowled the streets looking for after dropping off his last load of 'shine.

"Oh, yeah," he moaned. "This could turn into a lot of fun."

The kids were a problem. Stuart had never killed a kid before.

CHAPTER FOURTEEN

I spent the afternoon driving around on the roads north of Staunton. Only the sheriff knew my truck, so I didn't worry much about anyone seeing me. There was a secondary paved road that ran along the west side of Pritchard's property. I turned onto it, heading north. The road ran straight as an arrow for three miles, crossing low hills and small streams before veering away to the west to start a series of switchbacks up the mountain, just like the dirt road farther to the west.

Halfway up the mountain, I found an overlook with a clear view of the valley several hundred feet below. I pulled into the small parking area and climbed out of the truck with my binoculars. In front of the truck was a short walkway with a safety rail to keep people from getting too close to the steep drop-off. I leaned against it and scanned the prosecutor's property. Finding his house far in the distance was easy. It was large, probably bigger than the four houses on my island combined. The grass around it was bright and verdant, with old-growth oak trees set away from the house at a considerable distance. Japanese maples lined most of the driveway, their fallen leaves creating a red and brown carpet along the edges of the drive. The branches were nearly bare, save for a few stubborn leaves left on the lower boughs.

I shivered as a cold breeze blew down from the mountain. I didn't like cold, unless it was a beer bottle. The temperature was hovering around forty degrees, but the wind made it feel quite a bit colder. Knowing I might be out at night in the cold, I should have stopped somewhere and bought better gear; at least a pair of long johns.

Pritchard's driveway turned to dirt once it passed his house. There was a white Mercedes SUV parked in front of the garage; probably the wife's. The dirt track led back behind the house to two buildings, one obviously a horse stable, with a grazing pasture behind it. The pasture was fenced with the same white rail fencing that spanned the front of the property.

The other building was barn-shaped, with the typical multi-pitched roof. Both were designed to tie into the architecture of the house; painted the same color and having similar doors, windows, and trim. The two outbuildings looked like they'd probably been constructed at the same time as the house. Chyrel had said his moonshine still was in his *old* barn, so it probably wasn't either of those two buildings.

I continued scanning the property, finding another track that led north, away from the house and outbuildings. I followed it with the binos and lost it a few times.

It wasn't very worn, so probably saw little use. It passed a cluster of trees, then disappeared into the hills. I followed it back slowly and studied the group of trees.

Through gaps in the mostly dead leaves of the oak cluster, I could just make out a rusted metal roof. I looked more closely around the base of the trees. The back end of a van was just visible.

"Gotcha."

I moved over to the far end of the rail, away from where I was parked, and took another look. The angle was a little better and I could make out more of the van. It was parked under the oaks, and next to it, I spotted the lower left corner of the building. The planks were older, unpainted, and weathered by years of sun and rain.

The old barn.

If the van was making daily runs during the week, the track should have been more worn. There was grass growing between the double tracks and even over them in places. A van driving up and down that trail twice a day would leave ruts and keep the grass clear.

Checking my watch, I saw that it was after 1600. It would be getting dark soon. I passed the binos over the rest of the property and saw little else of interest, but with one final glance at the old barn, I noticed the van backing out from under the trees, steam rising from its tailpipe.

The van turned west instead of following the track back toward the house. I quickly realized why I could see only the one trail. As the van moved slowly west, the tires and lower part of the body were hidden by tall grass that lined a second egress. I kept my eyes on the van as it headed toward the road I'd just driven up.

When the vehicle stopped, it was very near the middle of the long, straight, paved road. Someone got out of the passenger side and walked toward the front of the van, but they were too far away for me to get a good look.

I didn't need to see where the man was going. He'd gotten out to open a gate on the west side of Pritchard's property. I quickly ran back to the pickup and jumped in. Backing out of the parking spot, I turned left and started back down the hill. Odds were, the van was going to go south, toward the main road. I wanted to catch it and follow it.

When I reached the bottom of the hill, I floored the gas pedal and quickly reached 80 miles per hour. Keeping an eye out for the gate the van had just come through, I spotted the cattle guard first. The fence and gate were just barbed wire on this side of Pritchard's property. I checked the odometer to figure out how far the gate was from the main highway.

Topping a low hill, I saw the van in the distance, turning right. When I got to the stop sign a minute later, the van was half a mile west, just going around a bend in the road. I turned and followed it, checking the mileage again. The gate was a hair over two miles from the main highway.

Pritchard had said they used the van to make deliveries and it left at sunrise, five days a week. So, I had to assume that it being a Saturday, the van was being used for something else now. When I reached the curve the van had disappeared around, I caught sight of it again. So, I sped up to close the distance a little.

The van slowed as it neared the small town of Buffalo Gap—more a crossroads than a town. When I reached the intersection, there was a convenience store across the road and little else. The van had turned left.

I made the same left turn onto Parkersburg Turnpike—Highway 254—the same east-west road that went through Staunton. Apparently, the van was taking a different route back to town. I kept a good distance between us as it continued through the outskirts on the west side of town.

The van continued past the loop road, heading toward downtown. Finally, it turned into the parking lot of a tall, red-brick, colonial-style building. I slowed as I approached. It was a hotel—the Stonewall Jackson.

I needed to ID who was in the van, so I turned into the parking lot as well. It was risky, since it might be Pritchard himself driving, but I didn't think it would be. He struck me as a man who hired others to do everything. The van turned into a parking fairway and I went past it to the main entrance, then stopped short of the entry, as though I was waiting to pick someone up.

As I watched, the van parked, and two men got out. They started walking toward where I was idling and I pretended to be busy with my phone, which I was resting on the steering wheel. I managed to shoot several seconds of video of the two men as they approached. One of the men was talking, but I couldn't hear him. I'd never seen either man before.

The driver was an older man, gray-haired and intelligent-looking. The other man—the one who'd gotten out and opened the gate—was younger, probably in his mid-twenties.

Neither man ticked the box in my head for a weapon. Adversaries were logged into my brain under two categories and they were based solely on size. Under two hundred pounds, I didn't need a weapon unless they had one, and even then, maybe not. Over two hundred, I might need one. It was not a cocky attitude, just where I drew the line for the sake of prudence. At six foot three, 220 pounds, and highly trained in many disciplines of combat fighting, I could handle most armed aggressors without a weapon. The sheriff had proven that. But I didn't fight even odds if I could help it. If a man was close to my size, I wanted a weapon. Neither of these men deserved that classification. In fact, they looked like a teacher and a student.

After they went inside, I circled the parking lot and backed into a spot in the corner where there weren't any other cars. I always thought it strange how the best parking spots were seldom used. There were a lot of benefits to parking in the corner; aside from adding a few seconds of exercise, there was far less chance of someone dinging your door, fewer people noticed, and if they did, they were too far away for a positive ID. There was only one reason for parking close; laziness.

I sent the video to Chyrel, asking if she could identify the men.

It was full dark by then and I needed to get a room myself. One hotel was as good as another, I figured, and started to get out of the truck when my cell phone buzzed. I pulled it out and glanced at the ID. It was Tony. I'd assumed I'd be hearing from him tonight or tomorrow. Lane's plane had landed in Miami an hour ago.

"Got him on ice already?" I asked, without preamble.

"No," Tony replied. "But I'm pretty sure he made a drive-by, just a few minutes ago. Tom's sending pictures to you and Chyrel."

"Tom's there? Good. Tell him I'm sending him a video. See if he can tell what the men in it are saying."

My phone pinged and I put Tony on speaker before opening the email. The picture was grainy, obviously shot with night optics, and the upper and lower portions were practically whited-out by lights. But Stuart Lane's shaved white head was clearly visible in the backseat, looking to his right.

"A taxi came by and slowed down," Tony said. "Then a few houses past Eve's, it came to a full stop for half a minute."

"I'm pretty sure that's Lane, Tony. Did he get out?"

"Negative. I think it was just a recon. When it stopped, it looked like the driver was doing something on a small tablet mounted to the dash."

"I'm worried about Eve and Little Jesse," I confessed.

"Don't be," Tony said. "Deuce was here until the cab came by. He followed it to a nearby Hampton Inn, where he parked near the entrance and watched Lane go inside with a backpack. There's only the one way in and out of the parking lot and Deuce is camped on it."

I had to smile. "Thanks, Tony."

"Don't thank me till you get our bill," he said, but I could visualize his big, toothy grin over the phone connection. "Hang on. Tom's looking at the video now."

I could hear Tom's voice but couldn't make out what he was saying. Tom Broderick had once been my commanding officer. While he'd been in rehab after the explosion, his wife had left him and he'd about given up on everything. But it turned out that he had a natural affinity for lip reading and had learned fast.

"Tom says the older man said, and I quote, 'There's enough rye to make several men kings.'"

"He's sure?" I asked. "Moonshine is usually made with corn, not rye. And I doubt anyone could get *king* rich making hooch."

"That's what's buggin' me," Tony said.

Tony was sharp. Rarely did anything get past him.

"What's got you bugged?" I asked.

"Even at twice the scale you described, I'd bet both the lawyer and the sheriff make more at their day jobs. Why make corn whiskey? Why the risk?"

The same thought had been going through my head. The risk-to-benefit ratio was way out of whack for two men who had solid, professional careers and reputations as pillars in the community.

I heard Tony ask Tom if he was sure about the rye and this time, I did hear Tom's response. "He either said rye or oohrah, Gunny. And neither man carried himself like a jarhead."

I mouthed the name of the grain and the Marine exclamation and he was right. The mouth made the same shape for both.

"Rye?" I wondered aloud. "Rye whiskey, I guess. Maybe it sells for more. I don't know, I've never been much of a whiskey drinker."

"I'm a bourbon man, myself," Tony said.

"What else can you use rye for?" I asked.

It was a rhetorical question, but Tony had an answer. He'd grown up on a farm in North Carolina.

"We always grew rye in the winter," he said. "Not as a cash crop, though. It was just to prevent erosion and to add nutrients to the soil when we plowed it under every spring to plant corn."

"That's it?"

"You can make rye bread and crackers," Tony replied. "But that kind of rye is grown in Europe. In the Carolinas, it was just grown for ground cover."

"There has to be more to it," I said. "Ask Chyrel to see what she can find out about rye grown in central Virginia. I wasn't even aware there were different kinds of rye."

I ended the call and got out of the truck, looking forward to a hot shower. But later. For now, I was going to stake out the hotel's restaurant. The two men from the van had to eat sooner or later.

CHAPTER FIFTEEN

Aiden Pritchard paced the floor of his home office. Saturday was usually date night for him and Susan. When the babysitter had called earlier to say she was sick, Susan started to call her sister as a backup, but Aiden had stopped her, telling her he could skip tonight if it wasn't a big deal to her. He was behind on his work and could get caught up. She'd agreed, but only if they could watch a movie together after the kids went to bed. Saturday date night had always been important to her.

Stretch Buchannan was a problem. He'd Googled the man's name on his computer and found dozens of news stories. He seemed to be a mid-level player in the south Florida drug scene. Some stories cited rumors that the man had a violent streak.

They needed Stuart back in Staunton. But he hadn't checked in since just before boarding the third leg of his flight to Miami. The man thought himself a computer hacker, and he *could* get around some firewalled systems and access people's email accounts. When he couldn't, he knew others who could. These people had their own network and sometimes traded jobs. Some charged exorbitant fees for their time.

Aiden wanted to know who Buchannan had told and who had access to the videos he claimed to have. He didn't need the man to show proof of either—just the mention of the conversation around the firepit was enough, and Lou had confirmed that he'd seen the other. Once they knew who Buchannan had told, then those people could be eliminated, right along with the bothersome drug dealer from Florida.

When the phone on his desk rang, Aiden jumped, but he composed himself as he put the receiver to his ear. "ACA Pritchard."

"It's Lou. Have you heard from Stuart?"

"I was actually hoping you were him. No, the last time he checked in was when he was boarding at Newark Liberty."

"He should have gotten there hours ago," Sheriff Taliaferro said.

Aiden checked the antique grandfather clock by the door. It was nearly ten. "He probably went straight to work. You know how he gets."

"Yeah," Lou replied. "He gets completely off the rails if there's a skirt involved."

"I spoke to him before he boarded. No shortcuts, no tracks, and no fucking around."

"You should have sent Jeb."

"That old man?"

"He's done this kind of thing before, and he's level-headed. You know Stuart; you were his attorney the night he strangled the hooker and shot the—"

"I've told you not to bring that up, Lou."

"The man attracts attention," Lou said, scoffing. "That Uncle Fester head and face of his."

"On a Saturday night in Miami, he'd blend right in." Aiden didn't know why he was defending his decision to send Stuart to Miami. "He's probably at the woman's house now and will be back tomorrow."

There was a moment's pause.

"Are you really just going to let this guy muscle in and take over?" Lou asked, finally getting to the real reason he'd called.

"Absolutely not," Aiden replied. "You know me better than that. But right now, he's got our asses over the proverbial whiskey barrel. There's only so much digging around *you* can do without drawing attention from your subordinates. We need Stuart to find out who Buchannan has told. After that, we can put him down; Buchannan's the kind of man who doesn't leave many tracks, and nobody would connect a missing Florida drug dealer to anything going on here in the Shenandoah Valley, or to us."

"But he was right, wasn't he?" Lou said. "About the sloppy part. Those guys are ripping you off and selling locally. You don't shit where you eat, Aiden. Both our dads knocked that into us early."

"You're right," Aiden said. "We have to put them on a tighter leash. But we need their rye."

"How's that coming along?"

"I was down there earlier today," Aiden replied. "Brown has started the extraction or whatever it is. He's already produced nearly two liters."

"What's that in regular English?"

Aiden rolled his eyes. "It's about half a gallon."

How that backwoods hick got into, much less *through* college, he couldn't fathom. They'd been classmates since kindergarten, but Taliaferro's folks could only afford in-state college, and Lou had graduated from the military school just down the interstate in Lexington. After VMI, Lou had served four years as an Army officer. Aiden glanced up at the Stanford diploma on his wall. His own father had been an attorney, and Aiden had attended both his alma maters, University of Virginia for pre-law, and on to California for one of the best law schools in the country.

"And you have a buyer lined up?" Lou asked. "Who is it?"

"Yes, I do," Aiden said, his voice showing his exasperation. "And I told you before, the fewer who know, the better. That half gallon is worth sixty grand, Lou. In one day, mind you. Brown will be making about that much every day for most of the winter. Twice that, once we bring the second processor online."

"Almost half a million a week," Lou said softly. "All winter long?"

"And he's checking the rye yields from other farms all over the valley. Our three can't be the only ones with that fungus growing on it."

"Let me know when you hear from Stuart," Lou said. "I don't trust this guy, Buchannan. I want him out of my county."

"I will," Aiden said, then hung up the phone. "*Your* county," he mumbled, as he resumed pacing. "Maybe it's time for a change there, too."

His phone rang again and he snatched it up, thinking it was Lou calling him back with another question. "What now?"

"Huh," a voice said. "It's Stuart. You said to call."

"Yeah, hours ago. Where are you?"

"Miami," Stuart replied.

Knowing the man's penchant for speaking with as few words as possible, Aiden chose to let it go. "Give me an update. Have you made any progress?"

"Looked over the house," he replied. "Should be easy enough. Gonna head back after midnight."

"Tonight? I figured you'd wait till tomorrow and catch her alone."

"Why? It's just one man, plus the two women, and a coupla kids."

"Kids?"

"Yeah," the brute huffed. "Sneed's daughter has two kids."

This wasn't something Aiden had figured on. He knew Stuart was impatient and he'd known the woman's daughter was married, but killing a kid?

"You're going to do it tonight?" Aiden asked.

"Yeah."

"How?"

"Figured I'd bust in and knock the husband out. With him outta the way, the others will be easy. Then I can do him last."

Aiden Pritchard had risen to assistant prosecutor before he was thirty-five, partly due to his ability to tell when he was being lied to, and partly for being able to lie convincingly himself. Stuart wasn't telling everything.

"Remember what I said, Stuart," Aiden reminded him. "Do it quick and leave no trace. I need you back here for another job. A hacking job."

"I'll be back tomorrow," Stuart said, and then the line went dead.

CHAPTER SIXTEEN

After checking in at the front desk and getting a key card, I went straight to the restaurant, partly because the two men might have already gone there, but mostly because I was hungry. The thought of a man going after Eve and the kids kept niggling at my brain like a worm. I should be *there*, not here. But I knew the caliber of the men who *were* there on my behalf. It wouldn't surprise me if Deuce had the whole team deployed after Lane's plane touched down. He'd be driving back to the office soon enough with Stuart Lane strapped to the hood. I had to concentrate on what I was doing here and now.

A pretty waitress in her mid-twenties approached wearing a smile, and the traditional white and black outfit of a fine restaurant. She had tattoo sleeves halfway down her upper arms that her uniform only barely covered.

"Good evening, sir. I'm Tammi and I'll be serving you tonight. Would you like to see a menu?"

"Is there a steak on it, Tammi?" I asked.

Her smile brightened. "Your choice of a twelve-ounce or sixteen-ounce New York strip, served with a baked potato and your choice of vegetable."

"The sixteen-ounce," I replied. "Medium, with broccoli, water, and any IPA you think is good."

"There's a brewery just a few blocks from here called Skipping Rock. They make a New England-style pale ale that I really like."

"Sounds great," I said, as I saw the two men from the van enter the restaurant.

"Bottle or draft?"

"Draft," I replied.

Having written nothing down, Tammi left my table. It was still early, and the room was less than half-filled with diners. Most were at tables close to the entrance. I'd chosen one in a corner. The two men sat at a table two down from me and a moment later Tammi brought my beer, then went to get their orders.

My phone vibrated in my pocket. It was Chyrel.

"Find out anything?" I asked in a low voice to keep others from hearing.

"Where are you?" Needlessly, she whispered back.

"In a restaurant at the Stonewall Jackson Hotel."

"I wouldn't order a fish sandwich there," she cautioned. "How are you surviving so far from water?"

"Steak," I said. "What'd you find?"

"I only have information on the older man. His name's Walter Brown and he's a botanist."

"A botanist?"

"A PhD, no less. He's done a lot of work in and around the Appalachians, even wrote a paper on the Okefeno-kee. I haven't ID'd the other guy yet. Facial recognition only hit on Doctor Brown so fast because of the numerous papers he's published."

"Anything else?"

"Tony said you were asking what uses there could be for rye," she said. "Aside from baked goods, some beers, and rye whiskey, not much. Why?"

"The two guys in the video were at Pritchard's old barn," I replied. "Tom said they were talking about how they had enough rye to become rich."

"Uh-oh," Chyrel said.

"Uh-oh what?"

"The sheriff called Pritchard a little while ago. Pritchard mentioned Doctor Brown and said he'd made something worth $120,000 dollars a gallon."

"So why the uh-oh?"

"I thought they were just confused and I only now put the two together." I heard her nails on a keyboard for a moment. "The most expensive liquid in the world. There's a microscopic organism that grows on certain grains called an ergot fungus. Ergotamine can be extracted from the fungus. Lysergic acid is made through alkaline hydrolysis of ergotamine."

"Remember who you're talking to Chyrel."

"Acid, Jesse."

"You mean like battery acid?"

"No," Chyrel replied. "I'm talking about Lucy in the Sky with Diamonds, Jesse. Cid, vitamin A, like Alice in Wonderland acid; LSD."

"From rye?"

"From the fungus that sometimes grows on certain kinds of rye," she corrected. "It's rare and you'd need thousands of pounds of rye just to make a couple of pints of LSD. But it's worth six figures a gallon."

"How much rye do you think Pritchard, Lane, and Long can grow?"

"Definitely enough to make it worthwhile," she replied. "That is, if the ergot fungi is growing on it."

"Put together anything you think Stretch can use as leverage against Brown and send it to me within ten minutes. He's here in the restaurant."

I ended the call just as my steak arrived.

"Thanks, Tammi," I said, as she placed a perfectly grilled steak in front of me. "This looks almost too good to eat."

Tammi smiled, leaning a hip against the table. "Will there be anything else, sir?"

I smiled back at her. "Call me Stretch, Tammi. I'm not real big on formalities."

Her smile brightened. "How was the beer, Stretch?"

Tammi was pretty; tall and willowy, with dark blond hair pulled back in a ponytail that hung to the middle of her back.

"It was good, thanks."

"Can I bring you another one?"

"No thanks," I replied, setting my phone aside.

It always paid to be nice to bartenders, waitresses, and cab drivers. They were the *invisible* segment of society that most people didn't even notice, but they all often overheard conversations.

Tammi left my table and I enjoyed my meal. Just as I finished, my phone chimed an incoming email. I spent the next few minutes taking a crash course on the production of what was a very popular hallucinogen in the 1960s. Brown and the man I assumed was his assistant ate their dinner while I read.

When Tammi brought my check, I gave her my card and asked her to deliver two double-shots of their best rye whiskey to Brown's table and to include their meals on my check.

She came back a moment later, placing the two highball glasses in front of Brown and the other man. Then pointing, to me, she told them what was in the glasses. Or she might have said, "Oohrah."

When she brought the check, she said, "I might as well have pointed a gun at them, Stretch. The drink seemed to scare them. What's that about?"

"Just a joke," I said. "Thanks, Tammi."

I added a $50 tip and then sat back and waited for the fish to take the bait.

I didn't have long to wait. Doctor Brown rose and came toward me. "I'm afraid I don't know who you are, sir. Why did you pay for our meals?"

"Have a seat, Doctor Brown," I said, pushing a chair out with my foot.

Brown glanced back at the other man, who appeared worried. When he turned back to face me, I rose from my chair and extended my hand. "Stretch Buchannan. We'll be seeing a lot of each other. I'm taking over the distribution for Aiden Pritchard."

He only stared at me blankly, shaking my hand as the color slowly faded from his face.

"Th- the rye?" he stammered. "M- mister Pritchard said he had a buyer, but he also said we'd never m- meet him."

I smiled and motioned toward the empty chair. "And yet, here I am."

Brown looked back at the other man again.

"Have your assistant join us," I said. "The three of us need to talk."

Brown motioned the other man over and as he approached, I offered him my hand. "Name's Stretch Buchannan."

"Frank Millhouse," the younger man replied.

"Pull up a chair, Frank. Doctor Brown and I were about to talk about our futures."

"I don't get it," Frank said, sitting next to Brown.

"It's simple," I said. "Your boss is a sloppy operator. I'm not. He'll get you arrested or killed. I won't. He and I have already agreed on me taking over the liquor distribution. But that's not enough for me, you see. So, I'll be taking the cid off his hands, too."

"Cid?" Brown said, his eyes blinking.

I lowered my voice. "You discovered a gold mine, doctor. If there's as much ergot fungi on the rye here as I think there is, we don't need the sheriff or the bozos they have making deliveries now."

"B- but... they own the land," Brown said.

"And they'll get a good price for their harvest," I said, falling easily into my drug kingpin persona. "Aiden will see to that. It'll be way better than what they'd get working the corn through the summer heat. And they'll have zero risk. I know Wright and Long will go for it. But Stuart Lane will be a problem. I've already taken steps to convince him, and I should know later tonight if he's on board. I'm sure he will be."

"What about Aiden and Lou?" Frank asked. "They're the law in these parts; the sheriff and prosecutor."

When Chyrel sent me the bio on Judge Whitaker, I'd downloaded his picture and stored his phone number on my phone. I scrolled through it and pulled up the judge's picture, then showed it to Frank.

"Aiden and Lou are *just* the sheriff and prosecutor," I corrected him.

Frank shook his head. "No way, man. I know him. He's as straight as they come."

I took a chance that Ollie would recognize my voice, or at least the Florida Keys area code, and called his number, putting it on speaker with the volume low enough that only the three of us could hear.

"Hello?"

"Hey, Ollie, it's me. Sorry to bother you, but I was hoping to talk to you one more time tomorrow. It's about that big adventure we discussed. Can we meet for breakfast? You pick the place. My treat."

There was a brief silence on the other end before the judge responded.

"Yes, of course. There's a Cracker Barrel down by the interstate. Say, six o'clock?"

"Perfect. I'll see you then."

I ended the call and looked from one man to the other. They both seemed to open up after that, describing the interior of the old barn and how Pritchard had customized it to make moonshine. Brown told me about how he'd met Pritchard and discovered the rare fungus on the rye grown on several farms in the area.

"How did you get them to partner with you?" Frank asked.

"I didn't say I was partnering with them," I replied. "I'm taking over."

Before either man could respond, I stood and strode toward the lobby and the elevator. Once the doors slid closed behind me, I redialed the judge's number.

"What's going on, son? You in some kind of trouble?"

"Sorry, Ollie," I said, grinning at the memory of the old black and white TV comedy duo. "I hated having to do it, but I needed more clout than the sheriff or prosecutor. There's a lot more going on here than moonshine and murder. It involves illegal drug manufacturing and the amount looks like it could be in the tens of millions of dollars."

"So, we won't be talking about fishing in the morning?"

"No, sir. We'll be talking about LSD manufacturing right here in Staunton. On a huge scale."

"How huge?" he asked.

"One drop of LSD, soaked onto a tiny piece of blotter paper, sells on the street for ten dollars," I replied. "They're planning to make gallons of it. I'm not sure how many drops are in a gallon, but I bet it's a lot."

"About seventy-five thousand," he replied. "And you're certain that Pritchard's involved in this?"

"I just had dinner with the botanist who is making it in Pritchard's old barn, along with the moonshine."

"And you made it appear to him that I was working with you?"

"A judge trumps a prosecutor," I said. "I'm sorry, but I didn't see any other way to get the information I needed from the botanist."

"I see. What else will I need to do?"

"If you should get a call asking what your involvement is with Stretch Buchannan, would you mind playing along and call me back with what you learn? Be reluctant to talk about us at first, though."

"I've been thinking about this all afternoon," he said, his voice sounding almost jovial. "I'll help any way I can, legally."

The elevator doors opened on the top floor and I explained quickly how I'd muscled my way into Pritchard's organization and how I was taking over all of it. Then I told him about my conversation with the botanist who had the know-how to make the drug.

"At some point," Ollie confided, "I will have to bring in the Virginia State Police and the Attorney General."

"Wouldn't that be the Commonwealth Police?" I asked, waving my key card in front of the lock and opening the door.

The judge laughed. "Actually, no. In this case, it is state."

"You don't have to do that right away, do you?" I asked. "I think I've only exposed the tip of the iceberg."

"No, not right now. I don't think I'd be breaking any laws, or even bending one slightly, by just saying that yes, I am conducting a business arrangement with you. But I'll need to give you a deposit in the morning for the charter. That way, I'm not lying."

"My normal charter deposit is a cup of really good coffee."

"Ah," Ollie said. "You liked that, did you?"

"Yeah," I replied, switching on the light and tossing my pack on the bed. "I usually drink a Costa Rican coffee."

"Hacienda la Minita?" he asked.

I was impressed. "I especially like the Tarrazu blend."

"Very good, as well," Ollie said. "What we had earlier was Jamaican Blue Mountain coffee."

"I don't suppose they have that at Cracker Barrel?" I asked, liking the old man even more.

"I really don't know, Jesse. But my niece is the manager there. My sister's daughter who moved here with her husband years ago. She always has something special in the brewer for me on Sundays."

"Thanks, Ollie. I look forward to it."

Ending the call, I pulled my laptop out of my pack, and powered it up. It was time for a conference call.

CHAPTER SEVENTEEN

The inside of the van was dark, except for the soft blue glow from a pair of computer monitors in the back. The van had no windows—it didn't need any. A heavy black curtain was drawn, blocking the view into the van's cab.

A barrel-chested man sat in front of one of the computer terminals, the glow casting weird shadows on his face from his thick mustache. A noise from near the other terminal caused him to turn.

The man's partner extended a cup toward him, "Here."

"Thanks," Andrew Bourke said, accepting the cup.

The side door of the van opened, and Tony Jacobs climbed in. At his console, Andrew was watching a computer screen that showed four small windows.

"Are they coming in clear?" Tony asked.

"Five by five," the former Coast Guardsman replied in a deep baritone. "I'm even picking up what sounds like a television from inside the house."

"Smart thinking," Paul Bender said from his seat in the back. "Having eyes on the back of the house will alert us if the subject slips past Deuce and Julie."

"That's not likely," Tony commented, taking a seat next to Andrew. "That hotel only has one entrance to the parking lot. Trying to scale an eight-foot wall in the back would draw more attention than this guy would want. He hasn't done anything yet."

Andrew glanced back at Paul, who was watching the same four video feeds that he was. "Think he'll make his move tonight?"

"Yes, I believe he will," Paul said, not looking up from the screen. "I've studied everything Chyrel pulled up on the man. He's impatient and impulsive, prone to violent outbursts. I think he has a streak of misogyny as well. He sees Sandra Sneed as inferior and he also has a strong dislike of attorneys. He won't have a gun. Probably a knife or a piece of rope to use as a garrote. Yes, he'll make his move tonight. Probably after everyone is asleep."

Paul's computer beeped. "Incoming video link," he said, moving the mouse around and opening the conference app. "It's Jesse."

Andrew nodded. "Get Deuce and Chyrel on there, too. I'll watch the feeds."

"Hello, Jesse," Paul said to the screen. "Mind standing by for a minute while I get the others on?"

"Yeah, I'll wait."

Andrew heard the man's grumbled reply and grinned over at Tony. It hadn't been so long ago that Jesse McDermitt couldn't even send a text message on a cell phone without help. He was okay with the electronic navigation equipment on his boats, but communications technology had left him behind after the pager.

"Hey, Jesse," Andrew heard Julie's voice say. "Hey, Paul."

Chyrel chimed in, greeting the others, then Jesse asked, "Who's with you in the van, Paul?"

"Tony and Andrew, right now," Paul replied. "Tom will be here in less than an hour."

"You have everyone on this?" Jesse asked.

"Yeah," came Deuce's reply. "All but Charity. She's out of the country."

Though Andrew could hear the others talking, his eyes never left the monitors in front of him. The top two images were video feeds from two rooftop cameras; one looking ahead of the van, showing the front of Jesse's daughter's house, as well as the street beyond it, and the other surveying the street behind the van. The lower two images were from the two wireless cameras Tony had just set up in the back corners of Eve and Nick Maggio's backyard.

"How are things up there?" Deuce's voice came over the speakers on Paul's computer.

"Cold," Jesse replied. "There's a chance of snow tonight through early morning. Any change in Lane's status?"

"He checked into the hotel several hours ago," Deuce replied. "Julie and I are watching the only entrance to the parking lot. He hasn't left."

"I can confirm that," Chyrel said. "I hacked into the hotel's security system and I'm monitoring the camera on his floor."

"I'm at a hotel in Staunton," Jesse said. "The Stonewall Jackson. I just made contact with a couple of guys who work for Pritchard, a botanist named Walter Brown and his assistant, Frank Millhouse. They're making LSD in Pritchard's barn, along with the moonshine."

"LSD?" Deuce asked. "Are you sure?"

Chyrel fielded the question. "It's the only thing that makes sense, from what I've learned. The primary ingredient comes from a fungus that grows on some types of rye seed. And it's the only liquid I've found that commands the prices they were talking about."

"I told them I was taking over the operation," Jesse said. "Something I'd already told Pritchard and Taliaferro earlier today, but I was only talking about the whiskey then."

"I bet the prosecutor didn't like that very much," Deuce said.

"He doesn't know I told Brown I was taking over the LSD operation yet," Jesse replied. "But I'm sure he will soon. His reaction was puzzling when I said I was taking over his moonshine operation. He really didn't seem to care all that much. It made me think then that there was more going on than just moonshine. So, I went up to the hills to recon the property and that's how I found the botanist. I brought Judge Whitaker in on it, making Brown and his assistant think he was behind me muscling in. I made sure they overheard our conversation."

"And you're certain he's not a part of it?" Tony asked over Paul's shoulder. "Things could seriously backfire if the judge is in on this."

"No doubt in my mind, Tony," Jesse replied. "By now, Brown will have contacted Pritchard, and it's likely Pritchard will call the judge. I'm meeting the judge for breakfast at 0600, something else I made sure Brown overheard."

"You'll be watched," Paul said. "What's to stop Pritchard from killing you?"

"I made it clear to him," Jesse said. "I told him that all the evidence I have is also in the hands of someone else and if anything happened to me, it would all fall onto the Attorney General's desk."

"We'll take care of Lane," Deuce said. "Nothing will happen to your family; you have my word. What's your plan moving forward?"

"I expect Pritchard to contact the judge tonight. I told Pritchard I'd be picking up the first shipment at sunrise on Monday. Do you know anyone at an ATF or DEA regional office near here; someone who can spare a couple of agents and a cargo van? Even the FBI would do."

"I do," Paul replied. "And we've worked with her before. Special Agent Sheena Mason has contacted me several times to do forensic psychological profiles. She's working out of FBI headquarters in DC now."

"Contact her," Jesse said. "Explain what's going on and ask her to meet me and the Judge at 0600 at the Cracker Barrel in Staunton. It's near the interstate."

"On it," Paul replied. "But don't you think Pritchard will have someone watching?"

"I'm counting on it," Jesse replied. "That way, he'll think she's part of the crew, when she arrives Monday with another agent."

"Anything else?" Deuce asked.

"Sorry to interrupt," Chyrel said. "But your boy is on the move. Headed for the elevator."

"No, Deuce, that's it. Get this guy. I want him there when I get back."

"Okay," Deuce said. "Gotta go, Jesse."

Paul ended the video link and remotely turned on the team's earwigs, including Chyrel's. "Comms are up," he said.

"Comm check," came Deuce's voice over the tiny communications device Andrew had in his ear.

The other five checked in one by one.

"What about Tom?" Tony asked.

Just then, the side door opened, and Tom Broderick stepped into the van. Paul got up from his console and moved aside so Tom could get to it. He'd keep watch on the video feeds and the computer's voice-to-text app would keep him aware of any verbal instructions from the others.

Without a word, Tom sat down and looked at the monitor.

"Tom?" Andrew said, as he rose from his position at the other console. Tom's name appeared on his screen and he looked up.

"We're going now," Andrew said with a big grin, as the deaf man read his lip movements. "Stuart Lane is on the move."

"Oh," Tom said. "I guess I got here at just the right time then."

The others laughed as they climbed out of the van, then silently dispersed to their various positions.

"We're on the move," Deuce said quietly.

Andrew pointed to the screen and Tom looked down. He lifted a thumb in the air, then made a shooing motion with his hand. Andrew stepped out of the van and closed the door.

With Deuce and Julie following the subject on foot, Andrew casually crossed the street and took up his position in the shadows next to a boat and trailer parked beside an empty vacation home.

He knew that Deuce and Julie would appear to be just what they were—a married couple enjoying a late-night stroll hand-in-hand. In the Grove it was quite normal.

"On Aviation," Deuce said. "Crossing Trapp. We're on the opposite side of the street from him, half a block behind. He's dressed in dark jeans and a black shirt, carrying a backpack. Good camouflage if he didn't have that big, white pumpkin on top of his shoulders."

"I'm in position," Andrew said, peeking around the corner of the house.

"Me, too," Tony's voice declared over Andrew's comm.

A few seconds passed, then Paul said, "I'm in position, as well."

"We don't want to spook this guy, y'all," Chyrel said. "As soon as he turns the corner, Deuce and Julie start running to catch up. Tom, make sure to hit the strobe before they make the turn. Deuce's call on the flash."

"He's crossing Lincoln and still hasn't looked back," Julie said a moment later. "He's walking pretty fast for a hit man. One more block."

The seconds ticked past as Andrew waited in the shadows beside the boat. A dog barked on the next block and he could hear the heavy crunch of footsteps approaching.

"Got him," Tom said. "Just rounded the corner."

Andrew glanced up and saw a black-clad, bald man turn onto Tigertail Avenue. He looked back down at the ground and closed his eyes tightly, shielding them with his arm, knowing that Tom was about to push the button on his console that would activate a very bright light on top of the van. He wasn't worried he'd miss it; they'd practiced this tactic before, and he knew the light would turn darkness into daylight. It was like a flash-bang grenade, but brighter and without the bang. The light was meant to disorient the subject, temporarily blinding him.

"Now!" Deuce's voice came over Andrew's earwig.

Even in the shadows with his eyes closed tightly, Andrew could still see the light. It flashed for only a second, then Andrew charged out from behind the boat, pistol raised.

CHAPTER EIGHTEEN

*S*heena Mason, I thought, as I closed the laptop. I'd all but forgotten about her. She'd been the lead agent during the arrest of a United States congressman in Beaufort, South Carolina ten years ago. The congressman had hired a Jamaican gang to kidnap and murder his own daughter and mother-in-law. In the excitement of the chase and apprehension, I guess we'd both needed a distraction.

I wasn't overly worried about Eve and her family, though it weighed on my mind. I could call Chyrel and have her patch me into their comm, but Deuce and the others had practiced this kind of takedown many times. And even my anxious breathing would be a distraction. They had a huge technology and manpower advantage, and Stuart Lane had no idea that anybody was on to him. He might know that a Florida drug dealer named Stretch Buchannan knew why he was there, but I didn't think Pritchard would cancel things because of that. I felt certain that before I went to sleep, Deuce would let me know that Lane was hog-tied face down on the floor of the van and that they were headed back to Key Largo. I knew I wouldn't sleep until he did.

As I was unlacing my boots, my phone rang. I grabbed it up, thinking it was Deuce already, but it was Judge Whitaker.

"Did Pritchard call you?" I asked, without saying hello.

"Yes, he did," Ollie replied, sounding pleased. "I always wanted to be part of an undercover investigation."

"What'd the prosecutor have to say?"

"He sort of beat around the bush at first," Ollie said, sounding as if he was thoroughly enjoying himself. "Finally, he just blurted out the question, asking if I knew who Stretch Buchannan was."

"And what did you say?"

I could hear the judge chuckle. "I didn't tell a lie," he said. "Nothing I said could ever be used against me or you. But it was the *way* I said it. I told him that not only did I know who Stretch Buchannan was, but that I'd personally hired the man."

I grinned. The judge was a very smart man. By saying that he knew who Stretch *was*, he alluded to the fact that, unknown to Pritchard, he knew my real name.

"Good choice of words, Ollie."

"So, what's next?"

"There will be a third person meeting us for breakfast," I replied. "An FBI agent by the name of Sheena Mason will be coming in from DC."

"The FBI? I thought it would be the state police."

"Fifty gallons of LSD means interstate distribution," I replied. "Hell, probably worldwide. We'll talk to Sheena in the morning and see how she wants to include state law enforcement."

The judge laughed. "In this case it would be the collective *commonwealth* law enforcement. The state police is the only Virginia government organization with the word *state* in its title. Weird, I know."

"I'll never get used to it," I offered. "You don't mind meeting with the FBI, do you?"

"Not at all," Ollie replied. "I've met Special Agent Mason a few times."

This surprised me. "I've only met her once; ten years ago, down in South Carolina."

"Ten years ago?" he asked thoughtfully. "The arrest of former congressman Nick Cross?"

"Yeah. How'd you know?"

"That case made her career. Were you involved?"

"Yes," I replied. "I worked for Homeland Security at the time. The team I was with was tasked with rescuing Cross's daughter and mother-in-law from Jamaican kidnappers in the Bahamas. It turned out that they were on Cross's payroll and had double-crossed him."

"Good riddance, if you ask me."

"I agree." My phone beeped, signaling an incoming call. "I have another call. See you in the morning."

I switched over, thinking surely that it was Deuce calling. "Did you get him?"

"Get who?" a voice asked.

For a moment I didn't place it, then realized it was Pritchard.

"Is this Aiden?" I asked in a friendly tone. "I thought you were someone else calling."

"I heard some distressing news a little while ago."

I pushed my boots off with my toes and grinned. "I bet you did, Aiden. You were holding out on me. And here I thought we were friends."

"Obviously our earlier arrangement will have to be renegotiated." He was nothing if not focused.

"Oh, I don't know," I said. "Seven bucks a gallon sounds like a pretty good price to me."

"For the liquor, yes," he said, not losing his cool. I had to give the guy credit. "You and I both know that's not even a fair price for a drop of what Doctor Brown is making."

"I'm meeting my partners in the morning," I said, becoming equally serious. "You tell me what you think is a fair price and I'll mention it."

"Judge Whitaker?"

I paused a moment for dramatic affect. "So, you know about my relationship with Ollie, huh?"

"And I don't like it one bit," Pritchard said.

"I don't care if you like it or not, Aiden. That's not how this kind of thing works in the real world. What? You figured you could corner the market or something, without anyone finding out? Give me a number."

"I already have a buyer," Pritchard said. Then his voice broke ever so slightly. "I can cut you in. We'll call it protection. A few others will be pretty upset.

"Taliaferro?" I asked. "He's in on the murder cover-up just as deeply as you are. He tries anything funny, prison will be his *best* outcome."

"My buyer is willing to pay two million for the first twenty gallons."

"Like I told the doctor, Aiden, I'm taking over your whole operation. I can find a buyer easy enough. Probably for more than that. I have contacts in this world—you don't. All I want from you is a number that you can live with. And it ain't two million. I told you, I'm a fair guy. So, let's say... four times what your expenses are for the rye, the equipment to extract the ergotamine, and the manpower to do it. You spend or split that amount however you see fit." He didn't say anything. "Aiden?"

"I'm still here, though I should just hang up."

"Is that any way to do business, counselor?" I asked. "Let's not forget the videos and other evidence I have on you. I'm not a lawyer, but I bet it's enough to put all of you in prison for the rest of your natural lives."

When he spoke again, it was with a voice resigned to defeat. "I'll have to crunch some numbers."

"You do that, Aiden. Text me a number at six o'clock."

"In the morning?"

"Yeah," I replied. "I'm having breakfast with the judge and the person who will be making Monday's pickup."

"I'll text you," he replied. "But it won't be a negotiable price."

"Everything's negotiable, Aiden."

I ended the call and set my phone on the desk. Taking my ditty bag out of my pack, I went to the head to brush my teeth and wash up. My phone rang again, and I raced back to the desk to grab it. It wasn't Deuce, but I recognized the area code; Washington, DC.

"Hello?"

"Jesse McDermitt?" a woman's voice asked. "Or should I say Stretch Buchannan?"

"Special Agent Mason?"

"Oh, come now, Jesse. I think we went a little beyond titles the last time we met."

"Sheena. How are you?"

She laughed. "Much better off since we first met. I never had a chance to thank you."

"Thank me?" I asked.

"Being the lead agent in the arrest and subsequent prosecution and conviction of a sitting congressman was quite an accomplishment for my career."

"Oh," I said. "I didn't realize it was that big a deal."

"And now you have your sights set on an assistant state prosecutor in Virginia?"

It was my turn to chuckle. "Assistant *commonwealth* prosecutor," I corrected.

"Paul told me that he's involved in making moonshine and LSD," Sheena said, getting serious. "You're certain of his involvement? Neither is really the FBI's territory."

"True," I said. "The moonshine would be ATF and maybe the IRS. The LSD would fall under DEA. But since it involves the county's prosecutor and sheriff planning to distribute across state lines, I thought maybe the FBI would be interested. He's not just involved, Sheena; under the sheriff's protection, Pritchard runs the operation. Or, he did, that is."

"Paul said you had him convinced you're a drug smuggler and just muscled your way in," she replied. "Yes, the FBI would be most interested. When can we get together?"

"I'm having breakfast with Judge Oliver Whitaker. He's the circuit-court judge here in Staunton and says he knows you."

"I remember him," she said. "I was a witness in his court twice in the last couple of years."

That could present a problem. Pritchard has been prosecutor for longer than that and would obviously know her.

"You're there in Staunton now?" she asked.

"Yeah."

"I'm not far. I can be there in an hour."

I looked at my watch and thought of our last meeting and Sara at the same time. It was nearly 0100 now. Five hours until I was meeting the judge.

"The judge and I will see you in the morning at the Cracker Barrel," I said gently.

There was a hint of disappointment in her voice when she replied. "In the morning?"

"Yeah. It's been a real long day and I was just about to go to sleep."

"Okay," Sheena said. "Paul told me six o'clock. Is that right?"

"Yeah—oh and one more thing; can you wear a dark wig?"

"You don't like natural blondes anymore?"

"No—er—well, it's because…"

"Just busting your chops, Jesse," she said, laughing. "You're worried Aiden Pritchard might see us together, recognize me, and figure out what's going on, right?"

"Yeah," I replied.

"Don't worry," she said. "The two times I appeared in the Staunton courthouse, I was wearing a black wig, big dark sunglasses, pancake makeup, and enough lipstick to make a sailor blush, so I could maintain my undercover status. Coming as plain old me should be fine this time around. See you in the morning."

The call ended and I sat down hard on the edge of the bed. Sheena and I had had a brief affair, if you could call it that. It'd been more like a one-night stand that went on for a couple of days. She'd snuck into my room the night before we took down Congressman Nick Cross. I couldn't let that happen again. I was single then. Though my relationship with Sara was a little unusual emotionally, it *was* mutually monogamous. I didn't need to clutter my life with more than one woman. Two was completely out of the question.

As I started toward the head to get a shower, I got a text message from Chyrel.

Lane's on his way to Largo. No injuries.

I let out a breath I didn't know I'd been holding. Eve and the kids were safe. I texted her my thanks and said

I'd call her after meeting the judge. As I started to turn back toward the head, a movement outside my fifth-floor window caught my eye. I went over to it, drew open the curtains, and scanned the parking lot below.

It was snowing.

CHAPTER NINETEEN

On the north side of town, Aiden Pritchard entered a well-lit all-night diner and went straight to a table in the corner, where Lou Taliaferro sat. Sunday was the only day that Lou wasn't in uniform. Before sunrise there were only a handful of people inside.

"Find out anything since I called you last night?" Lou asked, as Aiden took a seat.

"Yeah, a lot. Stuart called last night. By now the job is done."

"You haven't heard from him this morning?" Lou asked.

Aiden dug his phone from his pocket. "No, I tried texting and he didn't reply, so I called. It went straight to voicemail, so he's probably still asleep or on the plane."

Aiden pulled up the picture his neighbor Keith Reed had sent him. "Ever see this woman around?"

"Whoa," Lou said, leaning in for a closer look. "No, I'd definitely remember her."

"That's one of Buchannan's people," Aiden said, worriedly. "The two of them are having breakfast down at the Cracker Barrel."

"So? As soon as Stuart gets back, he'll find out what Buchannan has on us and who else he's told. There's always an electronic trail."

"They're having breakfast with Judge Whitaker."

"Oh my God," Lou muttered under his breath. "This isn't good."

"It's not what you think," Aiden said. "The judge is with Buchannan. He must have found out what we're doing somehow and brought Buchannan in to take over for him."

"You mean they're in cahoots?"

"Yeah," Aiden said. "Brown overheard Buchannan talking to the judge last night in the hotel restaurant. Seriously? I think the old coot is behind everything."

"This is turning into a real shit show, Aiden." Lou studied his friend's face a moment as he sipped at his coffee. "What else?"

Aiden looked around the room and leaned slightly across the table. "They know about the other stuff, too."

"Dammit, Aiden!" Lou burst out.

Several people looked over at them, but quickly turned back to their food or conversations. Aiden and Lou met in public all the time, and both were well-known in the diner. They often discussed high-profile cases and the townsfolk knew to leave them alone.

"How the hell did he find out?" Lou hissed.

"He's staying at the same hotel Brown is in."

"Brown told him?"

Aiden shook his head as Madge poured coffee in his cup and hovered the pot over Lou's. Lou nodded and she topped his mug off, then walked away. She knew both men wouldn't be ordering food. They only came here to talk and drink coffee.

"No," Aiden replied. "From what Brown said, Buchannan already knew about it. He even ordered him and Frank an after-dinner drink—rye whiskey—before introducing himself. Buchannan told them that he knew about what they were making in my old barn and he said he was taking over the whole operation."

Lou looked out the far window at the snow-covered field across the highway. "What are we gonna do?"

"There's nothing we can do," Aiden replied. "At least not right now. Once we know who else he's told, we can send Stuart and Jeb after them. But until then, we're just going to have to take a loss."

"You mean—"

"Buchannan is expecting to pick up more than just the moonshine on Monday. He wants to know a price that will keep us in business and placated."

"How much has Brown made?"

"By tomorrow morning, close to six gallons. But Buchannan doesn't know that. Brown told me that he'd spilled the information to Buchannan that they'd already made two gallons."

"Then that's all he'll get," Lou said. "Tell him two hundred grand."

"He's no fool." Aiden sipped at his coffee. "He'll know that production is ongoing. And he made it real clear last night that he's not interested in retail or even whole-sale price. He wants to know just how much it will take to keep us productive."

"Okay," Lou said. "Tell him four gallons at fifty grand each. That's a loss of less than half, right? And we sell the other two gallons to your buyer at full price."

"That was my thought," Aiden said, as he picked up his phone. "But he's going to counter, I guarantee it."

"When it's time," Lou said, his voice low and menac-ing. "I want him all to myself." He stabbed a finger at Aiden's phone and said, "Jeb and Stuart can have the woman and I'll force Buchannan to watch until they're finished with her. Then I'll slit that asshole's throat from ear to ear."

CHAPTER TWENTY

When I got to the restaurant, there was a light dusting of snow on the grass, as well as the bare trees. It was still an hour before sunrise, but it was already light enough that I could tell the sky would be low and gray later on.

The pavement and patches of dirt and rock were just wet. I guess they held enough heat from the previous day to keep the snow from sticking.

The headlights of the rental truck swung across the long front porch of the building. As was usual for this chain, it was decorated with a collection of antique-looking odds and ends—rocking chairs and barrels with checker boards set up on them.

The lot was mostly empty, but there were several cars parked around the corner. I saw the judge's Buick out front and backed into the spot next to it. Ollie was behind the wheel. We both got out of our vehicles at the same time and shook hands at the front of my truck.

"Good morning," he said. "Hope you slept well."

"Yes, it is," I said with a ready smile. "And, yes I did. Sorry if I woke you last night."

"Oh, don't worry about that." He chuckled and smacked me on the back. "The older I get, the less sleep I need."

"I know exactly what you mean," I said.

"You seem exceptionally jubilant." Ollie snapped his fingers. "That's right, you're from Florida. Is this the first time you've seen snow?"

I laughed. "Not hardly. "'We have fought in every clime and place' isn't just a line from the hymn."

"Ah, that's right. You were a Marine."

I let the *were* slide. "Twenty years," I replied. "So, yeah, I've lived and worked in much colder places."

"So, what is it that has you so happy this morning?"

"Stuart Lane is out of the picture," I said. "Like you saw and heard in that video I showed you, Pritchard sent him to Miami to kill the woman who was with Kamren Steele when he was murdered. And as I mentioned, that woman is my ex-wife, and she's staying with my daughter and her family. Lane went there to kill them. He failed. So, yeah, that makes me happy."

The judge gave me a sideways glance as he led the way toward the restaurant's entrance but said nothing. He didn't need to; I knew what the question was that he didn't want to ask.

"My people were all over Lane before he even got close to the house. You might say that he's been kidnapped. But I say he's sitting on ice until I get back."

A black Ford sedan pulled in and parked next to my truck. The judge and I waited by the restaurant door. It was still five minutes before it would open, but inside, I could see a young woman look up and step out from behind a counter while still talking to another woman. Their body language showed that the younger woman was in charge.

Sheena Mason got out of the government-issued car. At least it didn't have government tags, and the big sedan looked a lot like the judge's car.

Sheena stepped up onto the porch with her hand extended and a big smile on her face. "It's been too long, Jesse. How are you, Judge?"

"I'm well," he said hurriedly. "That's my niece coming to the door. How shall I introduce you?"

"Stretch and Marsha," Sheena said. Then she smiled at me. "I was a big fan of the Brady Bunch when I was a kid."

The door opened and Ollie hugged the young woman, who opened it before turning to us. "This is my niece Carolyn. Carolyn, these are my friends, Marsha and Stretch."

"Pleased to meet you both," Carolyn said. "Y'all come in out of the cold. I have your usual table set up, Uncle Ollie, and the coffee is just about ready."

I studied Sheena as I held the door. She hadn't changed much. Her blond hair was cut shorter, just over the collar of her jacket. She still had all the same dangerous curves and her blue eyes sparkled. There was just the hint of faint lines forming at the corners of her eyes. My grandmother had called them laugh lines. Mam had a lot of laugh lines.

Carolyn led the way to a table near a corner. It was close enough to a roaring fire in the fireplace to feel the warmth, but far enough away that it wasn't too hot. She left us with three menus and said she'd be back with coffee. The judge shrugged out of his long coat and draped it over the chair next to him.

"You said you were from Pittsburgh," I said to Ollie.

"So, how do I have relatives in Virginia?" Ollie asked as he sat down. "My sister was much younger than me. She and her husband moved here when Carolyn was a toddler. When she was a teenager, I was already retired and the kids moved away. That was when I lost my sister and Carolyn lost her parents. They were both killed in a wreck. So, Josie and I moved down here, rather than make her pull up stakes at such a terrible time in her life." He cleared his throat.

"So, you're chasing drug manufacturers now, huh?" Sheena said, sitting in the chair opposite the judge and against the wall.

Ollie smiled as I sat down across from him. It dawned on me that there was a coat rack right behind him. Something I was sure he was aware of. He'd intention-ally claimed both chairs on one side of the table. It might have been an act of dominance, his being a judge, or a tactical move, to sit across from whomever he talked with. But the smile told me he just wanted me to sit next to Sheena.

"What's the biggest LSD bust you've ever heard of?" I asked her, getting straight to the point.

"Last year, the DEA raided a facility in Kansas," she replied. "They seized almost two hundred thousand tabs of blotter acid."

"How much liquid would that be?"

"About three gallons," the judge replied.

"How do you know this?" I asked him with a grin.

Ollie shrugged. "I remember numbers," he replied. "And have a way with them. I've been practicing or judging law for nearly half a century, son. In that time, there isn't much I haven't seen or heard. Most people don't think of a drop as a unit of measure, but it is. Or it was until the early nineteenth century. Sure, the volume of a drop is different for different liquids, depending on all kinds of variables, but the difference is very small. Most liquids are about seventy-five thousand drops per gallon. So, two hundred thousand drops would be close to three gallons."

I looked into Sheena's eyes. "These guys plan to make fifty gallons. They've already produced almost a tenth of that."

"Do you have any idea what liquid LSD sells for?" Sheena asked, her curiosity obviously piqued.

"Over a hundred grand a gallon," I replied. "They have a buyer for the first twenty gallons, at two million dollars."

I heard the door open, though it was out of sight in the general store section, and then I heard Carolyn greet someone. After a moment, two men followed her into the dining area and sat down at a table across the room. They made a point of not looking in our direction, which I found odd. Sheena was a strikingly beautiful woman.

I leaned forward. "Ollie, do you know those men?"

He held the menu up in front of his face as if reading it and whispered, "I've seen them around, and I know they own farms on the north side of the valley, but I don't know them."

I kept my voice low. "I made sure that Pritchard knew we'd be meeting here." Then I turned to Sheena. "They think you're part of my crew and I'm a Florida smug druggler."

She grinned at the play on words. "What do you need?"

"You and another agent," I replied. "In a heavy-duty van, with a briefcase full of money, at Pritchard's place at sunrise on Monday."

"How much money?" she asked, just as my phone pinged again.

I looked down at it, then smiled at Sheena. "A hundred thousand."

"In twenty-four hours?" she said. "That's gonna be difficult."

"Too difficult for the girl who sent a congressman to prison and is about to make the biggest LSD bust in history?"

She smiled back and pulled her own phone out. Her fingers flew across the miniature keyboard for a moment, then she put it away. "Consider it done."

"The man facing this way keeps looking at us," Ollie said, his mouth barely moving.

Sheena and I had our backs to the men. I was sure they wanted a clear view of Sheena so they could describe her to Pritchard. The restrooms were just beyond where the two men sat.

"Sheena, I think they need a better look at you," I said. "Why don't you go powder your nose or something."

She gave me a nasty look as she rose from her seat and took her jacket off. She laid it across the back of her chair, bent over and whispered in my ear. "You know damned well that I don't wear makeup."

Turning my head slightly as she walked away, I knew there was zero chance the two men could ignore her. She wore tight-fitting black slacks and a turtleneck that hugged her ample figure.

"They got a good look," Ollie said, as Carolyn brought three mugs and a steaming pot of dark brown coffee.

"This is from Kona, Hawaii," she said, as she poured it into the three mugs. "It's called Volcano Estate. You need a minute before I take your order?"

"Yes, just give us a minute," Ollie said. "Until the young lady returns."

When Carolyn left, the judge glanced toward the restrooms. "You said Lane was "on ice." What *exactly* does that mean?"

"He wasn't harmed," I replied honestly. "My friends are sitting on him until I return. Then I'll personally decide what to do with him."

"And you're no longer with Homeland?"

"Not exactly," I replied. "Besides charter fishing, I'm partners in a security firm that contracts for a large private corporation that is funded by the federal government."

It wasn't a complete lie. Armstrong Research did contract us from time to time, and they did receive some funding and occasional special requests, via the Department of the Interior, but the organization of men and women who ran it had more wealth than many countries.

That seemed to appease him.

When I heard the restroom door open, I glanced back and saw Sheena approaching the men's table as she typed something on her phone. They were both looking at her, but not at her face.

"Okay," she said, as she sat back down. "They both got a good look. One even took my picture as I came out of the lady's room. Perverts."

"That's good," I said, as I took a sip of the strong Hawaiian coffee. It was delicious. "That means they probably work for Pritchard."

"I took their picture, too," she said. "I just sent it to Craig. He'll run facial recognition on them."

I sent a quick message to Chyrel as Carolyn returned to our table. The waitress I'd seen her talking with through the door went over to the two men's table.

"Decided on breakfast?" Carolyn asked.

We placed our orders and she hurried off.

"Craig texted me back," Sheena whispered.

"Y'all are still together?" I asked.

Sheena had been partnered with an agent by the name of Craig Allen ten years ago. He was a few years older than her, but she was the senior partner.

"Yes," she replied. "We work well together. He said that the van wasn't a problem, but it being a Sunday, getting that much money together might be difficult."

"If you had it in the form of a wire transfer, can he find a place to cash it?"

"Well, yeah," she replied. "But who has that kind of money just lying around?"

I pulled my phone out and opened my banking app. "Where do I send it?"

"You're kidding, right?"

I grinned at her. "You should know I don't kid."

She removed a card from her wallet and handed it to me. "This is Craig's email address."

It took a few minutes to navigate the website, then I stuck the phone back in my pocket. "Tell Craig he's got mail."

"That's a lot of money to put on the line, son," the judge said.

I shrugged. "I know I'll get it back."

Carolyn brought our food as Sheena typed away on her phone. Then the three of us dug in. While we ate, I outlined a simple plan that involved the FBI and Virginia State Police picking up all the turd fondlers at the same time on Monday. Before we were half finished, the two men, having had nothing but a cup of coffee, got up and walked out, leaving us alone in the dining room.

My phone chimed and I picked it up to find a message from Chyrel. I read it and looked over at Sheena. "One of those guys' names is Keith Reed."

Her phone beeped and she looked at the screen. Then she looked up at me bewildered. "How'd you know that?"

I shrugged. "I guess our facial recognition program is faster than yours."

"But you would have had to… Did you hack my email?"

"Craig's," I said with a grin. "You gave it to me."

"I could arrest you for that," she said, then smiled. "It was that woman Chyrel Koshinski, right?"

I nodded.

"Craig said she was good, and that's a lot coming from him."

"Where are you staying?" the judge asked me, as he wiped his mouth and placed the napkin on his empty plate.

"I *was* at the Stonewall Jackson," I replied. "That's where I followed Doctor Brown to last night. He and his assistant are staying there."

"You should both go back there," he said. "It's a nice place."

"Why?" Sheena asked.

"Those two men left," he replied, then nodded toward the window. "But they parked at the store right over there."

I followed his gaze. "The silver Chevy?"

"Yes," he replied. "They've been there longer than necessary for a convenience store."

"And you think they're going to follow us?" I asked.

The old judge nodded somberly. "Wouldn't you?"

My phone chimed an incoming message. I pulled it out and looked at the screen. "This is from Pritchard," I said. "Giving me a price that he wants me to pay for his LSD."

"What's it say?" Ollie asked, as I opened the message.

"He wants fifty thousand per gallon," I replied, as I typed in a short reply. "He says he'll have four gallons by Monday."

I hit the Send button and looked from the judge to Sheena. "I just countered with half that or no deal."

CHAPTER TWENTY-ONE

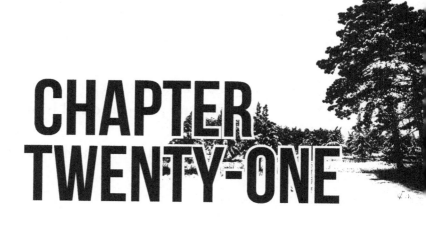

The judge left the parking lot before me and Sheena. We waited until he'd passed the convenience store before I started the truck. Reed and the other man in the car parked at the store didn't move, but as soon as I started to pull out of my parking spot, I saw vapor from their exhaust.

When we passed the store, the car pulled out behind another truck that was behind us. Sheena had left her sedan at the restaurant and rode with me in the rental truck. Craig would be on his way with the van before noon, and he'd bring another agent to pick up her car and take it to the hotel.

"I'm worried about Judge Whitaker," Sheena said, as we drove slowly north into town.

I nodded in agreement. "I was thinking the same thing."

Ollie had taken the same route but was now well ahead of us and out of sight. We rode in silence for a block.

"Are they still back there?" she asked.

"Yeah," I replied. "Two cars back."

"You should call the judge and tell him to come to the hotel, as well."

At the next light, I pulled Ollie's number up and called him.

"Where are you?" he asked.

"Downtown," I replied. "We think it might be a good idea for you to join us at the hotel, Ollie."

"Then get it in gear, son. I've been here for five minutes and was about to call you. I got three rooms, one for each of us—all adjoining."

I grinned over at Sheena as the light turned green.

"We'll be there in a few minutes," I said, then ended the call.

"What?" Sheena asked.

"He's already at the hotel waiting for us."

It only took a few minutes to reach the Stonewall Jackson. I'd been right about my earlier weather prediction. The clouds were low and gray, and there was an occasional snowflake that landed on the windshield, then melted instantly on the heated glass.

I pulled into the parking lot and drove straight back to the corner where I'd parked the night before. Sheena and I got out of the truck. We were both carrying tactical-style backpacks and slung them over our shoulders as we hurried toward the entrance. The temperature seemed colder than it had been since I'd left earlier, and I was eager to get inside. I'd experienced cold weather before, but not in a long time. I guess my blood had thinned since cold-weather survival training in Fort Drum, New York.

Out of the corner of my eye, I could see Reed's car drive into the lot and turn down the first parking fairway. The car pulled into a spot and the two men remained inside as we went through the main hotel entrance.

I spotted Ollie and stopped Sheena. "Take the judge on up. We have adjoining rooms. I'm going to stay down here for a minute to see if they come inside."

Sheena strode across the lobby to where Ollie was sitting, a small overnight bag at his feet, and they quickly moved toward the elevator.

I headed into the small breakfast restaurant, where I could see outside. I knew the windows were tinted and the two men couldn't see in. They just sat in their car.

"Would you like a table?" a frumpy, middle-aged waitress asked.

The car outside backed out of the parking spot and headed toward the exit.

"No, thanks," I said, watching the car turn right, headed out of town. "Just three coffees, please. To go."

While I waited, I texted the judge for the room number. When I got there, I had to juggle the three hot paper cups to knock on the door. A shadow passed over the peep hole, then the door opened. Sheena stood inside, her jacket removed and an empty shoulder holster under her left arm. In her right hand was a Glock 23, aimed down at the floor. The .40 caliber handgun was standard issue to most agents in the FBI, though some opted for the slightly larger G22. I knew that any agent who failed pistol qualification with either of those was issued a Model 19 or 17, which had slightly longer barrel lengths. The 23 in Sheena's hands told me that she knew how to use it. FBI range coaches were some of the best marksmanship instructors on the planet.

"Expecting trouble?" I asked, walking past her into the room.

"Always," she replied, holstering the Glock.

I placed two of the coffees on the table and checked out the window. "They sat in the parking lot for a minute, then left."

The judge was sharp; the room had an excellent view of the parking area and the approach road. The door to the adjoining room was ajar and I could hear him whistling a tune. A moment later, he stepped through the door.

"Were you planning to not go home?" I asked. "I noticed your bag."

"No," he replied. "I always keep a couple of changes of clothes, a spare robe, and other necessities in the trunk, just in case I spill something. Josie always insisted I make a neat impression."

"What do we do for the rest of the day?" Sheena asked.

"We wait," I replied. "Your partner should be here with the van around noon, and I need to check in with my team down in Florida. None of us got much sleep last night, so getting a nap might be a good idea."

"That's what I was just going to suggest," Ollie said. "I've unpacked and that bed looks pretty inviting."

Without waiting for a reply, the judge turned and closed the adjoining door behind him. He'd left his coffee on the table.

Turning away from the window, I found Sheena watching me. "So, is this your room or mine?" I asked, hoping she hadn't been reminiscing about our last encounter.

"You've changed, Jesse."

I rubbed the stubble on my chin. "Yeah, I guess I've let a few habits fall by the wayside."

"I like the hair," she said, reaching up and pushing it off my forehead. "I see enough crew cuts. Scruffy looks good on you. But I wasn't talking about a physical change."

"What do you mean?"

Twin pale blue orbs looked me deep in the eyes, searching from one to the other. "You're off the market, aren't you?"

"I...uh, have a girlfriend, if that's what you mean," I replied, eyeing my pack. "That's a ridiculous word at our age, isn't it?"

"Boyfriend and girlfriend?" she said, smiling sweetly. "Yeah, but what other term fits? Woman friend? Man friend?" She paused. "Lover?" She picked up one of the coffees. "You never remarried?"

"No," I replied. "I decided some time ago that I just wasn't husband material."

"What's the lucky woman's name?"

"Sara," I replied. "Sara Patrick. We started out working together, and when her dad was injured in a submersible accident, I took his place and she helped train me."

"Submersible? Long hours under the sea, huh?"

"Something like that," I said. "You never married?"

"Most agents are married to the job," she said, turning toward the other adjoining door. She opened it and turned to face me again. "This is your room, Jesse. I'm through here."

When she closed the door, I stood looking after her for a moment. We'd only been together a couple of nights—at a friend's house in Beaufort, South Carolina. I remembered the immediacy of Sheena's lovemaking.

I pulled my laptop out of my pack and plugged it in to recharge. Then I called Deuce to check on our Florida visitor's status.

"Hey, Jesse," Deuce said, when he picked up on the second ring. "How are things going up there?"

"I met with the judge this morning, and Sheena was there."

"I know. Chyrel intercepted a text message to Pritchard containing a picture of her. They had someone watching you, just as you predicted."

"They followed us back to the hotel," I said. "Once we came inside, they drove away."

"Chyrel also intercepted a message from Pritchard to the sheriff, telling him to 'meet me at the diner' at 0600."

I remembered telling Pritchard to give me a number before 0600 and he'd been a few minutes late with it.

"So, they were together when Pritchard sent me the text about the price." I ran my fingers through my hair and glanced over at the door to Sheena's room again. "Wish I could have been a fly on the wall when he read my counteroffer. How's Lane enjoying his stay?"

"He's not," Deuce replied. "I hope you don't mind, but I had Andrew take him out to your place on his boat late last night. It wouldn't be good to keep him here at the office."

"Good idea," I said. "Nobody'll know he's out there but Jimmy and Finn."

"What's your next step?"

"Tomorrow morning, I'll be with Sheena and two of her people when we meet at Pritchard's old barn for the first pickup."

"Will Pritchard and Taliaferro be there?"

"Pritchard will be," I said. "I doubt the sheriff will. As soon as money changes hands, Pritchard and anyone else there will be taken into custody. Judge Whitaker will have the state police arrest Taliaferro at about the same time."

"Did it ever snow?" Deuce asked, satisfied that it was about over.

"A dusting last night," I said, walking toward the window.

When I opened the drapes, I realized that last night was just Mother Nature's opening act. Big dry flakes fell straight to the ground, not a breath of wind to guide them. The blades of grass that had been left poking up through last night's snow were now covered and parts of the parking lot between cars were beginning to turn white.

"Call me in the morning for an update when you're on your way there," Deuce said as we ended the call.

I continued to stare out the window at the falling snow. I remembered seeing snow for the first time when I was just a kid, about five or so. Dad couldn't come home for Christmas that year, so we went up to Camp Lejeune. It'd started snowing two nights before Christmas. Mom had awakened me and the three of us had watched it fall outside the window for hours. Then, the next morning, Dad had surprised me with a sled, saying that the snow hadn't been forecast to come until after Christmas. Mom and Dad took me to the only hill on base, near the entrance to French Creek, so I could ride on it.

The snow outside was beautiful, but I also knew its dark side. Slippery, muddy, frozen ground and slick hidden rocks.

CHAPTER TWENTY-TWO

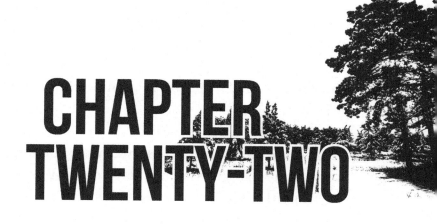

"How can we be sure what's in the containers is LSD?" I asked Craig Allen, who was sitting in the passenger seat of my rental truck.

We'd left the hotel well before daylight. Doctor Brown's van was still there. Sheena's partner rode with me and would act as the leader of my team. Sheena would be the driver of the van and the other agent who came with Craig was the tech guy, rounding out the judge's little team of *criminals*. Sheena had only introduced the new agent as Nigel before we split up into my truck and their heavy duty 4x4 conversion van. Where they got it, they didn't say, but it looked capable of handling any terrain with a heavy load.

The road was covered by more than an inch of fresh snow. Fortunately, the temperature was well below freezing, so even though it was covered, the road's surface was at least dry and ice free. Sheena followed us in the van.

"It's a simple test," Craig replied, not looking up from his phone. "A drop of the LSD on a dish will appear clear.

Adding a drop of a special reagent will make it pink to purple in color."

"What color's the reagent?"

Craig chuckled, put his phone away, and looked over at me. "The bad guys would have caught on by now if the reagent was pink or purple. It's also clear."

I concentrated on the road ahead. With no lines for visual reference as to where the lanes were, I just stayed on the highest part of the road's contour and kept my speed down to just 20 miles per hour. I was probably driving right down the middle of the road, but it didn't matter; no other vehicles were using it. Sheena followed right behind us. Ours were the only tracks on the road at this early hour, but I wanted to allow plenty of time.

The GPS told me to make a sharp right just ahead. I remembered the intersection from the day before. It had once been a Y in the road, but engineers had changed it, making a curve at the end of the intersecting road so that it formed a T.

"We're going to be early," Craig said.

I passed the intersection and turned left into the closed convenience store. When I'd made a complete circle, Sheena pulled up next to my side, rolling her window down.

"We're early," she echoed. "It won't even start to get light for another thirty minutes."

"Brown will come this way," I said. "And if Taliaferro decides to make it easier for us, he'll likely come this way, too."

"He won't," Ollie announced from the back seat of my truck. "The state police have his house under surveillance. There aren't even any lights on."

"So, we wait," Sheena said.

And wait we did. For nearly an hour. "Hurry up and wait" had been a sort of mantra when I was in the Corps. The structured lifestyle agreed with me. Hurrying wasn't in my nature.

Finally, just as the sky was starting to lighten to a soft gray, Brown's white van made the turn onto the road where most of the suspects lived. The sound of the tires crunching on the new-fallen snow seemed unusually loud against the stark black and white background. He accelerated too early and the rear tires spun for a moment.

"Let's give him a few minutes," I said, checking my watch. "It's twenty till eight."

After five minutes, I put the truck in gear and crossed the highway onto the intersecting state road, Sheena following right behind me. The going became a lot easier—all I had to do was follow the tracks of Brown's van. After a few miles, it turned onto the road going up to Buffalo Gap. When we reached the turnoff on the west side of Pritchard's property, the gate was open, and Brown's tracks turned through it.

"I guess Brown saw us waiting," Craig commented.

"We'll leave it open," I said. "In case we need to make a hasty retreat. Let Nigel know."

On either side of the twin rut road were deep ditches to channel rain runoff. The snow followed the contour easily, but with everything white, the road looked unusually narrow, even with the tracks of the van as a guide. I stopped and shifted the truck into four-wheel drive.

"For a Florida man," Craig said, "you drive in this stuff pretty good. Me? I hate snow."

"Never make assumptions," I said.

"What do you mean?"

"Ever since last week, when I decided to come up here, everyone's been telling me I'm out of my element." I looked over at him and grinned. "I was a Marine during the height of the Cold War. We all assumed the next big land battle would be in Siberia or China. So that's what we trained for. I went to the Keys to get away from ice and snow."

As we came around a bend in the road, the barn came into view. A concrete area in front of it had been swept clear of snow and a forklift stood ready to load three blue barrels. They were lying on their sides, stacked in a pyramid, and strapped to a wooden pallet.

Brown stood off to the side with Pritchard. Frank Millhouse was nowhere in sight.

"Brown's assistant isn't here," I said. "Young guy, dark hair. Keep your eyes peeled."

He repeated my warning to Sheena and Nigel. I backed in next to Brown's van and Pritchard's Dodge, allowing Sheena a wide spot to turn the cargo van around.

"The signal will be when one of them picks up the briefcase," Craig said. "Not before then."

I looked over my shoulder at the judge, sitting in the backseat. He had his phone to his ear. "Stay here, Ollie. Is that the state police?"

"I have no intention of getting out," he said, with a smile. "I like taking part, but I know my limitations. Yes, I have the trooper in charge at the sheriff's house, waiting for me to give the go ahead."

Ollie had already issued bench warrants, sending them to the Virginia State Police and the Attorney General. He'd personally called both offices, bringing them up to speed on the corruption in his county.

Craig and I got out and strode toward Pritchard. My eyes scanned the area. I saw no tracks outside of the immediate area, so Millhouse wasn't off in the distance, hiding behind a tree with a rifle. I looked up at the barn and saw no movement or indication of a hidden shooter. The door opened and Brown's assistant stepped out carrying a box.

"Did a cocaine truck turn over in your yard, Aiden?" I asked, striding confidently toward him. "I almost wrecked three times driving up here in this white crap."

Sheena backed the van into place and got out. Moving to the back, she opened the doors, swinging them out to the far sides. Nigel was inside, sitting on a small stool, a folding table in front of him.

"Can we do this quick?" the young man in the van asked. "It's friggin' cold out there."

"Bring that over here," I said to Millhouse.

He looked to Pritchard, who nodded. Then he carried the box over and placed it on the floor of the van. It looked large enough to hold four gallons.

"I'll get the other ones," Millhouse said.

"What other ones?" I asked.

He stopped and looked back and forth between me and Craig.

"Those are the empty jugs," Pritchard said, pointing to the ends of the barrels. "Reuse the ones you pick up at each stop."

The barrels were slightly raised at the opposite end and each one had a tap with a valve in it at the lower end. "Not too shabby," I said with a grin. "But reusing the empty bottles is hardly sanitary."

Doctor Brown laughed. "Trust me, nothing can live in what we make. That's eighty percent alcohol."

"One hundred and sixty proof?" I asked. "Whoa!"

Pritchard placed a hand on the top barrel. "Our customers blend it with non-alcoholic mixes or even water."

I took a small metal cup from my pocket and held it under the tap, cracking the valve slightly. The amber liquid in the shot glass had a powerful, almost clinical smell, but there was a trace of the oak and cherry. Though it was only half a shot, it burned my throat going down, and landed hard in the middle of my belly, spreading a warmth more than capable of battling the cold air.

"Dammit, man!" I said, holding my chest. "They'd *better* cut it, that's for damned sure."

Craig went with Millhouse to the door of the barn, where another box sat on a hand truck. Craig stood aside as the young man carefully tipped the hand truck and rolled the second box toward where Sheena and I stood.

I opened the box already in the truck and pulled out one of the empty glass jugs. Then I opened the box on the hand truck and lifted out an identical one, except it was full.

"That's pretty smart," I said. "If your guys got busted, the cops might think this is just hooch."

"Not if they taste a sample like you did," Brown said. "That same twenty milliliters would kill two people."

I turned and carried the jug toward Pritchard. "It's not hooch in here, is it?" I extended the jug toward him. "Or water, maybe?"

"You're a suspicious man, Stretch," he said, grinning. "I like that in a business partner. I see you brought a little extra muscle."

"And I see you didn't," I said, patting him on the shoulder. "I think we understand each other."

His smile wasn't one of mirth. "Yes, I think we can do business together. But we're going to have to make different financial arrangements. You get your terms this time. But after this, we're partners, not suppliers. Me and you. And we cut everyone else out."

So, he wants to get rid of the sheriff and the others, I thought. This was a man with a single goal: money. He had no aspirations of gaining power in this deal—he got that from his day job. Greedy people were easy to figure and easier to manipulate.

"Can you bring that over here?" Nigel asked. "I'd still like to test it."

Brown took the container and carried it over to the cargo van. "You're using Ehrlich's reagent?"

Nigel placed an empty jug on a scale beside him on the floor of the van, read the weight, and punched at his phone's screen. "Yes, as a presumptive test."

He put the empty back in its box and took the full jug from Brown, placing it on the scale. He then punched at his screen again and said, "The weight is accurate for a 3785-milliliter sample."

Sheena looked over at me and smiled. "That's a gallon, Stretch."

Nigel put on a pair of latex gloves and opened the jug. Using an eye dropper, he extracted a small amount, placed one drop on a dish on the table, and then put the rest back in the jug, tapping and squeezing the dropper several times. From his pocket, he took a small jar and unscrewed the lid. It had a dropper attached to it. He added one drop of the contents to the dish and the clear liquid immediately turned pink, then slowly darkened to a light purple.

"It checks," Nigel said.

"Go get the money," I told Craig.

Craig walked over to my pickup and opened the back door. When he returned, he had a briefcase in his hand, which he placed on top of the barrels of moonshine.

"Four gallons of acid and a hundred and fifty of liquor," he said, grinning at me. "Enough to light up South Beach for a couple of days."

Craig opened the case and turned it toward Pritchard. "That's a hundred grand for four gallons and a thousand and fifty for the three barrels. Total is $101,050.00. The judge said to round it off to an even $102,000.00."

Pritchard looked at the stacks of money, picked two up and set them aside, then lifted one at random from the bottom of the case and fanned it. He put it back, re-arranged the stacks and counted them. Then he looked up at me.

"I'm serious," he said. "This bullshit strongarm stuff doesn't mean a thing. Next week, the price is fifty grand per gallon. And you have to take out the sheriff. Other-wise, I just shut down and walk away."

His hand moved to the briefcase's lid and stopped, waiting for me to reply.

I slowly let a grin spread across my face. "I like you, Aiden. You know a good business opportunity when you see it. Eliminate the share that goes to the good sheriff and give it to me, huh?"

He nodded.

I pretended to mull it over. "No deal," I said. "I want the others' shares, too. Here's what I'll do: after this good-faith gesture, I'll pay you forty thousand a gallon, not a penny more. And you can keep the moonshine. But to kill Sheriff Taliaferro, well, that'll be a hundred thousand in cash, half up front."

Pritchard eyed me for a moment, then took five bundles from the briefcase and placed them on the barrel next to it. He closed and latched the case, then picked it up with his left hand, extending his right to me. "You have a deal, Stretch."

The handshake is a gesture that goes back to medieval times, as does the military salute. The extended or raised hand shows the other person that you are unarmed and friendly.

Our response to his proffered hand must have shocked Pritchard. I drew my Sig from under my jacket and pointed it at his chest. Instantly, Craig, Sheena, and Nigel produced weapons to also cover the three men.

Sheena stepped forward, took her wallet from her pocket and placed it face-up on the barrel, showing her badge and FBI identification.

"Aiden Pritchard," she said, as Craig turned the stunned lawyer roughly and forced him up against the barrels, "you are under arrest for conspiracy to commit murder, for the sale, possession, and manufacturing of illegal alcohol, for the sale, possession, manufacture, and intent to distribute hallucinogenic drugs across state lines, suspicion of capital murder, and intent to defraud the Internal Revenue Service. Probably a bunch more, but that's just off the top of my head."

"You can't—I'm the prosecutor in this county!"

I heard the truck door open and looked over. Judge Whitaker walked toward us, putting his phone in the inside pocket of his jacket. "The state police just apprehended Sheriff Taliaferro, Jesse."

I looked back at Pritchard as Craig was Mirandizing him, then leaned in close to his face. "My judge trumps your prosecutor."

CHAPTER TWENTY-THREE

Stuart Lane lay on a bed in the dark, one ankle handcuffed to the foot railing. It was hot and humid, and he was inside a house of some kind. He'd been similarly hog-tied for most of the night, though he didn't know how long. They'd taken his watch and everything else; even his belt, shoes, and shirt.

A big guy with a deep voice had brought him here in a boat from the outskirts of Miami. The trip had seemed to take hours. They'd cuffed him behind his back and he'd had to endure the boat ride lying face down on the deck with a bag over his head. It smelled of dirty laundry.

Once they'd arrived, the man had pushed him across what seemed like a mile of loose sand, then up a flight of steps, where he'd tossed him roughly onto the bunk. There, he'd pulled the bag off Stuart's head before stripping him down to his pants and handcuffing his foot with two sets of cuffs linked together.

The people who'd grabbed him never said who they were, but there were at least four of them, all with guns.

Stuart was pretty sure they weren't cops. They'd taken him straight to the boat instead of to a police station. And none of them read him his rights, like cops are supposed to do. Whoever they were, Stuart believed they were professionals.

He wasn't able to see much of anything after turning the corner to the house where the Sneed woman was staying. A bright flash of light had blinded him and his vision didn't return fully for a long time. By then, they'd put the bag over his head and carried him onto the boat. But not before he'd seen the guns.

He couldn't see much in the total darkness, but the guy had a huge chest and his shoulders were as broad as a lumberjack's. The big, bushy mustache was still very apparent, though.

He knew he was on the second floor of somewhere, but the room had been too dark to see much. The man had a big yellow dog with him. Stuart didn't like dogs; never had. When he was a kid, he'd been bitten on the leg by a big dog. Big dogs scared him and that one was huge. So, Stuart had done whatever the man told him.

After they left him alone, Stuart's eyes became a little more accustomed to the dark. There were other beds in the room. Six sets of bunk beds. But it didn't look like any were occupied. There were windows between each set of beds, as well as beside the entry door at the far end of the room. The bed he was lying on was by another door.

Stuart looked around, straining his eyes. The door at the end of his bed was next to his left foot, the one with the chain on it. Across the room, next to another bunk bed, was a white box of some kind.

He rolled over to put his right foot on the floor, curling his restrained left foot under him. Then using the bed above for support, he managed to stand. The two sets of cuffs on his ankle were just long enough for his toes to reach the floor, and by keeping his left foot in place, he was able to stretch and get close enough to the box that he could reach down and touch it.

It was a cooler. He opened it and felt around inside. There were six plastic bottles, but no ice. It was too dark to read the labels, but he took one out anyway and hopped back to the bed to sit down. After unscrewing the cap and sniffing the contents, he smelled nothing, so he tossed the cap on the floor, and put the bottle to his lips for a tentative taste—water. He chugged the whole bottle.

The sky outside was beginning to lighten, giving Stuart at least some indication of time and direction. He stood again and tested the doorknob by the end of the bed. It was unlocked, and when he opened it, he saw it was a bathroom. The toilet was close enough to the door that he could probably sit on it with his left leg wrapped around the open door frame. But he'd have to stand cross-legged in front of it. He lifted the lid and unzipped his pants, then pissed in the direction of the toilet.

"If you fuckers gotta clean it up," he mumbled to himself, "it's your own damned fault for chaining me up like a dog."

Back in the room, he moved as close as he could to the nearest window and looked out. The sky was dark to the left, but far to the right, it was lighter. He looked across the room toward the other window. He could see darkness to the right there, too. The door at the end of the room faced east or maybe a little northeast, he decided.

Outside the near window were a bunch of trees that he could see over, but he could see nothing beyond them. He could hear the sound of water lightly surging on a shore and realized he was probably looking out over the ocean, just beyond the trees.

He remembered that after he'd been forced onto the floor of the boat, the big man had navigated several turns at low speed. The last turn had been to the right as he started to accelerate. After that, the boat had bounced along at a fast speed for some time. Stuart figured the boat had gone south from Miami.

What's south of there? he wondered. Then it hit him: *Key West.* That was the only place he knew of that lay beyond Miami.

Looking through the opposite window again, Stuart saw more trees, but farther away, and there was a clearing of mostly sand in between. As it grew lighter, he sat down and studied the cuffs and the bed. The end of the cuffs were attached to the big upper bar of the metal-framed bed. The bunk itself reminded him of those in the barracks, back when he'd been a soldier. The cuff could only slide a few inches either way until it was stopped by vertical bars.

He looked around the immediate area. If he could find a stiff wire, he might be able to pick the lock on the cuffs. Then what? Swim to Miami?

Wait, he thought, remembering having read once about a long bridge that connected Miami to Key West. The ten-mile bridge or something like that.

If he could get loose, he could find his way to the bridge and flag down a car or something. But to get loose, he needed a wire. Looking up, he extended a hand. The springs of the upper bunk were too thick.

Hearing someone coming up the steps, Stuart climbed back on the bed and pretended to be asleep on his side. The door opened and someone came in. Stuart cracked an eye open and saw a man approaching. It wasn't the same guy. This one was skinny, with long hair. At least he didn't have the dog with him. The man was carrying something.

"Wake up," the man said, stopping in the middle of the room.

Stuart didn't move.

"Breakfast is here, dude."

At the mention of food, Stuart's hunger pangs hit him. He resisted until the smell reached his nostrils. He couldn't help it; he opened his eyes fully and looked up at the figure standing in the dimly lit room.

"Where am I?"

"I was told not to tell you anything," the man replied.

"Where's the other guy?" Stuart asked.

"Sleeping," the skinny man responded, moving a step closer. "Got you some scrambled eggs, toast, and some fresh mango, man."

Stuart half-rolled and sat up, then pointed to the cooler. "Can you slide that over here?"

As the man bent and placed the tray on the cooler, something fell from his pocket. It was a pack of cigarette rolling papers. And not just any kind.

Stuart's eyes went wide when he recognized the brand. They were the same as he used; papers with a thin wire that allowed a person to hold the end when the joint got so short it would burn your fingers.

The man swept the pack up with his hand and scooted the cooler close enough that Stuart could use it as a table, then stuffed the papers back into his shirt pocket.

Without hesitating, Stuart launched himself, extending his whole body in the direction of the man's head as his right fist came up. He'd only get one shot and knew that it had to be a good one. He caught the guy completely off guard. The punch connected with the side of his head and the skinny man staggered back a few steps before falling to his knees and then onto his side. He didn't move.

Stuart shook his hand out; he could feel the sting of the blow all the way up into his wrist. He lunged toward the fallen man but couldn't get close enough to reach his pocket, so he grabbed the guy's wrist and pulled him closer. He knew the wire in the paper wouldn't be stiff enough, but several of them twisted together might work.

After grabbing the pack out of the man's shirt pocket, he opened it and sat down. It was half full. Stuart began pulling the papers out, stripping the wires from them and laying them on the cooler. Finally, he twisted about ten strands together and went to work on the cuffs.

A friend in high school had once owned a pair of real policeman's handcuffs; he'd said that he'd stolen them from a cop in a scuffle in Roanoke one time, though Stuart didn't believe that part. But the guy had shown him how easy they were to pick, especially if they were an older pair. He'd said the tumblers in the lock had a memory and carefully pushing each one in, you could feel where the key stopped them.

It took quite a while, but Stuart finally released the cuff that was around his ankle. He crossed to the window on the other side of the room and looked out. The sun was just becoming visible off to his left. There was another house across the clearing with a deck around it and a big water tank above the roof. Far to the right, he saw a third house on the west side. Beyond both houses, he could see water. In fact, he could see water just about every direction he looked.

He was on an island, but Stuart didn't think it was Key West. It was way too small—no bigger than his two-acre horse pasture.

Turning back to the man on the floor, he checked his other pockets and discovered a cheap disposable lighter and a small wooden container. He slid the top off the box and the scent hit him instantly; weed. He closed it and shoved it and the lighter into his pocket, then pulled the man over to the bed and latched the empty cuff around his ankle.

Pausing for a minute, he raked the eggs into his mouth and chewed while he looked around the rest of the little house. There wasn't much, just the six bunk beds, the bathroom, and a desk by the exit door. He rifled the desk's drawers but found them to be completely empty. The same was true for the bathroom cabinet. The place was set up like some kind of fishing camp or something, but aside from the furniture, and the cooler with the water bottles, there was nothing else in it.

Before leaving, Stuart closed the windows. The long-haired guy was still unconscious but breathing. He should choke the asshole to death, but he needed to move fast. The guy had told him that the big man was sleeping. For how long, Stuart didn't know. But he wanted to take advantage of that time, and the closed windows would keep this guy from being heard if he started yelling when he woke up.

Stuart did take the guy's sandals and shirt, though the sandals were too big and the shirt too small. Outside, he saw that there was another house next to the one he'd been in. All four were about the same size and raised on tall, concrete stilts. Moving behind the two houses, he found a dock, but no boat.

He needed transportation. While there might be something of value in one of the houses, he didn't know which one the bigger man was sleeping in and he didn't want to take the chance with that big dog around.

Stuart quickly followed the shoreline to the west. The house on that side had a big front porch and a small sand beach in front of it.

When Stuart reached the house with the water tank on the south side of the island, he found another pier, and this time he got lucky. A big twin-engine boat was tied to the dock. He walked out toward the yellow boat, constantly looking back over his shoulder. The engines on the Yellowfin center console looked odd and didn't have a name or anything on the covers.

Stuart knew a little about boats; he had an eighteen-foot bass boat that could scream across the lakes at more than 40 miles per hour. But he'd never even been on one this big. It had to be close to thirty feet long.

Stepping down into it, he studied the controls but couldn't find an ignition key anywhere, just two silver buttons below two switches between the twin tachometers. He pushed them and nothing happened. He flipped the switches and pushed the buttons, again to no avail. He flipped a couple more switches and nothing came on, not even the bilge pump or radio.

The battery! he thought. His boat had a switch to turn the battery off so it wouldn't go dead when the bilge pump discharged rainwater all week while the boat sat on the trailer.

At the stern, he found two small doors in the transom, both with key locks. Fortunately, the second one was unlocked, and that was where Stuart found the battery switch and not one but two big marine batteries.

Switching both batteries on, he heard the bilge pump start up, whirring loudly but not pumping any water. He moved quickly to the helm and shut it off, looking around and up at the house. He heard nothing. When he pushed one of the buttons again, one of the engines started up. He looked back at them. The weird-looking engine *sounded* strange, too; whining, but quiet.

The other button started the second engine, and he shifted over to the side of the boat and quickly untied the lines holding it to the dock. The water surrounding the boat appeared to be deep, but just a bit farther away, it seemed shallower. Probably too shallow. He'd have to be careful.

The front of the boat pointed away from the island, as did the dock it'd been tied to, and the water ahead looked deeper.

Stuart put one of the engines in gear and let the boat idle away from the dock and the island. Every fiber of his nerves wanted him to push the throttles down and haul ass. But one look at the sandy bottom just a few feet to his left told him that he'd need to be cautious. In front of the boat, he could see that the deep water reached a T where he would have to turn left or right because there was shallow water beyond it.

A glance toward the sun indicated which direction to head in, so Stuart steered the boat to the left, staying in the deeper water. Not far to either side, he could see the sandy bottom, just inches below the surface. The compass on the dash said he was going northeast, which he assumed would eventually get him to Miami, or at least back toward civilization.

Ahead, and a little off to the north, a flash caught his eye. He stared hard in that direction for a few seconds and saw it again; a flash of green light against the early morning sky just above the horizon. He knew what a green marker was for.

Stuart put the other engine in gear and pushed down on the throttles. The expected roar of the outboards wasn't there, but he *was* pushed firmly back against the seat. The quiet whine of the twin 577 horsepower outboards suddenly rose to an ear-splitting, high-pitched scream.

CHAPTER TWENTY-FOUR

Before the sun was fully up, there were half a dozen state police cruisers and SUVs parked around Pritchard's barn. The three men had been hand-cuffed, kept separated, and put into the backs of three different cars.

Sheena was in her element, directing the other two Feebs and the newly arrived state police troopers. The judge and I kept out of the way.

"She's a very efficient young lady," Ollie noted, as a large box van pulled into the yard from the direction of Pritchard's house. It had *Forensics* written on the side.

"Yeah," I agreed. "She's a good cop."

"Speaking of which," Ollie said, turning toward me. "I want to thank you for bringing this to my attention. I had my share of dirty police officers up north."

"It's not a geographical thing," I told him. "There are good and bad people everywhere and they work in all occupations."

Ollie laughed. "Are you sure you're just a charter boat captain?"

I grinned at him. "And not everyone is in the same occupation their whole life."

"The folks from the State Police Office of Internal Affairs arrived at the sheriff's office at the same time Lou Taliaferro was arrested. There will be a full-blown public investigation. Any deputies found to be involved in this or any other criminal activity will be fired and prosecuted."

I nodded. "As it should be, Ollie. I doubt you'll find any involvement outside of the sheriff. This whole thing reeks of good ol' boy cronyism."

The judge jumped slightly, reached into his pocket, and pulled out his phone. "This thing makes me feel like I'm having a heart attack every time it does that. Excuse me."

With his phone pressed to his ear, Ollie stepped over to the forensics van and shook hands with a man who climbed out of the passenger seat. A moment later, he returned, gesturing to his phone. "Jeb Long and Luke Wright were picked up by state police troopers and are being transported to the county jail. The only one un-accounted for is Stuart Lane."

That reminded me: I'd told Deuce I'd check in when we were on our way to Pritchard's barn. I'd been so intent on getting there in one piece in the snow that I'd forgotten.

"I think I can fix that," I said to Ollie, taking my own phone out.

Before I could pull up Deuce's number, the phone in my hand chirped, displaying his name as an incoming call.

"I was just about to call you," I said. "Everything's under control here, and all the players are in custody."

"Lane escaped, Jesse," Deuce said.

Though the air was crisp and cold, I felt beads of perspiration forming on my forehead. Sounds became more acute and my vision narrowed.

"When? How?"

"Jimmy took him something to eat," Deuce said. "He got too close and Lane knocked him out, then he somehow unlocked the handcuff on his ankle and stole Andrew's boat."

"Is Jimmy okay?" I asked, as I started toward my truck.

"Yeah, Lane cuffed *him* to the bed and when Jimmy came to, he got Finn's attention, and Finn woke Andrew up. Jimmy said it happened at sunrise, so maybe an hour ago. It was slack tide and Andrew took one of your boats and could still see the line of disturbed water heading northeast. He's giving chase, but you know what his boat has for power compared to *El Cazador*."

"Northeast?"

"That's what he said," Deuce replied. "He also said he didn't have much gas in the boat."

"I'm on my way," I said, spotting Sheena and angling toward her.

"They had two more gallons hidden in the lab," Sheena said as I approached her. "It's official; the biggest

LSD bust in history. Right here in tranquil Shenandoah Valley."

"I have to leave," I said. "Stuart Lane is loose in south Florida, bent on killing my ex-wife."

I didn't wait for her reply but turned and started toward my truck.

"Craig, you got this?" Sheena shouted urgently.

"Yeah," he called back. "What's up?"

"I'll text you," she yelled back, then came running up alongside me with her pack slung over one shoulder. "I'm going with you."

I didn't argue. Having her along might expedite a few things. Minutes later, the truck was bouncing down the double rut toward the side gate, all four tires chewing and spewing snow and mud.

Powering onto the paved road, I left the truck in four-wheel-drive and drove faster than would be prudent on the snow-covered road.

"Do you plan to drive all the way to Florida?" Sheena asked. "I can arrange a plane."

"I have a plane," I said. "Just a few miles away, at the airport."

"I can get a faster one," she said. "But it's at Reagan."

Did Lane know the waters of Florida Bay? Nothing in his bio suggested he did. When looking at a map of south Florida, northeast would be a straight line between my island and Miami. But it was forty miles of open water, some of it not very deep, just to reach the mainland. Then it was another fifty across the southern half of the Everglades. No, he definitely didn't know the water.

244

"Yours can't go where we need to go," I told Sheena.

"We can go into any airport in the country unannounced."

"There isn't an airport where we're going," I told her.

"Where's that?"

"The Everglades."

She turned in her seat to face me. "You have a seaplane?"

"An amphibian; a 1953 deHavilland Beaver and she can take off and land on a field or lake the size of a football field."

"How far away and how fast?" she asked, typing on her phone.

"Almost a thousand miles," I said. "We'll have to stop once to refuel, but we can be there in six or seven hours."

"We have a G550 available at Reagan. It can be in Miami ninety minutes after taking off. Is there someplace there to rent a seaplane?"

She had a point, but I had a better idea. I pulled my phone out and handed it to her. "Find Billy Rainwater in my contact list and put him on speaker."

"S'up, Kemosabe?" Billy answered.

"I don't have a lot of time, Billy. Driving fast on a snowy road. Can you have your Beaver warmed up and ready in two or three hours?"

Billy understood the urgency in my voice and didn't ask unnecessary questions. "Yes. Do we need any special gear?"

"Have a rifle on board," I said. "I'll give you a precise ETA when we're wheels up out of DC."

"Headed over to the airport now," he said, then ended the call.

"Where is your friend?" Sheena asked, as I turned onto the loop road around Staunton.

"Tell your Gulfstream driver to come to Shenandoah Regional to pick us up," I said. "Have him file a flight plan to LaBelle Airport. It's about halfway between Miami and Tampa, on the northern edge of the 'Glades."

She typed on her phone some more, then paused for a moment. It pinged and she looked up. "The Gulfstream will be there in twenty minutes."

Once on the interstate, we could make better time. There was little or no snow; it was all piled up on the shoulder, apparently by a snowplow.

When I turned into the airport's general aviation parking lot, I saw the Gulfstream business jet taxiing toward the fixed base operation terminal. I could also see *Island Hopper*, her red aluminum skin glowing against the overcast sky. I loved the old bird, but she *was* slow in comparison to the Gulfstream.

When Sheena and I walked out onto the tarmac, the Gulfstream was parked right next to *Island Hopper* and the pilot was walking around her.

"Is that yours?" Sheena asked me, as the pilot turned and came toward us.

"Yeah," I said. "She might not look like much, parked next to that jet, but she goes where I need her to go."

"She's a beauty," the pilot said, extending his hand. "Bruce Carson."

"FBI SAIC Sheena Mason," Sheena said, shaking the pilot's hand, and flashing her credentials. "This is my associate, Jesse McDermitt. You have the airport we need to get to?"

"LaBelle," he said, leading the way to the boarding ladder. "Already programmed in. We'll be there before noon."

The turbine engines started to whine as we climbed up the ladder. The interior was luxurious compared to *Island Hopper*, with comfortable-looking tan leather seats for ten people. Carson pulled up and latched the door as the plane began to move.

"Have a seat anywhere and buckle up," Captain Carson said. "We'll be at cruising altitude in just a few minutes. Maybe then, Mister McDermitt, you can come up and tell me about your plane."

"Sure thing," I replied, looking past him toward the open flight deck. "Love to check this baby out, too."

I was only in my seat a moment when the jet turned onto the taxiway heading toward the downwind end of the runway. A few minutes later, the engines roared and I felt myself being forced hard against my seat back, as I'd never experienced before. It seemed like only seconds before we were airborne and climbing rapidly at a very steep angle. Instantly, the plane was enveloped by the low-hanging snow clouds, but that only lasted a few seconds until we blasted out of the clouds into clear blue sky. Within five minutes, we'd leveled off well above them and a moment later, the hatch to the flight deck opened.

The co-pilot came back to where Sheena and I were seated. "Mister McDermitt, the captain asked if you'd like to join him on the flight deck."

"What's our plan when we get to LaBelle?" Sheena asked.

I looked out the window beside her. We were at least eight miles above the ground. "We'll fly a lot lower and slower over the 'Glades and Florida Bay until we find Lane."

Sheena started typing on her phone screen, and I rose and went forward.

"Permission to enter, Captain?" I asked at the hatch.

"Have a seat," Carson replied. "I had to get out when I was on the apron and admire your Beaver, even if only for a few seconds. When I was a kid, my dad fl ew one in Alaska. Is she all original?"

Sliding into the co-pilot's seat, I looked over the array of gauges and switches, noting our airspeed and altitude. Gazing through the windshield, it was impossible to tell that we were traveling at nearly 600 miles per hour.

"I doubt there's an all-original Beaver anywhere in the world," I replied. "*Island Hopper* has her original engine, controls, and instrumentation, but the interior has been modernized. I use her to take fi shermen into hard-to-reach places."

"Exactly what they were designed to do," Carson said. "My dad swore it was the best bush plane ever built.

I remember him taking off from a snow-covered field behind our house. He'd be airborne within a hundred yards. So, you own a charter business?"

"Yeah," I replied. "Are you with the FBI, too?" I asked.

"Me? No. From what I gather, the FBI only has a few planes. They have contracts with several companies for when they need one. Our company sometimes works with them and other government agencies. The boss bought this a month ago and we just finished the trials. He wanted it just in case we need to move someone a long distance really fast."

"It's a beautiful aircraft," I offered. "Who do you work for?"

"We're actually a research company," he replied. "But you probably never heard of us. Armstrong Research."

CHAPTER TWENTY-FIVE

The boat was incredibly fast. Once Stuart passed the green marker showing the entrance to the channel, he gleefully pushed the throttles farther until the boat was racing along at 50 miles per hour. And there was still some throttle left.

On the dash in front of the helm was a large, covered instrument screen. He removed the cover and saw that it was kind of like the GPS and fish finder on his bass boat, but a lot bigger.

Stuart slowed a little and studied the screen. When he turned it on, a map appeared showing his location as a boat-shaped icon near the bottom of the screen. It didn't show much of anything else, though.

He turned the large knob at the top and the map image zoomed out, showing a group of islands behind him. He zoomed out further until he could see all of south Florida. The place he'd just left was in a cluster of small islands north of the center of a long line of them extending from the southern tip of Florida. The map showed Miami and he was headed straight toward it.

It also showed an area of light green between his location and the city. He assumed that was shallower water and he'd have to slow down when he got near it. But it looked like the shallow water extended all the way to the western edge of Miami.

The water had only a light chop, kind of like the lakes back home. Stuart kept looking back but saw no other boats. After fifteen minutes and what he guessed would be almost fifteen miles from where he'd stolen the boat, he felt sure that nobody was following him.

Looking at the map again, he noticed a panel beside it that listed a bunch of numbers. He got closer and saw that one box gave his location in degrees, another showed the boat's speed, and another gave his heading. At the bottom, a steadily decreasing number showed that he was in only fifteen feet of water.

How could the ocean be this shallow so far from land? he wondered, as the numbers ticked down to ten feet.

"Holy shit!" Stuart shouted, as he looked ahead and saw a sea gull standing on an exposed sandbar.

He spun the wheel and pulled back on the throttles too hard, nearly swamping the boat. His wake passed him and washed up onto the sand, causing the gull to take flight, crying out loudly at the intrusion.

Stuart looked at the map. He was in only four feet of water and in danger of going aground. He zoomed in until Miami disappeared from the screen. The sandbar, along with a bunch of lines, appeared. The lines on the map had numbers, and he guessed that they were lines showing depth, since he was between the one that read 5 and the sandbar now lying fifty feet off to his right.

He'd have to be careful and keep the map zoomed in to show detail. He studied the lines and saw that the five-foot depth marker curved away to the south, blocking him from reaching Miami. He'd have to go back a considerable distance and then go east to get around it. The other way, it curved closer to the green area.

Green, he thought. Not shallow green water, but land. He zoomed back out until he again saw Miami.

"So why no roads or towns?" he asked aloud.

The gull landed on the sandbar again and cried out, as if telling him to go away.

Stuart realized that if it was a map for boats, there was no reason for it to show roads and towns and stuff. It'd just show the water and the outline of land.

He zoomed out again until he could see where he'd started from. He was more than halfway to land. He just had to go around this shallow spot.

Putting the boat into gear again, he steered due north, zoomed in on the map until he saw the depth lines, and then followed the ten-foot line. He soon felt comfortable enough to go a little faster and pushed down on the throttles. Once the boat got up on plane, he could see the color change as the shallow, greenish-gold water to his right dropped away to darker blue on the left.

Finally, the ten-foot line swirled back to the east and he could resume his northeasterly course. He kept the map zoomed in so he could check it now and then for other shallow places.

Ten minutes later, he could see palm trees ahead. Dry land. He could ditch the boat, find a car, and make it to Miami before nightfall. The people who'd stopped him the night before would probably be watching the house again, but he'd find a way to get past them. There was always a way.

He thought again of the hot, older woman who was staying with her tall, hard-bodied daughter. He'd find a way, and he'd make sure that he was compensated for the extra time and humiliation of being caught and tied up like a dog.

One of the engines sputtered and the boat suddenly slowed. Stuart pulled back on the throttles and looked at the gauges, just as one of the tachometers dropped to zero. The engine had died.

Then he saw why. The gas gauge was bouncing on empty. With just the one engine running, he kept going toward shore, the beach now just half a mile away.

The water got shallower. He looked at the gauges and hoped he'd have enough gas and water to reach shore. A beeping sound came from the map thing on the dash. The depth number was flashing 4 and when he looked over the side, he could clearly see the sandy bottom.

Stuart had no idea how shallow the boat could go but knew that the propellers were probably the deepest part. Finding the engine tilt controls, he raised the engine that wasn't running until it was all the way out of the water. Then he raised the other engine so the prop was just below the surface and continued onward. Still several hundred yards from shore, the other engine died.

"Dammit!" Stuart shouted, as he looked around. The beach was vacant, which struck him as odd. He thought all of Florida's beaches were covered with girls in bikinis and surfers and backed by high-rise condominiums. There was none of that here, just miles of empty beach.

Stuart looked down at the bottom. The water was only three feet deep, but the boat was now drifting away from shore. He needed some time to figure things out and he didn't need to spend that time moving away from his destination.

He moved to the front of the boat and studied the anchor. It was resting on a pulpit, but the chain fed through a round thing, then down through the top of the boat next to a hatch. Stuart opened the hatch and saw the chain was probably thirty or forty feet long and was tied to a heavy rope of what he guessed was a hundred feet or more. There was a release lever on the side of the mechanism and when he flipped it, the anchor fell into the water with a splash.

The anchor reached the bottom almost immediately, but the chain continued to rattle up and out of the storage area. Stuart waited until nearly all of the chain was out and flipped the switch back to lock. A sudden silence fell all around him.

At the helm, he zoomed the map out until he could see Miami again. He'd made it less than halfway and would have to continue the rest of the way on land. Stuart looked toward shore. All he had to do was find a car. He glanced back down at the map.

The beach ahead was called Cape Sable.

CHAPTER TWENTY-SIX

J ust an hour after we took off, the plane started its descent toward tiny LaBelle Airport. Noting a handset in a cradle, I pointed to it. "Is that a satellite phone?"

"Yes, sir," he replied. "Would you like to make a call?"

I took my own satellite phone from my pocket and pulled up Jack Armstrong's number. "Yeah, if you don't mind. I don't want mine to interfere with your instruments or anything."

Carson lifted the handset and gave it to me. I punched in the numbers from my phone and waited.

"It's me, Jesse," I said, when Jack Armstrong answered.

"I was just thinking about you," Jack said.

"Why's that?" I asked. "Because I'm on your plane?"

There was a brief pause, and Carson looked over at me.

"I knew the FBI was using it," Jack said. "Are you with them?"

Quickly giving him the information about the bust at Pritchard's barn and Stuart Lane being on the loose, I asked if he could have the Gulfstream stand by in south Florida for a while.

"I don't see why not," Jack replied. "Is the pilot available?"

Grinning, I handed the phone to Carson. "Mister Armstrong," I said. "He wants to talk to you."

The pilot took the phone and spoke into it. "Captain Bruce Carson."

He listened a moment then said, "Challenge word: insomniac." His eyes went wide as he heard Jack's response, then he said, "Yes, sir, Mister Armstrong. As long as you like."

Finally, he ended the call and looked at me. "I never would have guessed you were ARMED."

"I think that's the intent," I said. "I've been a contractor for Armstrong Research's Mobile Expeditionary Division for a couple of years."

As I rose from my seat to rejoin Sheena in the cabin, Carson picked up the radio mic and declared his intention to land. Leaving the flight deck, I could hear the rush of air as the landing gear doors opened and the gear was lowered. The co-pilot rose from where he'd been sitting across from Sheena and passed me on his way to the cockpit.

"I thought *you* were going to land the plane," Sheena said with a smile. "I made sure to put my belt on nice and tight."

"When we land," I said, "the Gulfstream will wait in Miami. We can bring Lane back to Staunton in it."

"I wouldn't count on that," Sheena said. "These charter companies don't usually let their planes sit for long."

"This one will," I said. "It's owned by the company I work for."

She gave me a sideways glance. "You're an enigma, Jesse."

I sat down beside her and buckled up. "Not sure what that is. Do I wanna know?"

She only smiled. A minute later, the jet came over the runway threshold and touched down lightly on the runway. I checked my watch; well before noon. Looking out the window, I could see the new hangar Billy had mentioned building some time ago. His Beaver was on the apron just outside it.

"Grab your gear," I said to Sheena as I unbuckled my seatbelt and stood in the aisle. "Our next ride is waiting."

I picked up my own pack from the seat across the aisle and started forward as Carson taxied the Gulfstream to a spot off to the side of the hangar. The co-pilot came back and opened the door just as the plane came to a stop.

Carson quickly joined him, handing me his card. "Here's my number. Mister Armstrong said to ask you what to do from here."

I pocketed his card. "Head to Miami and refuel," I said. "We might be a few hours or a few days. Grab a cab to the South Beach Marriott and keep your phone close."

"Nice to meet you both," Carson replied. "Thanks."

I followed Sheena down the boarding ladder to find Billy standing just off to the side of it.

"We're all set," he said extending his hand to me. We gripped forearms in the Calusa way he'd taught me so long ago, then turned and smiled at Sheena, extending his hand. "Billy Rainwater, ma'am."

"Billy, this is very special agent, Sheena Mason, with the FBI."

Billy rarely showed any kind of emotion, but I caught a glimpse of surprise in his eyes. I doubted Sheena saw it.

Billy was a lot of things. Among Native-Americans in the south Florida area, he was considered the acting chieftain of the Calusa people. His father was the rightful leader and probably the last of the pure Calusa. The old man had been like an uncle to me, but he hadn't spoken a word since his wife died many years ago. Billy's mom was half Calusa and half Seminole, giving Billy more Calusa blood than probably anyone on the planet. Billy was also an attorney, a hunting guide, 4x4 expert, and an occasional arms dealer—the reason he blinked at Sheena being a federal agent.

"We're looking for a killer, Billy," I said, as we started toward his plane. "He left my island just after sunrise, headed northeast."

"Northeast?" Billy said. "Ain't nothin' for him that way but bugs and sun."

"He's not from around here," I said.

"I'm guessing he's from somewhere that gets that snow you mentioned on the phone," he said, opening the back door of his Beaver. "You're a bit overdressed for here."

Billy was right. My heavy jeans, boots, and jacket were already becoming uncomfortable after the luxurious, air-conditioned comfort of the Gulfstream. Sheena climbed in back and Billy pointed out the headsets hanging on the plane's bulkhead. I shrugged out of my jacket and stuffed it and my pack under one of the seats.

Five minutes later, Billy taxied the antique airplane to the upwind end of the runway. He announced his intention on the airport's UNICOM frequency, and advanced the throttle. Any air traffic in the area would be monitoring the universal communications frequency and respond with their location and intent. The old bird gathered speed quickly and was airborne in seconds.

"Where should we start?" Billy asked over my headset, as I took my phone from my pocket.

"Head toward Flamingo," I replied, as I pulled up Deuce's number. "That's the only place he could go in the direction he took."

I lifted my headset and put the phone under it.

Deuce answered immediately. "Where are you?"

"Just took off from LaBelle with Billy and Agent Mason," I shouted over the engine noise. "We're headed toward Flamingo and will start searching from there."

"Andrew is on the water in your Winter," Deuce said. "He's headed there, too. Chyrel has him on satellite comm. I'll have him turn a little north and head for the Ten Thousand Islands area. He said his boat didn't have enough gas to get any farther than that."

"Hold on," I said, then reached into my pocket. I took two small boxes out and handed one back to Sheena. I opened the other and showed her how to activate the earwig, then stuck the communication device in my other ear, under the headset.

"Tell Chyrel to connect my two earwigs," I told Deuce, and waited.

A moment later, I heard a click from the device in my ear and removed the phone from under my headset. Deuce had already disconnected.

"Jesse's headed there by air," I heard Chyrel say. "Turn north toward Everglades City. Okay, Jesse's on now."

"Hey, Chyrel," I said, looking back and getting a thumbs-up from Sheena. "I have Agent Mason of the FBI on my other comm."

"Sheena?" Chyrel said, excitedly.

"Hello, Miss Koshinski," Sheena said. "Are you hearing me okay?"

"Five by five," Chyrel replied. "Deuce, Andrew, and Tony are on here with us."

Billy had a long, thin mirror mounted above the windshield. Looking in it, I could see myself, as well as Billy and Sheena. The whole cabin could be seen from either front seat.

Sheena smiled brightly. "Brings back fond memories. I never got a chance to thank any of you ten years ago."

"No thanks needed," Deuce said. "Jesse, what's your ETA to Flamingo?"

I looked at the GPS app on my phone and glanced at the air speed indicator. "Twenty minutes," I replied.

"If he held his course," Andrew said, "and went fast, he'd run out of gas before he could get to Flamingo. If he puttered along, he might make Shark River, but not much farther."

"You told Deuce you saw his disturbed water," I said. "I don't think he's the kind of guy to take things slow."

"I lost track of it after about ten miles," Andrew said. "He kept a northeast course the whole time."

"What if he turned east?" Sheena asked.

I looked up in the mirror and saw her studying her own phone, obviously looking at a map of the area.

"He'd be stranded on a mud flat somewhere in Florida Bay," I replied. "Chyrel, if he *did* hold that course the whole way, where would he make landfall?"

"Between East Cape Sable and Flamingo," Chyrel replied. "About midway."

"He'd run up on First National Bank before he got there," I said. The less-than- clever name for the shoal waters around Sandy Key Basin was nothing compared to the bank just to the east. "That is, if he didn't know the water and I don't think he does. That would be the place to look. Where are you, Andrew?"

"West of Sandy Key about eight miles."

"Let's switch," I said. "You head for First National and we'll run out a couple miles off Ten Thousand Islands and head south. That bright yellow boat of yours should be easy enough to spot from the air."

Billy banked to the right and a few minutes later, I could make out Tarpon Bay far off to our left and the Gulf just ahead. He banked back to the left after we crossed over the wild, southwest Florida coast we both knew so well.

I'd grown up just a little north of this part of Florida, just outside of the small town of Fort Myers. Billy had grown up in LaBelle, a little east of us, and we'd gone to school together ever since I was eight years old, and he was seven. We were blood brothers in the Calusa way.

"It's beautiful down there," Sheena said.

"That's the real Florida," Billy replied, glancing up in the mirror. "Just like it was before the Spanish came."

"You know the area well?" she asked.

"Take a look down there at that coastline," Billy replied. "Anywhere you see a sand beach, me and Jesse have camped and fished it."

"Coming up on First National," Andrew said. "Nothing here but a lone sea gull. I'll slip through the cut to the basin, on the off chance that he found it, then run up to Flamingo."

"Roger that," I said, looking out over the water under our wings. "We're approaching Shark Point now."

"Still a lot of ocean down there," Billy said.

With my hurricane hole on the eastern horizon ten miles off to the east, we could see a twenty-mile wide swath of the Gulf and the Everglades, with Cape Sable coming up ahead of us.

"There!" Sheena said, pointing straight ahead through the windshield.

I followed her finger and saw a flash of yellow and white fiberglass. It was just off the beach beyond a finger of sand pointing out into the Gulf. "Middle Cape Sable, Andrew," I said. "Your boat is about a hundred yards from shore, just to the east of the point."

Billy throttled back and banked away to the west to bleed off speed. Then he banked back to the left as we slowly descended. It was Andrew's boat, all right. The large, unusually shaped outboards on the transom were a dead giveaway. A friend of his had been part of the engineering team with Seven Marine, the company that set the benchmark for high-horsepower outboards a few years ago when they debuted the engine at the Miami Boat Show. Andrew had bought the prototypes when they were finished with testing.

As we flew over at less than 80 miles per hour, all three of us looked down. I saw no sign of anyone on the boat or in the water around it.

"I have you in sight," Andrew said. "Be there in ten minutes."

"Tony, where are you?" I asked.

"Just went under the Seven-Mile Bridge," he replied. "It'll take me an hour to get there in Rusty's boat."

"Keep coming," I told him. "We don't see anyone aboard. This might turn into a foot search. Circle downwind, Billy," I instructed. "Put us down as close as you can get us to the boat."

Billy banked way over to the right, sliding the plane lower, then pulled out just fi fty feet over the water and half a mile from the boat. He lowered the fl aps and reduced power, checking that the landing gear lights showed the gear up and locked for a water landing, then let gravity do its will.

The plane descended toward the water and Billy decreased power further. As soon as the fl oats touched the glassy surface of the shallow water, Billy increased power and pulled back on the yoke to keep the nose up and the fl oats planing as the Beaver slowed down. Finally, about one hundred yards from Andrew's boat, he cut power to an idle and the plane settled slightly into the water.

"Get the anchor," Billy directed, as he steered toward the boat.

I hung my headset up and popped the release on the door. The prop wash pushed back against me and the roar was deafening as I pushed the door open. I stepped out onto the float and with one hand on the wing strut, opened the anchor locker.

Billy shut down the engine while we were still about one hundred feet away, and I pulled the anchor out and held it ready to drop into the water.

"It's cleated at fif ty feet," Billy said, exiting the plane on the left side. "Drop it here and let the line pay out."

"Would he be fool enough to head into the 'Glades?" I asked, scanning the beach.

Billy shrugged. "I thought I saw where something went ashore when we flewover. "

His seeing the guy's tracks didn't surprise me any. When we were kids, we'd done a lot of hunting, and I believed then and still do today, that Billy could track a lizard across solid rock or a fi sh through the swamp.

Off to the west, I could hear the familiar sound of *El Cazador's* diesel engine, and the steady swoosh of her bow wave as she approached the shallows. Looking under the belly of the plane, I could see Andrew bringing her down off plane as he neared us.

"Where do you suppose he went?" Sheena asked, standing on the float beside me.

I was surprised to see that she was wearing a red tank top and khaki shorts. She'd been wearing black slacks and a jacket when we boarded the plane. Clipped to her belt was her badge and sidearm.

She shrugged. "I was told we were overdressed."

"Him," Billy said. "You'd look good in a potato sack."

Sheena smiled at him.

"My guess is he ran aground," Billy said, as he reached inside the plane and pulled out a pair of binoculars. "Tide's rising, but it's still only a few feet deep here."

The anchor line became taut and slowly spun the plane around to face into the current, the wingtip on Billy's side nearly over the foredeck of Andrew's boat.

"Don't see anyone," Billy said, glassing the beach. "But I can definitely see where he went ashore."

Billy scanned the beach for a moment more, then lowered the binos and looked over at me. I'd known the man nearly all my life. Though he was the epitome of the stoic Indian, I could read subtle signs in his face.

"What is it?" I asked.

"No 'coons."

Usually, racoons would flock to the beach when a boat was in the area, or whatever the equivalent was to a big group of *banditos*. Over the years they'd become so bold they would follow beachcombers. One handout and they felt entitled for generations. I knew what the lack of racoons meant.

Behind me I heard a splash as Andrew dropped *Cazador's* anchor. When I turned to look, he was in the stern, already climbing down the ladder into the hip-deep water. Sloshing through it, he moved past us toward his boat.

"Keep a sharp eye out," I called to him. "There may be a croc around. Billy didn't see any racoons on shore. And there're always sharks here."

He nodded and kept looking around constantly as he moved over toward the stern of his Yellowfin and climbed aboard.

"A crocodile?" Sheena asked, scanning the water.

"Saltwater croc," I replied. "About the only thing that'll keep the racoons off the beach."

"Fuel switch is still on main," Andrew called over. "If he didn't use the reserve, the boat can make it to the fuel dock in Flamingo easy enough."

Billy climbed back into the plane and headed to the passenger cabin, where he opened a small storage compartment in the floor.

I watched Andrew as he checked out his boat. After opening an overhead compartment in the T-top, he looked over at me. "He's armed, Jesse."

"What with?"

Andrew moved back to the stern and stepped down into the water. "He's got my Beretta 92FSR, suppressor, and four mags of ammo."

"Here," Billy said, extending a scoped Sig-Sauer AR-10 rifle through the door. "Zeroed at 200 yards."

I took the rifle and looped the sling over my shoulder. Then I pulled my pack out, removed one of my holstered Sig 9mm handguns and clipped it to my belt. Billy stepped down on my side with his father's old Remington.

"Let's go," I said, stepping down into the water and throwing my pack over my shoulders. "Fan out and don't bunch up. Head on a swivel."

CHAPTER TWENTY-SEVEN

Stuart had watched the airplane circle around. It had pontoons to land on water. He remembered an old guy up the valley a way who had one like that and he'd taken Stuart and a group of other men up to a hunting lodge on a lake in northern Virginia once.

Hiding behind the dune, he watched the plane come in and land. Behind him, all he saw was more water. He wasn't on the mainland at all, just another damned island. Beyond the water, he could see trees on the far bank. And through gaps in the trees, he could see tall grass blowing in the wind. The grassy field extended to the horizon.

When he glanced back out to his stolen boat, he saw the plane heading toward it on the water. Farther out, he spotted another boat heading his way.

"Who *are* these people?" he wondered.

The meddling tree-huggers weren't that important, but the people who'd attacked him and took him away from the house the woman was staying in were obviously professionals. Now they'd tracked him across the water to wherever the hell he was. The boat he'd stolen probably had a tracking device or something.

Stuart took stock of what he had. His pants were soaked from wading ashore. The long-haired guy's shirt was way too small; he couldn't even button it, but it was keeping the sun off his back. His feet were sliding around in the sandals, even though he'd pulled the straps tight. He had the guy's weed, papers, and lighter in the shirt pocket. He was looking forward to getting away from all this water and trying it out. The long filet knife and gun in his pants pockets were both hanging out at odd angles.

He pulled the gun out and looked at it again. Stuart was a hunter and knew guns. The one in his hands told him that the guy who'd owned the boat, the big guy with the mustache—he knew guns, too. And this worried him.

Before leaving the boat, Stuart had looked through all the cabinets and drawers. He'd found the knife first and had stuck it and its leather sheath into his back pocket. Then he'd found the 9mm Beretta in a case in one of the overhead compartments. The case also held a silencer and four magazines, all fully loaded. He didn't care about being quiet, but the length of the silencer added a lot of accuracy to the already-very-accurate handgun.

On the beach, he could clearly see his tracks. They were the only ones there, and again, he was puzzled by the lack of anything man-made. He hadn't bothered to hide his tracks because he hadn't thought anyone would be looking for him so soon.

Because those tracks were so visible to him, he was sure the people out there could see them, too. His footprints in the sand led off to the east along the shoreline, until the point where he'd quickly come up the dune after hearing the plane. If he stayed where he was, these people were sure to find him.

Stuart had been hunting white-tail deer, turkey, pheasant, and occasionally even bear, since he was as tall as his first rifle. Two centuries earlier, hunting was how his ancestors had put food on the table. He knew his skills were as sharp as any man's in the Valley.

Stuart looked around again. *This ain't the Valley*, he reminded himself. *Friggin' water's everywhere.*

He figured he should continue east and leave no tracks. The people looked like they were preparing to come ashore. When they found his tracks over the dune, they'd assume he would have doubled back. That's what most people on the run would do, but Stuart wasn't on the run; he had a destination.

Stuart looked behind him at the calm lake. If he moved in the water, they wouldn't see his tracks, so they'd go west. He should do the opposite and continue east.

The big man was on the boat that had just anchored and was wading toward the boat Stuart had stolen. He could make out three people on the plane. One of them was obviously a woman.

Stuart felt a stirring at the sight of the blonde's tight-fi tting red tank top and long, tan legs. She looked a little like the woman in Miami he was going to kill. But this one was taller.

Stuart looked left and right. The dune was unbroken and the water along the edge of the lagoon—or lake, or whatever it was—had a sandy bottom and little vegetation. It wouldn't take him long to circle around it and lose these people in the woods. He was a master in the woods.

The guy standing on the plane's float with the woman looked tall and rangy, with sandy brown hair over his ears. There was another man inside the plane doing something. He was darker and had long black hair, tied back at the base of his neck, and hanging down his back. Both men wore jeans, plaid shirts, and boots. The black-haired man handed something out and the tall man took it, slinging it over his shoulder with prac-ticed ease. It was an assault rifl e.

Stuart backed away from the dune, moving toward the lake, crouching low. When he reached the water, he moved along the shoreline to the east— toward Miami and his quarry. Looking back, he was satisfied that nobody would be able to follow him in the water.

In minutes, after wading through an exceptionally deep part, he reached the trees. They weren't on land, though. They had hundreds of small roots that went below the surface of the lake. Farther to the east, Stuart could see a group of tall, stately-looking pine trees of some kind. They were in a large cluster in the middle of the grassy field. He knew pines only grew on high ground and he wanted to get out of the water.

The water trees, or whatever they were, provided some cover, but he couldn't move through them—an impenetrable tangle of roots blocked his way.

So, Stuart followed the tree line, wading in waist-deep water again. The stand of pines was beyond the water trees and across the grass field, about a quarter mile away. If he could reach the safety of the pines, he could find cover and easily pick off all four as they got close.

Well, maybe not the woman.

Finally, he found a gap in the trees and pulled himself through the roots toward the grassy bank. Except it wasn't grass at all. At least not any grass he'd ever seen. It was growing in waist-deep water, too. Just like the trees. And there wasn't any bank.

The pines were closer; only a couple hundred yards away. The people following him would have to wade ashore and walk at least that far down the beach. The water trees would block their being able to see him. He could easily make the pines before they found the way through the water trees to this side.

The water was clear as he brushed the grass aside and waded into it. The bottom was very soft and spongy, unlike anything he'd ever felt. Stuart pushed further into the tall grass.

"Dammit!" he hissed, pulling his hand back.

The edges of the grass were like razor blades. Stuart looked at the trickle of blood coming from a thin, almost surgical slice in the meaty part of his palm.

He moved forward more cautiously, trying not to touch the edges of the grass by pushing it aside from the backside of the blades. This proved fruitless, as other tufts of the sharp-edged grass were pointed in different directions and he received more cuts to his hand, wincing with each one.

The water was cooler than the ocean he'd waded out of and it wasn't seawater—he could tell because it didn't sting the cuts on his hand. Stuart stopped and smelled it. It was crystal clear and had a bit of an earthy smell, like filtered water from a deep well or a high mountain stream. He cautiously put a tongue to it for a taste—no salt.

Stuart had neglected to take any of the water from the cooler with him, so he drank deeply of the cool, fresh water. Then he moved on.

The grass was above his head, so he felt he was pretty invisible except from directly above. He'd be able to hear the plane if one of them took off to search for him from the air.

Pushing deeper and deeper into the tall grass, he received more cuts on his hands and arms, even across his belly and exposed ankles. No matter how careful he was, he was being sliced to ribbons.

"Oh, that bitch is gonna pay," he mumbled, thinking of all he was going to do to the meddling tree-hugger when he got to Miami.

Stuart could see the tops of the pine trees ahead and kept moving toward them. He used his hands and knees to gently push the grass apart, then used his sandaled foot to mash the grass out of his way. He figured he was halfway there.

He made it another ten or fifteen yards when he realized the bottom was starting to rise up, and he could see over the grass. Looking back the way he came, he could make out the water trees about a hundred yards away. There wasn't anyone there.

Moving forward, Stuart kept his head down, just in case they did find the way through the water trees. The grass was a pain and the cuts hurt like all hell, but it also provided great cover. When the water only reached his knees, he paused and looked back again, slowly lifting his head above the surrounding grass.

There still wasn't anyone in sight. As he started to turn back toward the pines, however, a movement caught his eye. It wasn't back at the water trees, but about halfway there, the grass was moving. It wasn't the wind, which moved the grass like undulating waves. No, this was unnatural movement and it was headed toward him.

Who are they? he wondered again. Had they found the place he'd crossed through the water trees while he wasn't looking, and were now hidden in the grass and about to catch him? He studied it another moment. There was definitely someone coming. And they were moving the same way he'd pushed through the grass.

Turning, Stuart moved faster toward the safety of the pines and dry ground while whoever was following him was still in the tallest part of the grass and couldn't see him. The grass was less than chest-high where he was. He sloshed forward, using his knees to push through the dense grass.

Suddenly, Stuart's right knee struck something solid. He winced in pain and felt around cautiously, keeping his weight on his left leg. There was a log sticking up from the bottom. It felt kind of smooth and rounded at the top, and very solid.

Glancing back, Stuart could see that whoever was following him was getting closer. Ahead, he spotted the stand of pines, only ten or fifteen yards away. In front of the pines, where the grass ended, were dozens of stumps, some short, and some a foot taller than the grass. They had smooth, reddish-brown bark and were rounded at the top, like the one he'd kicked. Above, he noticed a bunch of white birds in the branches. They had long necks and legs.

All this was foreign to Stuart. The mountains, he knew well, but all this water was beginning to grind on his nerves. The strange trees and birds were unlike anything he'd ever seen.

The water was still knee-deep as Stuart neared the stumps. The pines weren't the same as those back home either; they didn't have needles but looked almost like bright green ferns. The base of each tree was massive compared to its trunk. And to his dismay, they were also standing in water. He couldn't see far into the stand of pines, but what he could see was water. Everywhere he looked; water, dark and black.

Pine trees and grass growing in water?

He looked back again. There was unmistakable movement in the grass now, just fifty yards behind him. And more grass moving off to the north, indicating another pursuer on an intercept course with whoever was behind him.

"Where'd you come from?" he wondered under his breath, as he watched the newcomer.

The second pursuer was moving faster and didn't seem to disturb the grass as much, which struck him as weird. Even if he'd been wearing leather gloves up to his armpits, Stuart didn't think he could move that fast.

Pulling the Beretta from his pocket, he pointed it toward the person who was closing in from behind as he moved cautiously backward toward the pines. He tripped over another stump and nearly fell, sloshing sideways to regain his balance.

As he did so, there was a loud splash and just ten yards away, the grass parted quickly as his pursuer came at him with unexpected speed. Stuart suddenly realized that at that distance, the grass was only about waist high—not high enough to hide in.

The grass suddenly parted just a few feet in front of Stuart, and a massive alligator lunged toward him, its long, narrow jawline bristling with enormous sharp teeth. He stifled a primal urge to scream and fired five rounds at the huge reptile, the gun making a light, cracking sound as it bucked in his hand.

The alligator stopped and stared at him. Stuart didn't know how many of his shots had found their mark but felt certain he'd hit the animal. It was only ten feet away. The eyes looked lifeless, but he just couldn't be sure.

Stuart started to move backward and the thing raised its head, opening its mouth wide to display a white throat. Stuart fired three more rounds into the gaping maw.

The alligator thrashed wildly, when suddenly something huge caught one of its legs and rolled the beast. It was a giant snake. Stuart had never seen a snake so large. It was easily as big around the middle as he was.

Thrashing violently, the alligator was rolled again, as the snake coiled more and more of its body around the massive reptile.

Transfixed by the horror right in front of him, Stuart nearly missed a flash of red against the dark background of the water trees. He looked up from the grisly scene playing out ten feet away and saw the tall man and the woman standing in the gap between the water trees. The man raised his rifle to shoot, but the woman put a hand on it, pushing it down.

Suddenly the thrashing and roiling intensified, moving closer. The snake- wrapped alligator lunged toward Stuart, intent on making a meal out of him even if the snake killed him afterwards.

Stuart heard snapping and popping sounds coming from the mortal combat between the two giant reptiles as the snake pulled the alligator under. He staggered blindly and tripped over another stump. As he struggled to get back up, he saw the snake's head rise to the surface as its body uncoiled from the dead alligator.

Just as Stuart turned and started a headlong dash through the last of the grass, he felt something clamp down hard on the back of his good left knee.

CHAPTER TWENTY-EIGHT

We'd found Lane's tracks where he'd disappeared over the dune into Lake Ingraham. Of all the places for a person from Virginia to try to escape to, Cape Sable and the Everglades was way at the bottom of the list. The area was primordial and for the most part, wild and untouched by humans. It was a dangerous place for even the most skilled guides.

Billy studied the water at the shore of the lake closely. "This way," he said, and started moving along the bank to the east.

"Are you sure he didn't double back, hiding his tracks in the water?" Sheena asked.

"He's sure," I replied, following behind my old friend, who was one of the best trackers in the state.

We stayed on the sandy bank as Billy followed whatever he was seeing in the water. We had to wade across the man-made canal that connected the lake to the Gulf.

"There." Billy pointed toward a gap in the mangroves.

Beyond the opening, even I could see the disturbed sawgrass where someone had pushed through. I winced a little, just at the thought of trying to slog through it; it was called sawgrass for a reason.

When we reached the opening, I went through first. The gap was tight, and the mangrove roots were a tangled trip hazard, but I managed to get through.

"Keep one hand on the branches," I told Sheena, helping her squeeze past.

We emerged together just as I heard five popping sounds. I ducked instinctively and looked out over the sawgrass.

What I saw was like something out of a horror movie. Lane was standing among a bunch of cypress knees, pointing Andrew's suppressed Beretta at the water. The wide back of a large saltwater croc was visible just a few feet from him. He fired three more times, and the thing began to thrash around.

"Big bull croc," Billy said from behind us. "Saw his sign back on the beach."

Suddenly, something else was there, too. I couldn't believe the macabre scene we were witnessing; a giant anaconda wrestling with an equally large crocodile.

I raised my rifle, just as Lane looked toward us.

"Don't kill him," Sheena said, pushing the barrel down.

Lane and the embroiled reptiles were only a couple hundred yards away. The battle was a complete puzzle to my way of thinking. I knew that the snake could easily kill the croc, but why? The croc was way too big for the biggest snake to swallow. The croc could eat the snake in chunks—if he could kill it, that is. Wrapped in the snake's powerful coils, it was obvious to me which animal was going to die. It was just a matter of time.

"I wasn't going to shoot Lane," I said, raising my rifle once more. "Only the croc has a right to be here. I'm going to shoot the snake."

I looked through the scope. Where was the head?

The coils were massive—as big as a man's waist, but the croc was even bigger around, probably thirteen or fourteen feet in length. Why would the snake attack something it couldn't eat? Suddenly, I realized what the term invasive species meant.

The snake would kill the crocodile because it was a competitor for the snake's food supply—in this case, Stuart Lane.

"Where's the damned head?" I muttered, as Billy and Andrew joined us.

"It will drag the croc under and crush the wind out of him," Billy replied.

He was right. The snake and croc were writhing deeper. Stuart looked up and saw us, then started running toward the relative safety of the cypress stand.

The thrashing ceased and finally the head of the snake appeared. It was already halfway to Lane, uncoiling quickly from the dead crocodile.

Stuart stumbled and went down before I could bring my sights to bear. In an instant the anaconda was on top of him, grabbing the back of his leg in its powerful jaws and rolling its body up and around the man's torso, crushing his left leg across his chest and left shoulder at an unnatural angle.

Stuart screamed in pain and went under as more of the giant snake coiled in on top of him, dragging him to the shallow bottom. It was over in an instant.

"Oh my God," Sheena said, huddled close to me. "We have to help him."

"There's no helping that man," Billy said. "If he's not dead, most of his bones are broken and he's dying of suffocation. We'd never get there in time."

As we continued to watch the gruesome scene unfold, the snake uncoiled its body from its victim. Through the magnified scope, I saw Stuart Lane's lifeless face look up at the sky. The snake's head appeared, moving toward Stuart's. I'd never seen a snake that big but knew they grew up to forty feet in length in the Amazon and were more than able to swallow a person whole. This one made a python look like a garter snake.

I breathed in and exhaled slowly, relaxing my body as I took the slack out of the trigger. The crosshairs were on the snake's head, moving only a fraction of an inch with each beat of my heart. Instinctively, I felt the wind on the side of my face and made a Kentucky windage adjustment, moving the reticle just a little to the side of the snake's head.

The recoil of the heavy .308 rifle wasn't quite as powerful as my own M40A3, though it was the same caliber. The Sig AR was a semi-auto and much of the shock was taken up by the recoil spring as the bolt slid backward, extracting the empty cartridge and chambering another round.

The scope barely moved when the round left the barrel. The giant snake's head exploded in a mist of pink spray, just inches from Lane's own lifeless head.

Sheena started to move in Lane's direction, but I put a hand on her arm, stopping her. "Too dangerous."

"We can't just leave his body," she said.

"Jesse's right," Billy said. "Let the dead bury the dead."

Sheena turned toward him. "What's that supposed to mean?"

"That croc wasn't the only one around," Billy replied. "It's suicide to walk out there."

"Not all that safe here, either," Andrew added.

"He's right," Billy said, pointing. "Look."

I followed his finger and saw several places where something, probably more crocodiles, were moving through the sawgrass toward the scene.

"There's nothing we can do," I said, turning back toward the lake. "Let's get out of here."

Andrew stood there, looking out over the 'Glades for a moment. Soon, the dead man, the dead snake, and the dead croc would provide a bounty for others in the area.

"You coming?" I asked him.

Andrew glanced over at me. "I really liked that gun."

CHAPTER TWENTY-NINE

We made our way back to the beach, nobody saying anything about what we'd witnessed. The struggle for life and death in the wild is very real and seldom seen, though it is a constant battle for survival. We, as humans, are ill-equipped to match the merciless ways of nature, with or without our weapons and tools. Nature doesn't recognize their strength and will do what nature does anyway.

We crossed the dune and started wading out toward where the boats and Billy's plane were anchored, shuffling our feet to avoid stingrays.

"Is there a tow line on *Cazador*?" Andrew asked, as we sloshed through the water.

"No need," I said. "Take your boat to Flamingo and fill it up, and I'll take *Cazador* back to my island."

"*Your* island?" Sheena asked.

I pointed toward the southwest. "It's about thirty miles that way."

"And you own it? The whole island?"

"Yeah," I replied. "It's not big, just a couple of acres of sand and mangroves."

"I'd like to see it," she said. "I can have the plane moved to someplace closer, to take us back to Virginia. You need to pick up your plane. Besides, I need to get statements from all of you about what happened."

"I fl ew the plane down here and landed in the water," Billy said. "End of statement."

"I drove Jesse's boat up here to retrieve my stolen property," Andrew added. "Not much more than that, I'm afraid."

Sheena stopped a few yards from Andrew's boat. "Are you stonewalling the FBI?"

I turned to look at her. "Come on with me. I'll give you a full statement and we can go to Marathon Airport, where *I'll* call and have the Gulfstream moved to. But really, what they said is pretty much the extent of their involvement."

Sheena put her hands on her hips and glared at me. "There is the small matter of how Stuart Lane got down here."

"I think if you check the flight records," Andrew said, climbing aboard his boat, "you'll fi nd that he fl ew a three-hop from Virginia to Miami. Outside of that—" he shrugged "—he's a tourist, or at least he was; they get lost all the time."

Billy stood next to his plane's float and extended his hand. "Thanks for the adventure, Kemosabe."

I gripped his forearm and he gripped mine. "I'll get your anchor. Send me a bill, okay?"

He only grinned, then pulled himself up onto the float and climbed inside. He passed my jacket to me and I returned his rifle, then closed and latched the door.

With Sheena behind me, I followed the anchor line and pulled the hook loose from the sand. As I coiled the line, I pushed and nudged the plane toward deeper water before dropping the anchor and rode into the box and closing it.

"We better head toward my boat," I told Sheena.

When we were beyond the wingtip, I checked the area. Andrew had his engines running and was pulling his anchor. He was far enough away.

"All clear," I shouted.

Billy waved to me from the open window and then started the Beaver's engine. He pointed her away from shore and the plane moved downwind. Once clear of the point, he turned upwind and the engine roared. By the time we got aboard *El Cazador*, Billy's plane was a disappearing dot to the north, and Andrew's boat a disappearing dot to the south.

"Déjà vu," Sheena said. "Do your friends always take off so quickly?"

"What do you mean?"

"Ten years ago," she replied. "When I turned around, you were all heading away from the dock, disappearing."

I just shrugged. "When the job's over, it's over."

"What are you going to tell your ex?" Sheena asked, in the quiet stillness that was Cape Sable. "I mean, Lane killed her boyfriend. What will you tell her about how he died?"

I helped Sheena climb up the ladder. For a second, I looked up at her standing on the swim platform, silhouetted against the bright blue sky. Her red tank top and khaki shorts were soaked and clinging to her body. I climbed up and joined her, with just inches between us on the small platform.

"We've been divorced a long time," I said with a lecherous grin. "She doesn't need to know anything."

Sheena punched me in the shoulder. "You know damned well what I'm talking about."

"She's an environmental activist," I said with a shrug. "Lane messed around with the environment and got what he deserved. She'll understand."

I went to the helm and started the engine, checking the gauges. "There are some towels in the side locker," I offered. "Port side, under the console."

As I pulled the anchor up, Sheena dried off and then handed me a towel. "You must be dying of heat in that flannel shirt."

I draped the towel over the rail and took my shirt off. Putting the boat in gear, I turned toward deeper water and let the engine idle as I dried off. It was good to get out of the cold and return to the heat and humidity I enjoyed.

When I turned, Sheena was watching me, smiling. "If I said how uncomfortable those jeans looked, would they come off, too?"

I felt my face flush, even though I was already sweating heavily.

"Kidding!" she said, smiling brightly. "Oh, you should have seen the look on your face!"

She joined me at the helm, and I pushed the throttle forward, heading almost due west, to give the shoals a wide berth. I could feel the heat from her body as we stood against the leaning post. Occasionally, our hips or bare shoulders touched as the light chop bounced us around. It was a sure bet that Sara would ask about what had happened. I wasn't real confident about how much I would tell her.

"You're lucky you can take your shirt off," Sheena said. "Mine smells like sweat and swamp."

I opened the port side overhead compartment in the hardtop Bimini and pointed to the stack of Gaspar's Revenge Charter Service T-shirts. "Help yourself," I offered.

Sheena stretched and riffled through the stack till she finally picked out a yellow women's shirt. Then she moved around in front of the console with the shirt in hand and sat down on the forward-facing seat. Before I could say or do anything, she pulled her tank top over her head, then looked back at me, smiling again. She unhooked her bra and let it fall to the deck in front of her.

No tan lines. At least not on her back.

Dammit woman! Do you not know what you're doing?

After pulling the low-cut T-shirt over her head, she lifted her blond hair out and let it fall down her back. Then she gathered up her dirty clothes, stuffed them into a side pocket of her pack, and rejoined me at the helm.

I found myself scanning the horizon, and each time my eyes drifted her way, I could see the effect the bouncing boat had on her braless form.

To distract my thoughts, I recounted to her the events since last week's Thanksgiving visit from Kim, and the revelation that Sandy's boyfriend had been murdered.

Sheena went into professional mode, asking pertinent questions if I didn't divulge enough information. She overlooked some of the things that bordered on illegal, like Chyrel hacking into computers and files.

When we neared my island, I called Deuce and told him what had happened.

"Your son-in-law spilled the beans to your ex," he said. "She's in my outer office now, demanding to see you."

"She lost her right to make demands on me a long time ago." As soon as I said it, I realized what a position that statement would put Deuce in. "Tell her how to get to the *Rusty Anchor*. I'll be there in an hour."

"Trouble with the ex?" Sheena asked, smiling coyly when I ended the call.

"No trouble," I said, slowing the boat as we approached the south dock.

Jimmy and Finn were waiting there. Both looked surprised to see me. Or maybe they were surprised to see me with a strange woman.

I introduced them and asked Jimmy if I could use his shower, so Sheena could use the one in my house.

"I don't want to put you out," she said, as we grabbed our bags and headed toward the foot of the pier.

"No put out, *mi hermana*," Jimmy said over his shoulder. "*Nuestra isla es tu isla.*"

She looked at me for a translation. "Our island is your island," I said, as we reached the top of the steps. I opened the door to my house and waved Sheena inside. "You and Sara are about the same size. She has a few things in the top drawer in the back room."

"Are you sure?" she asked. "I know I'd be pissed if my boyfriend let another woman wear my clothes."

"She's got a lot of clothes," I said, "she won't miss anything. Most of what she has here, she's never worn."

"No need?" she asked, then went inside, and closed the door.

Twenty minutes later, we were back aboard *Cazador* and heading toward the Seven-Mile Bridge. Even in the wind, I could smell the fresh scent of her hair. It wasn't anything of mine, so I figured she had stuff in her pack for just this kind of situation. She smelled good. Not a perfume smell, just a clean scent.

Passing Sister Rock, I backed down on the throttle, and turned *Cazador* into Rusty's channel. The back door of the bar opened and Rusty came running toward the docks. For his size, the man could move pretty quickly when he needed to.

He grabbed the line off the bow rail and quickly made it fast to a dock cleat. "You're not gonna believe who's here."

"Sandy," I said, helping Sheena step up to the dock. "I know."

"Sandy?" Rusty asked. "What the hell would she be doing down here?"

When I stepped up beside him, I looked toward the bar. Sara was coming out the back door, hurrying toward us. She stopped about twenty feet away, looking from me to Sheena. Then she looked Sheena up and down. There was no doubt that she recognized her own clothes on the woman.

"What's going on here?" Sara demanded.

I looked from one woman to the other, trying to come up with a coherent sentence. Sheena moved toward Sara, pulling her ID from her pocket, or Sara's pocket, as it were.

"You must be Sara," Sheena said, extending her credentials. "I'm Special Agent Sheena Mason with the FBI. Jesse has told me so much about you. I'm afraid my clothes were ruined chasing a suspect up on Cape Sable. Jesse was kind enough to let me borrow something of yours. I hope you don't mind."

Sara took a few steps closer as I approached her. In an uncharacteristic manner, she stepped into my arms and pulled my head down to hers, kissing me passionately. I recognized it for what it was, even if she didn't; she was marking her territory.

When Sara hugged my neck, she whispered in my ear, "Do something like that again, and I'll cut off your balls."

"Did you catch the guy?" Rusty asked.

"Not exactly," Sheena replied. "He was killed by a snake."

"You're kidding," Sara said stepping back. "What kind of snake?"

"I'm pretty sure it was an anaconda," I replied.

"Anaconda?" Rusty said. "Not many of those up there, thank God. Pythons are the big problem. They have regular snake hunts these days. Pythons, boas, and the occasional anaconda are squeezing out native species." He chuckled at his own unintended joke. "No pun intended."

As we started toward the bar, Rusty pulled me aside. "It wasn't Sara I was talking about, bro."

"What do you mean?"

He pointed to the end of the canal, where a big Grand Banks trawler was tied to the side of his barge, the name *Sea Biscuit* visible on the stern. "Sara just got here a few minutes ago. Savannah's been here since yesterday."

Savannah? Here?

I'd first met Savannah Richmond a couple of years after I retired from the Corps. Our time together was short but had produced a child; a daughter she'd named Florence, following a family tradition of southern city names. I'd only learned about Florence a couple of years ago, but so far all we'd done was talk on the phone occasionally.

I stopped in my tracks as the back door opened and a tall young woman stepped out. We'd sent pictures back and forth by text message and talked on the phone, but I'd only seen her a few times when she was a young girl. Florence had her mother's blond hair and blue eyes. Though no more than seventeen, she was probably taller than Savannah, who was five-ten.

"Fl-Florence?" I stuttered.

She looked me in the eyes for a moment without answering, then let her own eyes move across my face, studying me. "I thought you'd look older."

"So, who's this?" Sara asked.

Florence looked at Sara and Sheena, as if seeing them there for the first time. "I'm his daughter," she said. It sounded so natural. Then she looked at me again. "You're my father." Without a word, the girl stumbled into my arms. "It seems like I've waited for this moment forever."

Holding Florence close, I stroked her hair. "I can't believe you're here."

"We tried several times," Florence said. "Either you were away, or we had to be somewhere."

"I know," I said, holding her out at arm's length to look at her again. "And I'm sorry."

The door opened again, and Savannah stepped out onto the deck. The last time I'd seen her was in the Virgin Islands. Florence had been about ten or twelve. I'd gone looking for them, to find out once and for all if the girl was my daughter. But I'd spotted Savannah in the arms of another man and for nearly two years after that, I'd tried to kill myself with pot and rum. I'd nearly succeeded several times. She was still as beautiful as the day we'd met.

"There's nothing to apologize for, Dad. Mom told me what you do." She paused for a moment and I could sense fear. "Is it okay if I call you that?"

I pulled my daughter into my arms again. "I'd love it if you did, Florence."

"We just happened to be in the area," Savannah said, extending a hand to Sara and Sheena. "Hi, I'm Savannah."

I introduced everyone and suggested we go inside. Rusty led the way to a table in the corner. "I bet y'all are hungry," he said. "I'll get Rufus to make some fish tacos. That be all right?"

"Yum!" Florence said, as we all sat down.

Sara and Florence sat on either side of me, as Naomi, Rusty's step-niece, brought over a bucket of beer. There was also a bottle of wine stuck in the ice, and several bottles of water and soda. The bucket sat on a tray with a half dozen glasses.

I didn't realize how hungry and thirsty I was. Savannah and I reached for the same bottle of water, our hands touching. I grabbed a different one, realizing that it was the first time I'd touched her since our time together so long ago.

"You haven't changed, Jesse," Savannah said, then smiled at Sara and Sheena. "Always with a beautiful woman on your arm. Or two."

"Sara's the girlfriend," Sheena said, obviously enjoying my misery. "I only work with him now and then."

"What kind of work do you do?" Florence asked.

"I'm an agent with the FBI," she replied. "I work out of Washington and your father was kind enough to bring us in on a big drug bust up in Virginia."

Florence's eyes went wide. "The FBI? A drug bust?" Then she looked at me in wonder. "Are you a spy, too?"

"FBI agents aren't spies," I said. "They're more like cops for the federal government."

"Yeah," Sheena agreed. "Now, the CIA? Those guys are spies."

"Deuce kept me up to speed on what was going on," Sara said.

"Who is it you work for?" Sheena asked her.

"I'm the one who approved your use of the company Gulfstream," Sara replied.

"Ah," Sheena said, nodding. "Is that how you met? Through Armstrong Research?"

I heard the front door open and turned, as Sara explained how she'd trained me aboard *Ambrosia*, Armstrong's primary research vessel.

A blond woman was standing in the doorway. When she removed her sunglasses to let her eyes adjust to the darker interior, I was pretty sure she was my ex-wife, Sandy.

Perfect, I thought. *Four women.*

"Excuse me," I said, and rose from the table.

When I turned toward her, Sandy spotted me and started my way.

"Sandy?" I asked, still not quite certain it was her.

"Sandra," she corrected me. "I stopped being Sandy a long time ago."

Rusty moved out from behind the bar, his wife Sidney joining him. He had a big grin on his face as he approached us.

"Sandy McDermitt," he said, coming toward us. "Is that really you?"

Sandy stared at him for a moment, unsure. Finally, recognition shone in her eyes. "Rusty Thurman?"

Rusty wrapped her in a big bear hug, though she was a couple of inches taller than him. When he finally released her, she was smiling.

"Sandy, meet my wife Sidney. Sid, this here's Sandy, Jesse's first wife."

Though Sandy was taller than most women, she had to look up at Rusty's Amazonian wife. The two shook hands and Sandy turned to me. "First wife?"

"I remarried in 2005," I said.

Sandy glanced over at the four blondes I'd been sitting with. "I'd like to meet her."

"She died the night we were married," I said.

Sandy, never one to shy away from any sort of encounter, had already taken a step toward our table, but stopped. "She died?"

"Murdered," Rusty said.

I saw tears begin to form in Sandy's eyes and couldn't help myself. I put my arms around my ex-wife and whispered, "I'm really sorry for your loss."

She stepped back and wiped her eyes. "That's why I came down here," she said. "Eve's husband told me that you caught the man who killed Kamren. Are you some kind of cop now?"

"Not exactly," I replied. "Come over here and I'll tell you all about it."

EPILOGUE

How does a man introduce his ex-wife to his current girlfriend, a female FBI agent with whom he'd had a one-night stand, a former lover, and his daughter with that former lover?

I'd been worried about Sara and Sheena; just two women. Now, there were four. Five, if I counted Florence.

I probably didn't handle it in the way I should have. Explaining the circumstances around Alex's death was no easier. I came to realize that her death was the most pivotal moment in my life. My parents made me, my grandparents shaped me, the Corps molded me into a warrior, but it was the loss of Alex that drove me to become the man I was now.

As the talk wore on, I felt Sara becoming distant. When she said she had to get back to the ship that evening, I knew it was over between us. She'd lost her husband in Afghanistan a few years earlier, and no matter how close we got physically, I was always aware that she was still in love with his memory. She was always the one who'd insisted she wasn't ready for an emotional commitment, and I'd gone along with it. But I sensed we had now reached some kind of turning point.

Sheena was married to her job and Florence was too young to have suffered loss. But Savannah, Sara, Sandy, and I were all widowed and broken because of our losses. Losing Alex was probably why I couldn't bring myself to commit, either.

Sandy did seem to understand when we told her what happened to Stuart Lane. She termed it Karma; just another snake killing a snake.

Later that night, after Sara had left to return to the ship, Florence asked if she could go with me to bring *Island Hopper* home from Virginia. Savannah said it was okay with her—she had some work to do on their boat and didn't like flying.

Sheena suggested that Sandy come along, as well. She would have to give a statement to the acting sheriff of Augusta County concerning the murder of Kamren Steele. Sandy agreed and drove back up to Miami to pack. She'd driven down in Eve's car.

I called Bruce Carson and told him to fly down to Marathon in the morning to pick us up, and that he'd have a passenger who would meet him at the Miami airport in the morning.

The next morning, when the plane arrived, Florence was nervous and said that she'd only flown a couple of times in her life. The flight to Shenandoah Regional only lasted a few hours and Florence and I soon found ourselves alone in *Island Hopper* and headed back south. She said she liked the fancy jet, but really loved my old bird, especially since it could land on the water.

We talked while we flew back to the Keys. I let her take the controls for a while. She wasn't quite the natural that Kim was at her age, but she didn't kill us.

The trip lasted nine hours and we had to stop for fuel twice and use the bathroom, so we had a lot of time to talk. She said that she preferred to be called Flo, instead of Florence, and went on to tell me about her life, growing up on the water and living on the old trawler. She'd said that although she'd been what she called "boat-schooled," her mom wanted her to spend a year in an American public high school and graduate with other kids before going off to college. When I'd asked her where she planned to go, she'd told me she was going to apply to University of Florida.

It was the mention of UF that made me realize that Flo knew nothing about her two half-sisters. I'd told her then that her sister Kim had gone there and then immediately called Kim and Eve and asked if they could come down to Marathon the next day.

The meeting of the three sisters had been a long time in coming. Flo was younger than Kim by a dozen years, and half the age of my oldest daughter, Eve. But the three of them hit it off instantly. It was amazing how much they resembled one another.

Two weeks later, I got a phone call from Judge Orville Whitaker. He brought me up to speed on the investigation, and also told me that Pritchard was singing like the proverbial canary. As it turned out, Stuart Lane had been one of Pritchard's early clients, when he'd worked in the public defender's office. Pritchard spilled everything about the sheriff's involvement in the cover-up of the murder of the hooker and the judge's wife later the same night.

Stuart Lane had strangled the hooker, and, still high on cocaine and the rush of the first murder, he'd shot and killed the judge's wife while driving down the street, not even knowing or caring who she was.

I again invited Ollie to come down so that I could help him get a marlin. He agreed that he'd come right after Christmas.

Life on the island returned to normal, though I did miss Sara. I knew we'd still see and talk to one another, but that would be it. Whether or not I'd crossed a line was irrelevant. She'd retreated into her work, like a turtle in its shell.

The morning of December 24th, I awoke feeling a touch of melancholy. Christmas had been a wonderful time as a kid, before I lost my parents. I became more so, when my first two daughters were kids. Now, they were grown and had holiday plans with their own families. I was a bit depressed by mid-afternoon. Jimmy had left the island to stay at Naomi's apartment.

As I debated whether to take something out for dinner, or the boat to the *Rusty Anchor*, I got another phone call. I could tell by the long stream of numbers that it was a sat-phone.

"Hello," I said.

"Dad, it's me. Flo."

I could feel my spirit rise at the sound of her voice.

"Did your mom get a new phone?"

"It's our new satellite phone," Flo said. "This is my first call on it."

"I'm honored," I said, and meant it.

There was a moment of silence, then Flo asked, "Will you come to dinner tonight?"

"Dinner? Tonight?"

"I know it's short notice."

"Does Savannah know you're asking?" I asked.

"She's right here, if you want to talk to her."

I heard shuffling and muffled voices. Then Savannah came on. "It's nothing special, Jesse. Flo and I usually have a feast the day before Christmas. We used to anchor far from shore, so we could watch Santa fly over, and she wanted to do it again this year. And she wants to share it with you."

"Where are you?"

"Thirty miles north of you," Savannah replied. "Anchored off Graveyard Creek. It'd mean a lot to her; that is, if you're not busy."

"Can I bring anything?"

"No, we have everything we need," Savannah replied. "Lobster and mahi."

My spirit soared, and I only considered the implications of the invitation for about half a heartbeat.

"I can be there in two hours."

THE END

If you'd like to receive my newsletter,
please sign up on my website:

WWW.WAYNESTINNETT.COM.

Every two weeks, I'll bring you insights into my
private life and writing habits, with updates on
what I'm working on, special deals I hear about,
and new books by other authors that I'm reading.

The Charity Styles Caribbean Thriller Series

Merciless Charity
Ruthless Charity
Reckless Charity
Enduring Charity
Vigilant Charity

The Jesse McDermitt Caribbean Adventure Series

Fallen Out   *Fallen Angel*
Fallen Palm   *Fallen Hero*
Fallen Hunter   *Rising Storm*
Fallen Pride   *Rising Fury*
Fallen Mangrove   *Rising Force*
Fallen King   *Rising Charity*
Fallen Honor   *Rising Water*
Fallen Tide   *Rising Spirit*

THE GASPAR'S REVENGE SHIP'S STORE IS OPEN.

There, you can purchase all kinds of swag related to my books. You can find it at

WWW.GASPARS-REVENGE.COM

ABOUT THE AUTHOR

Wayne Stinnett is an American novelist and Veteran of the United States Marine Corps. After serving he worked as a deckhand, commercial fisherman, Divemaster, taxi driver, construction manager, and commercial truck driver. He currently lives in the South Carolina Lowcountry on one of the sea islands, with his wife and youngest daughter. They have three other children, four grandchildren, three dogs and a whole flock of parakeets. He's the founder of the Marine Corps League detachment in Greenville, South Carolina, where he met his wife, and rides with the Patriot Guard Riders. He grew up in Melbourne, Florida and has also lived in the fabulous Florida Keys, Andros Island in the Bahamas, Dominica in the Windward Islands, and Cozumel, Mexico.

Wayne began writing in 1988, penning three short stories before setting it aside to deal with life as a new father. He took it up again at the urging of his third wife and youngest daughter, who love to listen to his *sea stories*. Those original short stories formed the basis of his first novel, Fallen Palm. After a year of working on it, he published it in October 2013.

Since then, he's written more novels and now this prequel in the Jesse McDermitt Caribbean Adventure Series and the spinoff Charity Styles Caribbean Thriller Series. These days, he can usually be found in his office above Lady's Island Marina, where he also keeps his boat, working on the next book.

Made in United States
Orlando, FL
31 July 2022

20384575R00180